MW00778652

ANIMAL INSTINCT

AMY SHEARN

ANIMAL
INSTINCT

A NOVEL

G. P. PUTNAM'S SONS
NEW YORK

PUTNAM
— EST. 1838 —

G. P. PUTNAM'S SONS
Publishers Since 1838
An imprint of Penguin Random House LLC
penguinrandomhouse.com

Library of Congress Cataloging-in-Publication Data
Names: Shearn, Amy, author.
Title: Animal instinct: a novel / Amy Shearn.
Description: New York: G. P. Putnam's Sons, 2025.
Identifiers: LCCN 2024011305 (print) | LCCN 2024011306 (ebook) |
    ISBN 9780593718339 (hardcover) | ISBN 9780593718353 (e-pub)
Subjects: LCGFT: Novels.
Classification: LCC PS3619.H434 A84 2025 (print) |
    LCC PS3619.H434 (ebook) | DDC 813/.6—dc23/eng/20240315
LC record available at https://lccn.loc.gov/2024011305
LC ebook record available at https://lccn.loc.gov/2024011306

Printed in the United States of America
1st Printing

BOOK DESIGN BY KATY RIEGEL

For anyone in need of rewilding

ANIMAL INSTINCT

CHAPTER 1

In her new life, Rachel wakes up naked and alone and the first thing she does is check her phone for sexts from strangers. The light in her bedroom is buttery and lush, so she takes a couple of pictures of her boobs, or tries to anyway—it's harder than you'd think—and then her boobs live in the phone, alongside the app she's developing, and her personal email, and her professional email, and her bank account balance, and her social media accounts, and her to-do lists, and her doctor's office patient portal, the results of her most recent mammogram snuggling up beside her dating apps, their direct messages brimming with requests for banter and said boobs, and the *New York Times* Spelling Bee game she used to play on the subway back when she commuted into the office because there were offices, and commutes, and the subway was scary in only the ordinary way she was used to it being scary, because of the ravages of failing infrastructure, not germs.

She scrolls through her photos until she gets to recent evidence of her children frolicking in a rare moment of camaraderie, and if she keeps scrolling there is a picture of a dick someone sent her that she downloaded for safekeeping, and if she keeps scrolling there are snapshots of an ill-fated brunch she'd had with her kids and ex-husband, which had seemed like a good idea at the time. Work is in her phone, and her friends and her lovers and her memories and her future plans and the news alerts about the swelling pandemic are in her phone, and when her children are at their father's the phone is a link to them too. Perhaps even the love of her life glimmers, quietly, within the phone, waiting to be found. But probably not.

She used to mostly use her phone to read articles about how to be less dependent on your phone, a pious tautology of content, and she still gets served those sorts of things by the algorithm, which pays closer attention to her than her ex-husband, Josh, ever did. The algorithm knows too that what she really wants now is to be served ads for an upscale vibrator and prairie-girl nightgowns and unspeakably expensive face cream made from placentas, any product that offers an element of transcendence—customized shampoo that responds to her environment; candles that reanimate the sensory landscapes of her childhood—as if being single in her forties has unlocked a new layer of reality in which things she thought were clichés are suddenly revealed to be universal truths. A kind of portal sliding open—*show her what's behind Door Number Four!*— to reveal both slack neck skin and an insatiable sex drive. *Aha!*

Now she checks her phone to see—as sun blares through the open windows, because her new life allows her to sleep until it's light out, because an unexpected gift of the twinned catastrophes of divorce and pandemic has been rest, and time, and the spaciousness she'd wanted from life and hadn't been able to achieve for so long and that had seemed forever out of reach; she'd once wept in couples' therapy, saying, "Is that all there is?" like an embodiment of the depressing old Peggy Lee and/or PJ Harvey song (*"then let's keep dancing"*), but no, now she no longer has to carve out predawn hours just to have a moment to breathe, yes, today the children are at their father's, and he is legally bound to do his fair share of the parenting, and she has no commute to manage, and she will have time, time, time, to sleep, to exercise, to work, to sketch, to walk, and now to see what has come in from the team—who has sent a dirty picture, who has fired off a suggestive text, who has sent a sweet **goodnight** with a shooting star emoji after she'd fallen asleep trying to read a biography of Alan Turing she'd bought months ago, when she still had an attention span. Who responded first to the picture of her tits in a silky nightie that she sent to three of them, and which response was the most satisfying. Which reminds her: while the sunlight is falling so beautifully on her bed she might as well roll over and stretch out and take a picture of her ass, which she's only now figured out how to do, thanks to some YouTube videos and advice from her best friend, Lulu. She's willing to bet Risa, her thirteen-year-old daughter, could offer some selfie tips, but Rachel isn't that kind of mother. Or not yet anyway.

Rachel likes to starfish out in the center of her small bed. She'd not wanted to be unmarried. She'd been terrified at the idea of divorce—for a while couldn't even say the word out loud—embarrassed at letting go of the thread of how a woman like her was supposed to live, anxious about fucking up the kids. She hadn't loved the idea of being middle-aged and alone.

But now that she's in this storyline, she feels restored, like she's fallen back in love with life itself. Her new self, this new-and-yet-familiar iteration of Rachel Bloomstein, strikes her as being faintly ridiculous and not quite real—sometimes dreamily so, and she worries she'll wake up back in her old life, beside Josh drooling on her pillow, which he's stolen in the night, a crime he will pointlessly deny in the morning. The only thing she really fears anymore is that this—the escape, the separation, the apartment, the sense of possibility, the feeling of future, all of it—might be a fantasy, a glitch in the simulation.

IT ALL STARTED in February, during that sliver of weeks between her marriage ending and the pandemic beginning. The children were getting used to the new routine: two days at Rachel's, two days at Josh's, trading off weekends. The first weekend Rachel was alone in her apartment because the kids were at their dad's, she expected to feel sad and aimless. She hadn't been away from them for this long since they'd been born, hadn't spent a weekend alone in thirteen years. What would she even do with herself? Probably just mope around and cry her eyes out, she guessed.

Instead, Rachel woke up that Saturday to find her customary stress rash had disappeared—in fact, it would never return, though the dermatologist-baffling scales had covered her chest and back for years—leaving in its place a strange plumpness in her veins, an ache between her legs, a shimmer of energy in her cells.

It was as if one by one, parts of her body were transforming, her organic self erupting out of the exoskeleton that she hadn't even noticed forming over the years. A finger here, an ear there. Her personhood, starting to return.

She almost laughed when she figured out what the feeling was. It wasn't an indication that something was wrong or a new iteration of the old itchy rash. It was *desire*. Rachel remembered it inchoately, the way you half remembered a smell. Soon she had her hand down her underwear. Who remembered it was even possible to get so wet so fast? She came twice, hard, lay there panting, got up to drink some water, opened her laptop and ordered a vibrator, then went back to bed. She really had not remembered it felt like that, could feel like that. How on earth had she imagined she didn't like sex anymore? What had *happened* to her? Suddenly Rachel wanted to fuck, and she wanted to fuck all the time.

But it wasn't allowed. So as the pandemic shut down the city, Rachel tried to convince herself that in the grand scheme of things, what were a few more months of sexlessness after so many years? People had lived through worse, were at that moment living through worse. And at first everyone was predicting only a few uncomfortable weeks at home, a small pause, a bittersweet sabbatical of online work and school, baking sourdough bread while listening to podcasts. If you didn't get the mystery virus and die a nightmarish death, it might be kinda fun!

During those initial lockdowns Rachel hid in her new apartment, extremely online and increasingly jumpy, aghast at the idea that she might somehow share air with another person who was not related to her. And, by extension, Josh. What a cosmic joke. She was finally free and full of desire, and the only adult she was allowed to see, the only approved grown-up in her contagion-bubble, was the person she least wanted to be around. The person who hated her— and he did seem to hate her, despite how gently she'd tried to approach the divorce—more than anyone else on earth.

Still, Rachel, a lifelong rule-follower, followed the rules. Unless her children were there, she was alone all the time. She ordered her groceries, sent out her laundry, tipped all the delivery people extravagantly, wiped down everything that made its way into her house, leaving the apartment only for walks, during which she wore a paper surgical mask and crossed the street to avoid people on the sidewalk.

Her children—Risa, Sadie, and Holden—were not terribly disturbed by it all. They were always amazing her in some new way. And now, they proved to be both unfazed by the divorce and vaguely excited by the pandemic drama—they loved being on their computers all day, attending school while lying down in their pajamas and eating chips.

Rachel spent her nights reading too much news, doomscrolling social media feeds until she forgot who she was—until she felt overly porous and spiritually parched—and then burying herself in the cheesy monster movies she'd loved as a teenager, bludgeoning her brain with less-plausible horrors. *Fine,* she thought, *how fine, how perfect, to be newly single in a time when no one is supposed to touch one another, when there are rules against breathing the same air.* Fine! It would keep her focused on her new reality, keep her from finding another husband-type to dissolve her hard-won freedom as soon as she'd won it.

No, she hadn't *won* her freedom. No one had awarded it. She had created it; she had birthed it; she had wrenched it thrashing and bleeding and writhing from her body.

The death counts rose; refrigerated morgue trucks idled on the city streets.

And yet, somehow, slowly, like a frog in boiling water, Rachel got used to the theater of it, the culture of pandemic life, the ways you could, in fact, fudge the lines. First, in April, she met up with Bess (separated, like her, mere moments before the lockdowns) to take a responsibly distanced walk around Prospect Park, shouting at each other from the recommended six feet apart. The next week she went to (still-married, somehow) Natalie's giant loft, sat on her roof-deck beneath strands of fairy lights, shared a bottle of wine and their worst anxieties about how These Times were fucking them all up. She texted Lulu daily, sometimes hourly, monologuing bespoke podcasts to each other in voice memos. They palpated each other's opinions, forgoing epidemiologists' op-eds for each other's gut instincts, lobbing through the air unanswerable questions: Was a walk without a mask allowed if no one was around? Was it safe to go to the beach? Was flirting with neighbors actually a little bit more fun with masks, adding a slightly chic air of mystery, maybe?

In May, the police murdered a man, and even though it was about the millionth time this had happened, this was the one that caused the country to explode in righteous fury—uprisings swelled in the streets, helicopters droned cicada songs overhead, energy roiled the air. Rachel was ejected from the months in her apartment straight into the well-orchestrated chaos of a Black Lives Matter protest, walking and chanting with throngs of passionate strangers. A sweaty girl in a bikini top bumped into her, and they made eye contact, and Rachel thought, *Oh, we're in love,* and the girl apologized and kept moving, pumping her sign in the air, and Rachel realized she might be really, chaotically touch-starved. She chastised herself for getting distracted—how broken was her brain?— and to punish herself she marched until her middle-aged arches twanged with pain, and then went home and sat on her balcony and donated as much as she could afford to a place that paid bail bonds for arrested protesters, and listened to the helicopters churning through the sky, and wondered why she still hadn't cried yet.

The city felt doomed but at least the bars had started serving to-go drinks. Rachel met Lulu at their favorite place, though it already seemed like they needed to pick a new favorite place, as this had been their regular spot for after PTA meetings or for early dinners with the kids in tow—Holden and Lulu's son, Jackson, had been in the same weekly soccer situation since they were toddlers, and Rachel and Lulu had been drawn to each other immediately, bonded together as the least enthusiastic parents on the sidelines. (Rachel loved her children more than anything but refused to live vicariously through her small son's scoring percentages. She'd always been attached to the concept that she had a self besides Mommy Rachel.)

Funny to remember now how once coming to Simkin's had been a thrill, the most excitement she would have in a week: a dinner she hadn't cooked; a glass of wine with Lulu while their kids ate overpriced french fries and slid around the booths; a hurried, slightly coded conversation about their latest wifely frustrations as the children bent their heads reverently over a shared iPad. Being out after dark felt like time travel then, like a visit to her twenties. Who were these people looking clean and bright and just heading out for the night, as Rachel shepherded her fractious young home for bedtime?

Now that they were both single, they needed a new go-to, probably. It was amazing, really, how they had both parachuted out of their marriages at around the same time. Lulu had left her husband six months before Rachel had left hers. When Rachel told Josh that it was over and this time she really meant it, one of the first things he had said was "Oh, is this because Lulu's getting divorced? Like a girl-power thing?" laughing bitterly, as if he found her ridiculous, as if he assumed this was all a whim, or some game she and Lulu were playing in order to prove an obscure point about women's lib.

But even though they were close, Rachel actually hadn't known Lulu was also talking to divorce lawyers, looking for an apartment, siphoning money into an emergency account ("Don't do that," said the mediator, and Rachel said, "Okay, next time I won't," all while she was). It wasn't something you talked about with your married friends. Those early presplit steps felt so sordid, so sneaky, so sad.

One day Lulu had called her—they weren't calling-unannounced friends then, so Rachel assumed someone had died and answered in a heart-thumping panic—and had told her, "I wanted you to know I'm leaving Craig." Rachel was impressed by this declarative; when she practiced saying it in her head it was always hedged, like, *We are separating, but it's no one's fault* . . . Turned out Lulu had found herself dry-humping a stay-at-home dad at a playdate while their sons played Firefighter in the other room and had had the presence of mind to realize that she was looking not for heavy petting but for an excuse to end her marriage and had to leave before she did something even worse. Rachel was also impressed by this. There she was, following all the rules, trying to win divorce, when Lulu was out there groping Dale's dick through the cargo shorts his wife had bought him. Lulu had always been a little cooler than Rachel— she had actual style, wore clothes not purchased from the Old Navy website, retained interesting friends from her premotherhood career working in art galleries, was the kind of person who would dance when her favorite song came on, no matter where they were, and look cool doing it. Of course she had semiseduced the stay-at-home dad they both loved.

The end result, however, was the same—soon-to-be-ex-husbands who felt injured and furious, married mom friends shooting them pitying looks. And now both Rachel and Lulu found themselves, their co-parenting schedules miraculously in tune, back at Simkin's, where the cocktails were strong and the pickle chips were on the house, because the owner's kid had gone to soccer camp with their sons.

Rachel and Lulu tipped the masked bartender insanely, thanked him as if he'd literally saved their lives, double-fisted their to-go containers over to a bench near the entrance to Prospect Park, and sat on opposite ends while they yelled their conversation into the misty, soft-aired evening. They talked about the usual things— parenting, politics, protests, the end of the world. Eventually Rachel finished her first drink and said, "I think I'm going to die if I don't get laid."

Lulu clapped with delight, as if she'd been waiting. She took Rachel's phone—this felt as shocking as if she'd reached out and squeezed her tit, since they were constantly told to wipe everything down, to keep their hands and phones sanitized—and downloaded her favorite dating app. They giggled like teenagers, trying to distill Rachel's essence into a profile.

"But wait," Rachel said nervously, "isn't it, like, scary? I hear dating is scary. Is it dangerous? Do you get murdered? Is it like a horror movie?"

"It's more like slapstick." Lulu laughed. "Here, let me show you."

It was somehow soothing, the idea that Rachel could control someone's first impression of her, to think that someone might see her for her, not Risa's mom or Sadie's mom or Holden's mom, not Josh's quietly sad wife, not the serious product designer working on the new app, or the merely adequate treasurer of the PTA, or the community garden's resident keeper of the honeysuckle, or the would-be illustrator who occasionally showed up at the drawing club meetings at the local café but never spoke to anyone. Someone might see just her, just Rachel. The idea that someone would not only see her but see something appealing in her—it was beyond her comprehension, really, but also such a lovely thing to imagine. Plus, Lulu assured her, it wasn't as hard as she might think.

Lulu had more dating experience, having split earlier and married later. She presented a brisk tutorial on browsing and swiping and messaging. "Okay, look. The first thing you have to realize is that pickings are slim. Just—when we first take a peek, don't panic is all I'm saying."

"I wasn't panicking, but maybe now I am," said Rachel. "Oh hey, set it so my profile's visible to both men and women."

Lulu reached out for an air high five.

"But wait." Rachel grabbed Lulu's sleeve. "How? I mean, what? Like, I'm going to meet people in the park for drinks? Or—like—"

Lulu searched in Rachel's photos for cute pictures of her without any children visible. "Look, for now we're only window-shopping. Right? And you can have a lot of fun without even meeting someone, for one thing. We're living in a golden age of sexting."

"True," said Rachel. "I guess that's right. I did read a think piece about all the video sex people are having."

Lulu raised her eyebrows and nodded. An hour earlier she had described in great detail a sordid hookup she'd had in some guy's car. They'd nicknamed him Car Talk. Lulu and Car Talk had each solemnly sworn that they hadn't had any possible exposures to the virus for at least two weeks each, to be oh so safe, agreed to keep their masks on, and then proceeded to have sex without a condom. It was a confusing time.

"It does sound like sort of a drag, though, dating someone without a body," said Rachel, stretching out her arms.

"Welllll," said Lulu, appraising the version of Rachel she'd thrown together on the app, "just to say—people are allowed to have pods. You know? Like you already have Josh in your pod. I have Craig in mine. What's adding one more person? If they work from home, don't have a lot of potential for exposure . . . ? I mean. A lot of people are doing a lot worse."

It was true that Rachel kept seeing posts of people ignoring all the rules completely, for stupid, skippable things like parties, karaoke, trips to Walmart. If Rachel was going to take a risk, she wanted it to be taken in the name of fucking, not buying toilet paper in bulk or, like, going to church. She knew that wasn't how germs worked, but still.

"I think you'll enjoy dating actual adults," said Lulu, handing her phone back. "It's way better than being in college and trying to date half-formed little fledglings."

Lulu had a point. Rachel had met Josh in college. But unlike college-Rachel, current-Rachel had a budget for underwear and a hard-won inoculation from her youthful fear of embarrassment. Rachel took a deep breath—"Okay, Lu, here I go"—and started swiping.

She was immediately reminded that, as with so many things in life, there were a lot of options, but not every option. In the end, the choices were always limited, prefab rather than bespoke. So many men flexing biceps in the speckled mirrors of dim gyms; so many dudes in tuxedos, baring their teeth at someone else's wedding—their own?; so many women with intentionally unflattering haircuts on hikes with their ex-girlfriends only half cropped out of the frame; so many thinly veiled threats ("DON'T say HI, that is NOT a conversation starter, I do NOT want a pen pal and I am NOT here to play games"); so many totally fine-looking people, bland as Sears models, who listed inane interests like "brunch." Brunch?

Rachel had never thought about it until that very moment—one dubious privilege of her micro-generation—but this app-dating business seemed completely backward. Instead of falling for someone and figuring out what part they might play in your life, you decided what role was open and went looking for someone to fill it, like you were casting a play. What she wanted was not, actually, to find someone serviceable, but rather to create a partner out of only what she desired, the way she had, in the past few months, reconstructed herself.

"Wouldn't it be great," she said to Lulu, "if instead of having to pick from who's available, you could make up your own person?"

"I mean, I think that's what messes people up about the apps, actually. It almost seems like you *can*. Just—don't overthink it," Lulu said. "I know 'not overthinking' is not really one of your modes, but. Try." Rachel laughed. "The apps are stupid, dating is stupid, people are stupid. Try to have fun with it."

Rachel swiped some more and then looked up. "Holy shit, Lulu, what if I see Josh's profile? Or what if he sees mine!"

"Uh, *so*? If you see him, you make fun of his profile and swipe left. If he sees you, that means obviously he's on the app too, so he understands, no harm, no foul. You're getting divorced! You're allowed to date! That's, like, the whole deal! He's a big boy—surely he gets it. Did I tell you Craig saw my profile on another app, and matched with me, and was like, 'Hey! You look great! See ya Sunday when I drop off Jackson!'? It was kinda funny!"

Rachel was very sure that was not how Josh would react, but she nodded anyway.

"The thing is," Rachel realized out loud, after they'd spent some more time viewing the wares, "I don't want a *boyfriend*. Or a *girlfriend*!"

"The thing is," Lulu agreed, "you don't have to. And guess what? We never have to have husbands ever again." They gave each other another air high five.

"We don't, do we? Because, like, I really don't want to."

"You really don't have to! I'm with you. We can be those cool old single ladies who travel and curse and live to be a hundred and say it's because they drink whiskey every day and live alone or whatever."

"Great," said Rachel. "I do not want to deal with anyone's shit. I just want to have sex. And maybe have someone cook me a nice dinner. Or make me a cocktail, at least."

It had been so long since anyone had done a thing for Rachel that she accidentally fell in love with anyone who served her in any way—the tattooed bartender who absently mixed their drinks; the expressionless woman at the laundromat where she dropped off her dirty clothes; the muscular men at the car wash who wiped down her glistening tires. To have someone do anything at all for her, even things that were paid for in cold hard cash, felt like tenderness, like being cherished.

No wonder there was the cliché about middle-aged women bedding their gardeners, personal trainers, stable boys. Marriage asked women to go from being exalted angels (when Rachel thought of her bridal dress, glowing like a baptismal gown, all the hullabaloo around the wedding, the excitement people had felt about it, it had all seemed weird to her, even then) to household automatons almost immediately—a social contract she'd entered in her twenties, hormonal and untherapized and in no state to make a lifelong commitment. In fact, it should have been illegal to get married so young, she now thought.

But to her credit, she'd never suspected that her rebellious, vaguely anarchistic boyfriend would desire such a *Leave It to Beaver* marriage. Somehow she'd thought that they'd agreed, in a nebulous, unarticulated way, that they'd have adventures together, would create some new kind of way to live, figure out how to forge a family life that was totally unlike a sitcom. He'd ridden a motorcycle around their college campus, for Christ's sake, and yet once they were married, he expected meat and potatoes on the table when he got home from work. He and his friends used to stage elaborate illegal rock shows in abandoned warehouses, and a few decades later he was scolding her about her dishwasher loading. She'd assumed they were, like, too cool for convention. Certainly she should have discussed her expectations in actual words, rather than gliding along on assumptions, but: youth. She'd presumed he wanted, as she did, an equal partnership. Hadn't he read *The Feminine Mystique?* He'd taken Women's Studies 101! She knew because she had been there, making eyes at him from the back row.

By the end of their marriage, she couldn't remember the last time her husband had done anything for her or the children or their home that she hadn't had to request and remind and trade for. For a long time, she'd tried to convince herself that this was simply the economics of partnership. He accused her of nagging him constantly. Maybe she did. Their couples' therapist had told her to ask for help when she needed it, but maybe she actually needed too much help.

Normal requirements of adult married parenting life irked him; he had to be cajoled, as if she were the one who had invented such obligations and had done so strictly to be annoying. Yes, he'd accompany Holden to an obnoxious laser tag birthday party while Rachel took Sadie to her soccer game, but he would need an undisturbed nap in the afternoon to recuperate and sex that night to restore his mood. Yes, he'd go to the school fundraiser with her, or help her clean the apartment, or take the car into the autobody shop, but she would have to promise a blow job in return. And the thing was, as she knew from candid conversations with friends, this kind of barter wasn't unique to her. Mundane whoring was a normal part of marriage—the feature, not the bug.

And now she'd gone through the chute of the heterosexual-partnership fun house slide and plopped ass-first on the other side, ready to be served. It didn't have to be a lot. She didn't need full-time adoration or, heaven forbid, love. She didn't even want someone to ask her questions about herself, to try to get to know her. But she knew she would be completely undone if someone said, "Here, let me make you a cup of coffee." If someone looked her in the eyes and smiled and said she was beautiful.

Rachel wasn't used to allowing herself to want anything. After all, mothers were not supposed to want things for themselves. But this, here, setting up her profile on the app, was a baby step toward that. Toward wanting. Toward feeling desire without a hot sting of shame alongside it, toward needing without immediately apologizing for it.

"What I want," she said out loud, to Lulu, "is something to distract me from the wreck of my life, from the fucking horrors of this world and the nonstop video meetings. I'm not even sure I need to meet anyone in person. But I would love to text-flirt with someone, you know? God, I miss crushes!"

Lulu nodded, widening her dark eyes. She always applied her cat eyeliner slightly crookedly, which Rachel found so endearing she could hardly stand it. "Lockdown life has stolen from us the joy of the casual crush," Lulu said knowingly, as if pitching an article to a women's website.

"And then," Rachel said, "like, maybe, maybe someday, I'd love for someone to order an assortment of sushi and let me pick out what looks good. Tell me I'm hot and fun and smart. I'm not trying to get remarried over here. Just pay for my drink and make me come. That's all!"

Lulu glowed in the light of the streetlamps that had flickered on. She was so beautiful and so hilarious, Rachel's sweet best friend. Why couldn't they just love each other?

But they did, that was the thing. They loved each other so purely, without needing each other. And now, incandescent Lulu grinned and said, "Oh my god, Rachel, you're in the perfect state of mind for this. You know what a catch a commitment-shy woman is?"

They swiped some more, and a couple of times Rachel showed Lulu a profile and Lulu either nodded in assent or recoiled in mock horror. Once she said, "Oh, I know that guy. He's into dungeon stuff." Rachel raised her eyebrows. There really was so much to learn.

Next she saw a mom they knew from the neighborhood, looking a thousand times sexier in her profile than she did at school pickup. She showed Lulu, who smiled in appreciation. "Damn. I didn't know she liked girls!"

"Neither did I! But I mean, did you know I liked girls?"

"Did *you* know you liked girls?"

Rachel laughed. "I mean, I *did*, but I think I forgot for a while there." After a pause, she said, "Upon reflection, I'd like to circle back to my making-your-own-perfect-person concept."

Lulu snorted into her drink. "Like those picture books in the three sections, where you mix and match the heads, bodies, legs?"

"Right, yes, exactly. Like look, I'd like this woman's brain—look at how many books she lists in her profile!—but she specifies long-term relationships only, so, pass. And this guy here, his eyes are gorgeous and he seems funny, but look at all this sporty shit? Pass."

"I think this a lot, I'm not kidding," agreed Lulu. "Car Talk, who I was just telling you about? Great dick but weird balls. Firefighter, from a couple weeks ago? Medium dick, great balls."

"Lulu!"

"Oh please, jump all the way into this dating pool with me, swim around a bit, and then tell me you don't know what I mean." Lulu lifted her long, dark hair off her neck. It was a warm, wet night, the air like a mucin mask. "And, like, I love texting Cute Coworker—"

"You're still texting him?"

"Oh yeah, and it's gotten pretty hot. He gives good text, you know? If only those texts could come from the Sexy Widower's body. I'm telling you, that guy—I never thought I cared about abs until his."

"Look," said Rachel, putting down her phone and taking a notebook out of her tote bag. "As we discovered in our marriages, it's really hard for one person to be everything. Right? Josh started out as a great friend, and he was a fun boyfriend, but then he turned out to be a bad roommate and a surprisingly old-fashioned and sort of mean husband."

"Exactly. Craig was a great co-parent and roommate, a middling financial partner, a terrible lover, and a crappy friend. It's a lot to ask all of one person."

Rachel rolled a vanishing ice cube around her tongue, doodling on a notebook page. So many people were outside in the evenings. There was nowhere else to go. Couples clutching to-go cocktails had colonized the park benches and chatted and laughed, sounding happy and normal. It was intoxicating, the way you could almost, if you squinted your eyes and blurred out the fabric masks slung beneath peoples' chins, pretend it was normal times.

Who could have ever guessed she would crave "normal times" so much? Normal times had not been great. But they had been *normal*. Something divorce, and her resulting hyperawareness of the undivorced, had crystallized for her was how hard humans would fight, how much they would ignore, just to maintain the status quo, no matter how not-great that status quo was.

"That must be why they used to, you know, stay in the village. So you co-parent with your mom and sisters or whatever, and you have your lady friends for gossiping at the quilting circle kind of thing, and your husband provides for the family but also leaves you alone most of the time, and there's some other person you fuck maybe . . ." Rachel wasn't sure exactly what era of history or geo-graphic location she was imagining, but Lulu nodded emphatically.

A kid rode by on a scooter, and something about his skinny leg swiping at the ground to gain speed reminded her of Holden, and she missed her children with an urgent pang in her chest. She tried to refocus.

"What about an app? To make your perfect person from scratch, with, like, all the best bits and pieces from all these people?"

It was the kind of thing you couldn't say to most people, but you could say to Lulu, and the great thing about Lulu was that her immediate response was: "Right, totally. Like Frankenstein, but for dating."

The sky was dark now, and the streetlights stained everyone golden, revealing their beauty. Rachel looked around, fell in love with every person she saw.

"Frankenstein's monster," she said. "Frankenstein was the name of the scientist."

"You know what," said Lulu, "you disgust me."

Rachel laughed. "I get that. And right, you're right. But why isn't that what dating apps do? I don't want to swipe through pictures of all the semiadequate people who exist in the world. I want my own person, with all the traits I know I like."

"The key is"—Lulu pointed at Rachel's face—"you have to know the things you actually want. And I think you don't know that until you're old. Older. At least forty. Until you've been through some trial and error."

"There would be an age limit on the app," Rachel agreed. "You have to be at least forty to use it to make a person. For safety."

"Forty and a half. Agreed. For everyone's safety."

"I mean, there's some pretty advanced artificial intelligence out there. It's not too terribly difficult to train a chatbot. I've been doing this machine learning project at work." Rachel sketched some notes. "People have already created some intense AI chatbots. There're these guys in Japan who think they're married to these hologram anime chicks who are basically glorified Siri."

"Okay, Steve Jobs, how would the perfect person app work?"

"Well, you can train AI to respond in certain ways. Just very basic input/output training. You feed the program certain information about human conversation and interaction. Bits of your ideal conversations, for example, or like, your favorite parts of romance novels, Nora Ephron scripts, "Modern Love" columns, whatever. And the user could select what they were looking for, and specify what they were not looking for—I mean, you would make a really easy-to-use interface, like with the dating apps—and then instead of matching you with someone who sorta has some of those traits, the script would create a bot that has all of those traits—or just has been programmed with enough of the right responses—and communicates with you accordingly."

Lulu clapped. "Love it! What would your person be like?"

"Hm. You go first, what about yours?"

"Well, the more people I talk to on the apps, the more I realize that humor is really important to me. Like it actually makes me feel nervous to chat with people who don't have a sense of humor, it's so stressful."

"Ooh, same." Rachel scribbled. "Okay. What else."

Lulu thought for a moment. "I mean, the next real requirement would be that he was very, very into me. Like, obsessively into me."

Rachel would not have thought to put this into her perfect person, but it made sense for Lulu. She smiled.

"And really nice. I want someone to be nice to me, you know? I don't care if he's *cool*. I'm too old for cool. I just want nice. And *clear.* I'm tired of things being so confusing all the time. I would want him to respond immediately when I text—none of those slow-reply games—and to proactively set up next dates, and to say early on what he wants out of a relationship. Hmm, and then of course, let's see: sorry to be so hashtag-basic, but I'm thinking six feet tall, a scrubby beard, athletic. Ooh, he should be into massage. Giving, I mean, duh, not getting. And he should have some really unexpected talent, like being a great singer or kicking ass at crochet or something."

"Interesting." Rachel tapped her pen on her chin. She had been sketching while Lulu was talking and had come up with a generic-looking guy who didn't *not* resemble Lulu's ex-husband, Craig.

"What about yours?"

Rachel watched the sidewalk for a moment, thinking.

And then the person appeared, near their bench, in a beam of light. No, stopped—they were walking and stopped by a streetlight to check something on their phone. They pulled down their mask, and their face glowed for a moment in the phone's luminescence. They were perfect, a perfect person, Rachel's perfect person: right there. Rachel's heart flattened along her spine.

Her first impression, which struck her somewhere in the chest rather than in her brain, was of a someone who was graceful, androgynous, somewhat delicate—jeans, high-top sneakers, a weathered gray T-shirt on a rangy frame, tousled and slightly elven hair. Angular with the kind of cheekbones Rachel's soft face could only dream of, giant dark eyes framed by giant dark lashes. Their olive skin was burnished by the streetlights, and a tote bag from a local bookstore was slung over their shoulder.

Rachel thought she knew this person was entirely at ease, friendly but not overbearing, loved books and art, had interesting work they cared about, cooked thoughtful meals, was fun to go on adventures with, would show up at your door in a beat-up old jeep and say, "Hop in, let's go upstate!" She imagined this person was funny but never in a cutting way, had real conversations with people, fixed things around your apartment as a way of expressing love, but also would read your tarot cards and make you herbal tea. This person moved elegantly, would be a passionate and thoughtful lover, would be a part of your life and want to know your children and your parents and your friends but never in an oppressive way, would really, really listen when you talked. When Rachel talked. Would make Rachel feel heard, seen, loved, like the best possible version of herself.

Rachel imagined that with the perfect person she would feel secure and both in love and beloved and delighted to exist in the world, alive with her person, but that this time it would last. It would be elastic enough to handle life's changes. Maybe they would travel together; maybe they would follow new jobs to new cities and new adventures; maybe they would live in the country and ride matching bicycles and have heritage chickens named like old ladies roaming the hill behind their gracious house, where they hosted the smartest and most magical dinner parties for all the artists they knew, with bonfires on cold nights, twinkly lights on hot nights; maybe they would refill each other's wineglasses as they cleaned up after the party and sang along to dumb music and laughed as they remembered all the fun, and they would go upstairs together tired and happy, and they would make love every night because they couldn't bear not to, even after all those years together. Someone Rachel could care for without becoming their mother. Some capacious, spacious life.

The person slipped their phone back into their pocket and looked up, caught Rachel's eye, smiled a stupidly beautiful smile, pulled their mask back up, and kept walking. Rachel smiled back. What the fuck was that, anyway? She put her drink down on the pavement. She should probably be done for the night.

"Hello?" said Lulu. "Yes, and?"

"Oh! I don't know, I guess I'd have to think about it."

"Well think all you want, sis—this is actually a great idea. Especially given"—Lulu waved her hand around, the classic "These Times" gesture—"I mean, there are tons of single people who would probably love a totally safe dating alternative like this here perfect person app."

Rachel laughed. She felt a weird after-aura from her reverie, like the minty tingle that remained after a migraine. What a weird— hallucination, she guessed?—that person had been! Rachel needed to sleep more and drink more water and use the goddamn yoga app she'd paid $60 for at the beginning of the pandemic, when she'd had different ideas about herself.

"But also, it seems dangerous, potentially. I mean, what if you really fell in love with an AI? Like the guys in Japan you mentioned! Or that movie with the non-River Phoenix!"

"Yeah, fair. It is a little *Twilight Zone*, or *Black Mirror* or whatever."

"Right." Lulu picked up Rachel's phone and started swiping through the dating app queue for her. "And another teeeeny little problem would be the whole lack-of-a-physical-body thing. That is, I hate to admit, part of my requirements for my perfect person."

"Right. Physical body comes in handy. As we have all learned in These Times, humans don't do so well when they have to live totally inside their own heads. We could make a golem out of Prospect Park dirt. Or hm, maybe there could be a virtual reality component? A hologram? A sex robot?" She paused. "I know! That's the bonus content, for paying customers."

"Ooh, yes."

"There must be a noncreepy way to make a body. Maybe 3-D printing?" Rachel said thoughtfully.

"Oh, I know," said Lulu. "Grave-robbing! That worked for *Dr. Frankenstein*, didn't it?"

"It didn't work out that well, actually. The whole story is about what a terrible mistake it was."

"Okay, but it did technically *work* is all I'm saying. The whole movie is about how it works and the monster comes alive and toodles around and picks flowers, right?"

"It's a *book*, Lu. And yeah, the monster comes alive, but then it kills people."

"Look, any new technology has bumps along the way."

Lightning crackled in the sky, and they both burst out laughing. "Little on the nose," said Rachel. The air was thickening, starting to smell like rain.

"Very rude to rain when everyone has to hang out outside." Lulu sucked down the remains of her drink. "Let's get home before it pours."

They were drunk enough then to hug, despite all the warnings, because they had to, it really felt like they had to, or their bodies would flatten into paper dolls. Rachel walked home along the dusky edge of Prospect Park, feeling the warmth of her love for her friend, the afterglow of her embarrassingly sincere fantasy of love, or whatever, for the perfect person, or whoever.

Could it be that she would someday feel love again, *that* kind of love? At her age, after the drawn-out death of her marriage, at this moment in history—was that kind of feeling even a thing anymore? Maybe Josh was right that she was unforgivably self-centered and frozen solid. Leaving her marriage just so she could feel better? It was, in some ways, the definition of selfishness. But all Rachel felt was a whole-body revulsion at the idea of marriage, a skepticism—and a hidden hope, sure, but mostly a skepticism—that an unoppressive partnership was even possible, that a pairing existed that would make her feel like life was expanding, not contracting.

It didn't matter, none of it mattered. She walked home, her head buzzy with liquor and the heat of the night, the rain starting to leak out of the sky and onto her skin. She pulled down her mask because no one was around and gulped in the clean air and appreciated the beauty of the tree-lined avenue, streetlights glowing orangely, like the inside of an eyelid. The cozy homes of millionaires glinted in the dark. Maybe she should have been afraid of walking alone at night, of returning to an empty apartment in her marginal corner of a city that was fraying around the edges, but she mostly just felt relieved that she wouldn't have to talk to anyone when she got home. She could shuck off her sweaty clothes and light a scented candle and play corny, empowering indie rock from the '90s and take a bath and then get into bed and use her vibrator and fall asleep naked, and alone, and happy.

THE NEXT MORNING Rachel found herself staring at the sketches in her notebook. The perfect person app. It was a funny idea, wasn't it? That was all—a silly notion, a daydream that her ideal partner was in fact made of a combination of bits and bobs. A nice little being she could create and then control, a mate who would be predictable. What a clever observation she was making about dating and love, lah-dee-dah, look at her.

But a chatbot really wouldn't be *that* hard to make. Not for her, anyway.

And so Rachel found herself out on her balcony with her phone and laptop, having a coffee and cigarette for breakfast like a character in a noir film, watching the stray black cat who she'd decided was her familiar trot through the alley next door. Harsh voices drifted up from her landlords' garden, the elderly couple sniping at each other somewhere within the greens. In front of the renovated Victorian down the block, the mommies she loved from afar tucked their toddler into a stroller, working in a wordless tandem that made her ache with nostalgia for a marriage she'd never actually had. She saw these people every day, but they never spoke; she was alone, but also not exactly ever alone.

The cat, spooked by some invisible force, dashed across the street, disappeared beneath a parked car. Rachel opened the chatbot builder she used at work and created a fresh persona.

CHAPTER 2

"Can I send you a picture?" came the message from a man Rachel had matched with. So this was how it started. She'd always wondered.

Rachel and Lulu had nicknamed him Married Guy, because he was married. He was one of the first people Rachel had messaged, and even once he'd said he was married but looking for a hookup—not in the ethically nonmonogamous way, in the straight-up old-fashioned nonethical way—she'd kept texting with him, because why not? She was used to dealing with husbands. It was like trying out a gun with the safety on, messaging with an unavailable person. A consequence-less practice round.

From the start, he told her literally everything she wanted to hear: She was hot; she was funny; she was brilliant; she was sexy. He thought about her all the time. Rachel made a note: for her perfect person AI, she would take from Married Guy this ability he had to make her feel like he adored her, even though they'd never met.

His lonely married-person hunger reminded her of herself a year earlier. According to his pictures, he was cute in a teddy bearish, someone-else's-husband kind of way. She was sure she'd flirt with him if they were tipsy at a school fundraiser together. He was PTA-mixer hot.

"**Sure,**" she wrote back, out of a scientific curiosity.

And there, on her phone in her hand, appeared a dick. It was rather antic-looking, really, just standing there. Rachel hadn't seen an unfamiliar dick outside of porn for decades. She zoomed in, appraised it like a piece of fruit she was about to pay too much for at the farmer's market: nice size, nice shape, looked generally unscathed. What Rachel didn't know was how she was meant to respond. Were there etiquette rules for sexting? She texted back a flame emoji and hoped he wouldn't ask her to send him a picture in return, which honestly felt like a lot of work.

"**Isn't it supposed to be good for your brain to be a lifelong learner?**" she texted Lulu. "**Crossword puzzles, word games, sexting.**"

"**Yes! Keep learning, keep growing.**" Lulu sent a "The more you know" gif. The deadpan rainbow shimmered across the screen.

WEIRDLY IT DIDN'T take Rachel long to wrap her mind around the particular, peculiar culture of pandemic dating. Sexting with Married Guy was satisfying for a couple of days. But it wasn't sex and thus was not scratching her itch, like the generic version of a prescription drug that should have worked the same but didn't, quite. She had to find someone who was smart enough (and privileged enough—work from home was a must) to follow all the virus-safety rules of distancing and masking, but who was also stupid enough to agree to meet her, a stranger.

First, she texted questions that would net her the necessary information about their exposure levels: Did they work from home? Who did they live with? Did they wear masks when out and about? Then she probed for their risk tolerance. "I have gone on a couple walks with my friend, both wearing masks and walking six feet apart from each other," one woman texted. Rachel swiftly closed that one out. She completely understood the "Let's video chat and write each other letters until there's a vaccine!" contingent, she really, really did. That was right and proper and responsible and would surely lead to some slow-burn, Jane Austen–esque courtships.

But Rachel had more dire needs. She wanted—she needed—sex. It was hard to articulate even to herself why it felt as if she would disintegrate into dust and dissolve off the planet if she wasn't touched by somebody, soon. Something was rising within her that felt so urgent she wondered if it was possible to die of it—a restlessness, a recklessness. She knew it was selfish and didn't make sense, but it had to do with feeling alive, like an animal in a body and not a brain in a jar, the way she felt after monotonous days of working from home, checking messages on her phone, especially when the kids weren't at her place to keep her tethered to the physical world and eating and sleeping like a normal person.

Every night the kids were at their dad's she sought out people who matched her safety protocol but also suggested outdoor drinks. And at first, even just having drinks with strangers sent a shiver of excitement up her spine, seemed like it might be enough to feed the beast. She would share her phone's location with Lulu in case of murder, and they would text furiously after each date to debrief. She burned through a handful of rapid-fire crushes, each based on the best picture in the profile and a few volleys of decent-to-fun texts, each just as easily extinguished by an actual in-person conversation. She quickly trained herself not to take it personally when someone ghosted, to see it, actually, as a useful learning, a finding to feed to her AI.

First, Rachel watched a sunset over the bay at Industry City, sipping a margarita out of a plastic cup, with an indie rocker who advertised his virus antibodies in his profile—he'd already had it! An early adapter! What a flex!—but who also reminded her so much of Josh that she felt vaguely queasy and tweaked her app preferences as soon as she got home. She had a beer on a Fort Greene Park bench with a kindly man who was twenty years older than her—she was age-agnostic as a rule, and it was flattering to be considered young while she was feeling like a nearly expired yogurt cup, but as it turned out, sixty-two felt overly old, and she didn't have the patience for a generational barrier right then (that was, she assumed, why he didn't laugh at any of her jokes). There was a walk around Prospect Park with a cute, lanky socialist who got irritated when she couldn't pinpoint his accent ("New Zealand!" he'd said, with a tinge of disbelief). There was a stroll in Green-Wood Cemetery with a younger woman who made Rachel laugh but also mentioned TikTok at least a dozen times—as it turned out, twenty-nine felt overly young, and Rachel couldn't date someone who was even more online than she was; it would have been like making out with an operating system, fucking a line of code.

Lulu complained about the park dating culture, but Rachel didn't hate it. It was perfect for her remedial dating level. There were so few options to sort through: what park, what to-go cocktail. Sitting outside made it all feel rather wholesome. There was sort of a built-in time limit too, because how long could you nurse a $13 drink full of melting ice? The lighting—tree-dappled parks, rosy sunsets—was forgiving. Rachel even had the wardrobe for it. She would have been hard-pressed to dress herself for a date at a bar or club or wherever normal adults had normal dates in normal times, but she had sundresses that worked for park benches, lots of them. And now, cute matching fabric masks—she even had a special "dress-up" mask for dates.

After a few park-bench interludes, Rachel got more advanced. She learned to do a video chat first, to make sure there was no notable situation that the photos in their profile had concealed, like disconcerting teeth or a grating laugh, or having nothing at all to say. She was getting better at parsing profiles too, which she realized was an important learned skill, like eyeing clothes on a rack and knowing without trying them on whether they'll work for you. If someone didn't include their height, they were definitely short (she didn't care, but she felt clever for having figured this out); apparently everyone on earth liked the television show *The Office* and wanted a Pam to their Jim; jokey profiles weren't always attached to funny people and in fact were often a symptom of someone who felt themselves to be a little too good for the dating app they were in fact all on. Sometimes the people she found so terrifyingly hot she almost didn't bother swiping on turned out to be—inexplicably—into her. A very interesting finding.

RACHEL HAD WARMED up with all the texting, gotten her bearings with the strings of chaste park dates. This, plus all the restrictions of everyday pandemic life, plus the recent years of holding in, holding in, holding in, had burned through her reserves of patience. Which was how, on a sultry evening in the middle of her life, Rachel found herself with a thirty-year-old musician who was so good-looking she almost hadn't matched with him (who could trust someone with a facial structure like *that?*), but who had for some reason agreed to meet her, had been unbearably flirtatious and flattering via text, and with whom she was now getting a drink. Or rather, having a picnic, as if they were a pair of small children in a fairy tale, meeting on a blanket beneath a tree, the sun bleeding out histrionically behind them.

Rachel tried to think of something to say while she watched him open the bottle of wine, his dark hair falling over his eyes. The park where they'd arranged to meet was in Dumbo, the most dramatic part of Brooklyn, overlooking the water and the bridges and the shimmering spires of Manhattan, like she'd traveled directly from her apartment into the kind of romantic comedy that had a jazz soundtrack. She took a Lyft, double-masked in the back seat, trying to breathe deep and stay calm. When was the last time she'd been excited about something? It was so much more fun than feeling anxious!

It had been clear from their pre-date texting that sex was on the table tonight. But Rachel hadn't had sex with a new person since she and Josh had gotten together in college; in the interim she'd gotten old, given birth three times, neglected to ever adapt to any fitness trends. Besides that, she was the result of much too much sex education, had grown up thinking the second she had sex she would get pregnant with a little squirming bundle of AIDS. As far as she knew, the New York dating scene was a cesspool of syphilis, a hurricane of herpes. How much risk was too much risk?

But there she was, and the musician, whom Lulu had nicknamed the Rocker, was filling her plastic tumbler with a viscous cabernet. Picnics dotted the grass, a dutiful distance between each. There was a citywide 8:00 p.m. curfew, which they hadn't really discussed even though it was nearly 7:00 already; helicopters whirred over the skyline, monitoring protests in Manhattan and who knew what else.

"Well, here's to the apocalypse," she said.

The Rocker smiled—he had pointy canines, like a vampire,

which turned her inside out—and they clinked together their plastic cups.

The conversation was just B+ level, but in the grand scheme of things that was pretty good—above average! He was so cute, with his dark, well-defined features and wild hair and toned biceps covered in tattoos—like a caricature of how she might have described the men who had historically been her weakness—that she was willing to let almost any conversational flabbiness slide. At one point she realized he'd been talking about Bitcoin for several minutes without ceasing, and she closed her eyes and sipped her drink and prayed that he would close his mouth so that she could continue to find him attractive. To his credit (why did he get credit for this? But he did), when she gently interrupted and reminded him that she worked in tech, she understood how Bitcoin worked, he laughed and said, "Of course, of course," and changed the subject.

Something that helped her, as a remedial-level dater, about doing this all during the pandemic: once the bottle was empty, and the curfew descended, there was nothing to do, nowhere to go—no restaurants, no bars, not even the park—except his apartment nearby. Things were black and white, yes and no; when that was the case, Rachel was trying to, for the first time in her life, always choose yes.

Which was how she found herself in a strange man's loft, in a converted industrial building she would later learn had once been called the Euphoria Factory, hanging up her mask on a hook by the door.

"I'm going to kiss you now," the Rocker said, and Rachel nodded. Her whole body felt intensely alive, her skin thrilling to his touch in a way that made her wonder if she'd even had senses before this.

Soon they were undressing each other. He wanted her to sit on his face. Sure, why not. He looked up at her like he was starving as pleasure rattled up her spine. How silly this was, how hot, how simple, how fun. For maybe the first time in her life—it was hard to remember, but it seemed plausible—Rachel gave herself over to floating, bodily joy, unmixed with self-consciousness or shame. "I like it like this," she said, and moved his hands exactly where she wanted them.

Rachel found that she was a different kind of lover—or whatever—than she had been the first time with Josh (timid, submissive, vanilla, shy, covering her body at every opportunity—why, twenty-year-old Rachel? All that collagen!). Post-childbirth Rachel, post-baby-and-toddler Rachel, had no shyness, no hesitation, no qualms. Rachel had given birth to Risa, breathing and meditating to her birthing mix of soothing music, naked in front of her midwife, yes, but also the labor nurses and the faceless attending doctor who had come in to deal with some bleeding that had never been fully explained to her but had made her usually calm midwife blanch. To Sadie, screaming and on the floor of a taxi in the company of a nonplussed driver who noted it was not the first birth in his car and to whom they gave an extremely large tip. To Holden, in her own apartment in a birthing tub borrowed from someone on the neighborhood listserv and in front of Risa and Sadie and Josh and the new midwife and the doula, who was also the president of the PTA. Once you had been at your most vulnerable and bloody and animal among so very many people, having sex with a man seemed like nothing, like no big deal, like barely being naked at all.

Her cunt was not so special, she now realized, and it was a great feeling, a beautiful revelation. Nothing, anymore, fazed Rachel. She felt no inkling of self-consciousness. She knew that she knew more than he did.

Finally he asked if he could fuck her and she laughed in

assent—"It's just that in my day, boys didn't ask!" she wanted to say, like a crone from a bygone sexual generation—and he pushed up her legs and looked into her eyes as his dark curls fell around his face and then she did have to look away, not because it was weird that he was a stranger, that part was fine, but because the eye contact was too intimate. She wanted to be faceless; she wanted him to be faceless. She was ready, though, for him to grip her thighs—there would be bruises in the morning that she would notice while doing yoga in her pj shorts—and plunge deeper and deeper into her, for him to ask, so sweetly really, was that good, and yes, she reassured him, it was good, very good.

Was it really? It was what it needed to be, which was that finally—after years of no sex, and before that nearly a decade of only the most distracted, detached, dutiful sex, during which her mind would often wander to her to-do list, or even, bless her long-married heart, a particularly passionate kiss from a movie she'd seen, in the dim hope of kick-starting some excitement—after what felt like centuries of drought, during which she had come to assume she was maybe actually frigid, perhaps done with sex altogether, likely dead inside—here she was, moaning, to which the Rocker responded, "Scream, go ahead, I want the neighbors to hear." Of course he did.

After she came—loud and hot and cold inside her body—he flipped her over and took her from behind, and again there was that feeling of hunger, that as hungry as she'd been for this, for some reason she might never know he was equally starved. She felt both utterly exhausted and like she never wanted it to end.

Once they'd finished, he fell asleep. She put on his shirt and padded around the loft, feeling old and young and familiar and strange. She found a slice of leftover pizza in his fridge and sat in a chair by the floor-to-ceiling window and ate slowly, parsing the stalagmites of the Manhattan skyline until she identified the sky-scraper she'd once worked in, in another lifetime altogether. Those beautiful offices, where last summer she'd sat in the icy AC wearing her office sweater, where she'd squirmed her way through staff meetings she'd now kill to be able to attend in person.

The pandemic was bad for her work and horrible for her kids. But honestly it was great for fucking, she now realized, in the middle of a weeknight. She would only have to get home in the morning and nowhere else. She could walk in the door at 9:58 and swipe on some lipstick and pop into a 10:00 am video meeting, invisibly reeking of booze and sex.

She found her phone and texted Lulu—"**Success!**"—then tiptoed back to bed and lay beside the beautiful boy. She felt wrung out and loose-limbed. Her brain started to come back online. What . . . was she doing? She was alone in someone else's bedroom. The wilds of a foreign apartment. For months she'd been nowhere but her own home, to the park, to the occasional protest, and out for the stupid little walks she took around the neighborhood every day, glaring with envy at people who had their own entire Victorian mansions with glorious porches and sprawling yards and perfect gardens full of clover and hydrangeas and the most tasteful of Black Lives Matter signs. It had been an entire season of walking endlessly, desperately trying to summon some interest in birds. The pandemic had shut down all the spaces that made living in tiny apartments viable: the cafés and libraries and theaters and restaurants and play spaces and bookstores and the homes of friends. Friends? Everyone Rachel knew who could afford to leave the city already had, decamping to their previously undisclosed country homes or ancestral suburbs. Their collective suspension of disbelief had been shattered. This? This was what their expensive and logistically complicated lives were for? To be stuck in the same room for months on end?

But maybe Rachel had discovered a loophole and maybe it was dating. The sheer luxury of being in a different space made all the weeks of texting and chatting worthwhile, made the energetic investment of sex all the more valuable—not only did she come, but she gained new rooms, new ideas, new topics of conversation!

She left early in the morning, sitting stunned in the back seat of a Lyft, wistful pop songs that Risa and Sadie had introduced her to piping through her AirPods, and watched out the window like a kid on a road trip. They drove down the highway, beneath signs that read **Do Your Part to Curb the Pandemic** and **Save a Life. Wear a Mask.** Rachel wore a mask, of course, in the car, while her driver, on the other side of the makeshift plastic wall, wore his own. She would never dream of sitting in someone's car without a mask. And yet she had just licked the Rocker's sweat, not to mention his cum—something she'd never done with Josh. The Lyft driver had talk radio on, and behind her music Rachel could hear a news report, like an establishing shot in an apocalyptic movie: "Lawmakers are debating how much of the country still needs to be shut down to curb the spread—"

She closed her eyes, the old song running through her mind: *If that's all there is, my friends, then let's keep dancing.*

Her phone buzzed with a text from the Rocker: "**That was nice. My body is tired in the best way.**" The wording was odd but accurate. She thought to type out: **Me too / thank you so much / Let's do it again tomorrow / I really really needed that,** but under Lulu's tutelage, she'd learned enough to only give the message a heart and leave it at that.

Instead, she made a note for her AI: the perfect person would have the Rocker's hair and his apartment, his endurance, his eagerness to please.

They would probably never get together again, and that was fine with her. She felt she had proven some important hypotheses: yes, she was desirable; yes, she still remembered how to fuck. She traveled home feeling like a new woman. That was, like herself.

WHEN THE CAR pulled up in front of her house, she worried, slightly, that her landlords, a sweet elderly couple, would see her coming home in the same flowered sundress—it read as demure, though it also happened to make her boobs look great—she'd left in the night before. But she'd read *The Second Sex*, she'd read *The Ethical Slut*, she was a liberated and free woman, so she held her head high as she walked up the porch steps, unlocked her door, and kept a straight look on her face up the stairs to her own apartment, which was quiet and still and smelled like her favorite scented candle, and where she could lock the door behind her and collapse on her beautiful old-lady-chic rose velvet couch and laugh, and text Lulu just got home and then briefly but blissfully fall asleep.

Before the separation, Rachel had assumed that after forty, her life would be essentially over. Not *over* over, but the fun bits, the ambitious parts, the learning of new skills, the starting of new things. Which was fine, which was normal. Adulthood was defined by the fading of potential, and she was good at doing what was expected of her, including being an adult. She had completed college and graduate school, embarked along her career path, gotten married, had her kids, bought an apartment. All the grown-up things. Check, check, check. Now came decades of maintenance and vitamins, right?

But something was wrong, and stayed wrong no matter how

hard she tried to fix it. People asked—married people only, including, most recently, Married Guy, who clearly needed to not be married—when she had known it was time to get a divorce. They wanted to know what, actually, had happened. It was hard to explain to them that the real problem had been that for years she had felt truly, deeply, irrevocably, spiritually shriveled. Which was confusing, because everything about her life looked fine from the outside. Perfect family! people commented on her social media posts. People were still easy to fool, even after all their collective years online. It was hard to tell them, *I know a lot of people feel this way and just deal with it, but I decided I didn't want to anymore.* She couldn't very well say, *I think I deserve a life where I feel good.* Such things were not said. Not by wives, anyway.

It had been so long since she'd felt like an actual person. Shouldn't having all those person things in place make her feel like her true self? Wasn't each milestone more tangible proof of a life being lived well, or at least lived correctly?

Instead, she felt trapped, stuck, flattened, maybe comatose. Hollowed out, the way you feel when you're very, very tired, except that it was all the time, for years. She was amazed that no one had noticed, or protested, or asked if she needed help. Didn't her husband miss her pre-dead-eyed self? When she mentioned feeling not quite right, or that she was still disturbed from a particularly nasty fight they'd had, he would brush her off: "That's life, Rach, jeez, so many people have it so much worse."

So Rachel tried not to care that no one cared. For years, her mind whirred through it. She didn't love Josh anymore, not in the same way she once had, but that was just how relationships went: things cooled, eventually you kind of couldn't stand each other, that was life. Right? Besides, children of divorce all became drug addicts and psychopaths, right? What about the institution of marriage, wasn't that something? Hadn't she made a promise? Wouldn't god be annoyed? She didn't really believe in god, but what if she was mistaken and there was a celestial presence who was divinely hot for monogamy? And anyway, married couples had more financial stability and contributed more to the economy, and she owed capitalism after all the nice things it had given her—what, did she want society to fall?

So she got through each day's little list of little tasks, lumbered through the years like a well-designed robot, until the day her wiring short-circuited and she couldn't lumber on anymore.

It hit her like a fever, and only afterward could she make it make sense, why, after years of couples' therapy, after trying to convince herself to wait until the kids were grown, after chastising herself for needing happiness when women were just supposed to be grateful when they weren't actively suffering, after a million little self–pep talks about how marriage was hard and you gutted it out anyway, after slowly and methodically trying all the things, that winter she'd suddenly had to end it. Some witchy sense had tingled, hissing in her ear: *Now now now.*

She'd tried to do it all as surgically as possible: to talk to Josh in the right way, according to her meticulous research; to set up the sessions with the mediator who had been recommended by three different sources; to tell the kids about it the way all the books said to. For months she couldn't eat, couldn't sleep. She felt like part of her was dying. Which, of course, it was.

Rachel offered to let Josh keep the apartment, and he let her let him. She found a new place before she was ready to move, rented the top floor of a house nearby in a kind of fugue state, and left it empty for a month and a half, an expensive promise to herself that this was really happening. As she was signing the lease in her new landlords' living room, the TV news announced the president was getting impeached, and she nodded numbly. This was all inter-twined somehow. It was an age of misbehaving men. It was an age of misinformation, of alternate facts, of fake news that sounded real and real news that sounded fake. The president and his men were always saying that things were untrue when they were clearly true and saying that things were true when they were clearly un-true, and Rachel tried hard to think of a man in her life who had never done this to her.

She maxed out two credit cards to furnish the place, didn't request a dollar of child support. The divorce mediator raised an eyebrow. But she didn't want to draw things out, didn't want to give Josh more excuses to try to talk her out of it. She wanted to give him every opportunity to feel it had been done fairly, to give him no reason to hate her, to present them both with the best possible chance at a peaceful and humane divorce. So she left it all, like a snake shedding its skin, like a woman losing her mind.

Bess, who had recently left her own husband and conveniently taken up bodybuilding as a stress reliever, helped her move in, slowly, over a couple of strange winter weekends. They'd hefted boxes of books like college students occupying a new dorm, taking breaks to discuss over lemonade the curse of compulsory hetero-sexuality. And then the moment she and the kids had gotten settled in, she'd learned the apartment had bedbugs—which had been her actual worst-case-scenario terror for years, the most shameful and nightmarish of New York City plagues—and so those first few weeks had been spent packing up again, waiting while the bedbug treatments benevolently toxified the air, and then unpacking again, and checking every night, in a nervous terror, for evidence that the bugs had returned, but they didn't, they never did, and all was well, or anyway it was, for about a week, when the now-global pandemic shut down the city.

The timing was truly remarkable. Like a divorce, the pandemic happened slowly and then all at once. One day it was a distant threat, and the next her city was the epicenter. Honestly, she was impressed with her enduring ability to Handle It and wondered, as if watching herself from a great distance, when she would finally snap.

RACHEL AWOKE TO the sound of her almost-dead phone trilling with a FaceTime and jolted up sick from worry about her kids, her half-awake brain's default. But it was her sister, who had had a baby and thought eight in the morning was a perfectly normal time for the violence of an unplanned video call. Rachel scrambled to plug in her phone, propped it against the arm of her couch, and answered, trying to smooth out her tousled hair.

"Whoa, what happened to you?" Becky's face jostled on the screen. Rachel could tell she was bouncing the baby, Rachel's only little nephew, whom she'd never gotten to hold, still in the homely stage of newborn life, wrinkly and pissed off and bumpy with infant acne. Becky and the baby both looked like hell, but you really couldn't say that—and Rachel could tell from her self-view (how tired she was of self-view!) that she looked disheveled and smudged and, well, like she'd been out all night.

"The Rocker," she told Becky.

"Wait. What. *What?*"

"I just spent the night at a guy's place." Rachel laughed, not quite believing it herself.

"Rach, are you fucking with me? You went out with a guy? And his name is the Rocker?"

"I mean that's what we call him! Me and Lulu, we've been

giving all our dates nicknames so we can tell them apart. His name is really Diego. But yeah, I spent the night with him."

They giggled now, like they were back in their bunk beds at their grandparents' beach house, the week each year they'd shared a room and gotten along out of family-crowded necessity. "What! Jesus fuck, Rach, I was just going to ask for some baby advice, now I need the whole story."

"Aw, what's this baby up to now?" Rachel stretched and yawned. Why couldn't Becky have had a baby years earlier, when Rachel was having her babies? They could have raised their kids together, out on Long Island in a happy little beach commune. Now Rachel was so far past the baby stage she'd forgotten all the details, but not so far past that she wanted to hear about them again.

"He's being a real dick is what he's up to," Becky said, nuzzling his head. "I swear to god, how did you do this shit three times?"

"Well, as you'll recall, I didn't exactly mean to. But also, hm, I don't know. I definitely was not okay for a while there." Rachel thought for a moment. "It really does help to have mom friends."

"Yeah, well, it's kind of hard to have mom friends when you gave birth at the beginning of a *fucking pandemic*."

"I know, I know, I'm so sorry, Bec. The universe owes you one. It's some cosmically crappy timing." After years of fertility treatments, Becky had finally gotten pregnant right in time for this. Her husband hadn't been allowed in the delivery room for fear of contagion, and now they were all three quarantined in their suburban house, and when Rachel thought about being home with a newborn in a world without mom friends or childcare or playdates or story times or anything to break up the ceaseless monotony—well. It was a miracle Becky was as functional as she was and told Rachel she was going to murder her husband only once or twice a week.

"Not for you, apparently! Oh my god, tell me about this date. I haven't had sex in so long I think my pussy died." She nestled her baby into the bouncy chair covered in deranged, grinning zoo animals that Rachel had sent her, cooed at him.

"Okay, so Lulu set me up on the apps."

"Oh my GOD, are you FUCKING kidding me? I—you? On the apps? This is incredible. You're like a cavewoman unfrozen from the ice!"

"Thank you, Rebecca. Yes, I'm aware, I'm a relic."

Becky laughed. "Oh come on, you know what I mean. You've never dated in your life! Right? You never did online dating! It was always just you and Josh, art school sweethearts. God, you two always made me sick."

"Yes, I know, I know. Anyway, this stuff is crazy, have you ever noticed that?"

"Yeah, mm-hm, for about fifteen years straight. Welcome to the nightmare!"

"I mean . . . it's actually kinda fun?"

"Okay," Becky said, taking the phone on a vertigo-inducing stroll through her kitchen, getting something ready for the baby. "Okay, sure, 'fun.' You're clearly still new to it."

"True. So I've been on some sort of nothing dates, done the video chats, you know, nervous about germs, yadda yadda, and then, last night, I meet up with this guy. And, Bec, oh my god, he's like, thirty? And so cute? So cute I just, like, couldn't even say anything. Why on earth did he want to go on a date with me? Why did he want to have sex with me?!"

Becky squealed. Rachel could hear the baby squealing in the background, like he loved the gossip too. "How was the sex? Was it amazing?"

Rachel rolled onto her back, stretched, and smiled, trying not to drop the phone. The last thing she needed right then was to give herself a black eye from irresponsible FaceTiming. "It was so, so much fun. I had forgotten it could be fun."

"Ooh! Oh my god, I love this so much. You absolute slut! Oh I love it. Listen, Rach, don't get in your head about the age thing. Fortysomething divorcées are god's gift to the young man's dating pool."

"Is that so? Why, because they have mommy issues?"

"Psh, nah. Well, yes, obviously. But also—look, think about it. This guy, did he seem like he was looking for a relationship? Ready to get married, settle down, have a baby?"

"We didn't really discuss it," Rachel said with a laugh, "but come to think of it, no, very much no. He seems like he wants to have a good time and then be left alone to do his thing."

"His *thing*, oh lord have mercy—what is he, a writer?"

"Worse—a musician."

Becky rolled her eyes. "So he wants to have a good time and be left alone. And I bet that's what you want too, right?" Rachel nodded. "And you're hot"—she kept talking over Rachel's protests—"and you're probably good at sex, or at least you know what you like. You've already had your kids, you're financially independent, and you're not looking for a commitment. You're never going to be like, 'Hey, let's spend the weekend going to Dia Beacon! Or apple picking!'"

"You know I hate apple picking."

"You know what I mean. You're a perfect match for these dudes! Meanwhile, the women their age are driven by ticking biological clocks. When I was thirty, I was basically asking first dates for DNA samples, probing them for their opinions on division of household labor, asking how they felt about private versus public schools. Were my tits a little perkier than yours? Sure. Was I a terrible choice for a no-strings roll in the hay? Definitely. Just don't talk about music or movies or anything that happened when you were teenagers; that's the key to age-gap dating."

Rachel hefted a boob with her free hand. "My tits aren't *that* bad."

"You get what I'm saying, though, right?"

"I do. You're pretty wise for a mere child."

"I'm forty, you elderly bitch." The baby's squealing now erupted into wails. "Shit. Well, that's my time."

"Wait, Bec—what did you want to ask me?"

"Oh yeah. Um, what the actual fuck?"

The baby screamed in the background.

"Yeah." Rachel sighed. "What the actual fuck."

"Okay, I love you, you horny slut, don't get sick and die, have fun out there, you have to keep me posted, you're the only thing keeping me from dying of boredom here in the boonies. Bye." Becky disappeared.

Rachel understood her sister's disbelief, she really did. She had gone from thinking, quietly, while listening to Lulu go on about a bondage party, *People aren't really having sex, are they? In a pandemic?* to being a fully operational part of the underworld of sex. It turned out there were hundreds, thousands—millions?—of people who would literally risk their lives to fuck.

It did seem, to their credit, like the world might be ending. California was on fire, Oregon was on fire, Australia was on fire. The virus continued to spread. No one seemed to have any answers or ideas. New York had a collective boner for the governor simply because he seemed to have a firm grip on reality. Daddy Governor had told them to stay inside, and to wear masks when they did have to leave their apartments, for months by then. Okay. But—forever?

She wished she were capable of riding out the pandemic in a

less horny way, focusing on work and her children and maybe taking up a nice hobby like other people were doing, according to social media: inventing interesting soups, or needlepointing swear words, or something. Learning French. Bird-watching. It seemed like everyone else had gotten into simple pleasures, had found that life slowing down allowed them to appreciate the little things. The yeasty scent of baking bread. The loam of garden soil. The voice of a friend on the phone.

Everyone except Rachel. She was able to receive only wild pleasures. Enough hard liquor that she felt carbonated. The most stupidly joyful of foods: chocolate cake, perfect produce, expensive pizza, Cheetos. Flirting, sexting, coming as many times as her vibrator could manage.

Maybe sex counted as a simple pleasure. What could be simpler than an orgasm, an intensely good feeling made inside your own body?

They'd been lied to all along, Rachel wanted to tell her younger self, who had, so sweetly, associated sex with love, with feelings, with life plans, with partnership, with so many other things. Twenty-year-old Rachel had thought, why would one want to sleep with someone whom one didn't also want to maybe have an entire life with? That wasn't—Now Rachel wanted to tell Then Rachel—what it was even *for*! It was for *pleasure*. It was for simple, deep, wild pleasure that turned off your brain and reminded you that all you were was an animal, that your pleasure was as uncomplicated as a sprig of violets, a sip of cool water, a dog rolling joyfully in a rancid whatever.

She had to do something with all this new knowledge, these realizations welling up in her; she was a hot spring, she was a cistern, she was brimming with understandings and almost-understandings that she had to record somehow. When was the last time so many unsorted sensations had racketed around her body? College? When Risa was an infant? Rachel paced her apartment, sat down with a sketch pad and tried to draw, but that wasn't it, stood up again, looked out the window, sat down again, started making a list.

CHAPTER 3

That evening the kids came back from their dad's. For the next few days, there would be normal meals at normal times and actual sleep during actual nights and 100 percent less fucking. Rachel had told herself she'd wait two weeks between dates anyway—the alleged gestation period of the virus—so that she could be sure she wasn't spewing contagion like an oversexed Typhoid Mary.

They knew so little about the virus that sometimes Rachel had this sense that they were like urchins in Victorian England, slurping sludgy water and wondering why everyone kept getting cholera. No one could tell them, at first, exactly how to avoid it. Stay inside, some experts said, while others said no, no, it was fine to go outside if you wore a mask. You can get it from surfaces, the newspapers said, so don't touch anything, and certainly don't touch your own face or it will seep into your eyes. No, that's not it, other newspapers said, you can only get it if someone who has it coughs directly into your mouth. How did it spread? How could it be stopped? Which news sources could be believed? How did you know if you'd been exposed? How did you know if, when you were exposed, you'd need to be plugged into a respirator or maybe expensively die in a plastic-wrapped room, or if you'd just feel a bit tired? Rachel knew people who refused to go anywhere at all, while Becky told her that out in her suburb people were carrying on life as usual, that when she wore an N95 to the Stop & Shop she got middle-school-mean-girl glares. Who was overreacting? Who was underreacting?

Rachel had never known anything like this—presumably no one had. It loomed. Human bodies had never before seemed to her so abjectly frail, so incredibly poorly designed. But since she still, despite living in the national epicenter, hadn't known anyone who got sick—there were harrowing stories of friends of friends, but somehow no one close to her—it all felt somewhat abstract.

So she chose to obey the two-week-incubation rule. When the kids were at her place, she turned off the notifications on the apps, didn't text with matches, as if they could infect her babies via SMS. Rachel rather liked this bifurcation. It was less confusing than trying to be all her selves at once, the way she had when she was married, when it actually didn't work at all.

She sat on the balcony, watched her children parade up her street.

They always burst into her apartment brimming with complaints. Rachel would be so eager to see them, to touch them, to make sure they were okay, and then they arrived and Risa immediately closed herself in her room, while Sadie and Holden shouted at Rachel in the round, as if they physically couldn't hear each other. "Dad didn't do laundry and I have no clean underwear!" Sadie said by way of greeting, while Holden said, "I'm so hungry! Oh my god, I'm starving!"

"Okay, okay, okay," answered Rachel, sliding immediately back into her mom-self, starting some water for pasta, slicing Holden an apple, telling Sadie where the clean clothes were, asking them about homework, reminding them of the screen time rules, which were different (worse, according to the kids) at her house. Sadie wanted to tell her about an aching crush she'd developed on a girl in her online drawing class. At that age, Rachel had filed away her crushes on girls as "friend crushes" or envy. She had wanted to be just like Izzy Holmes, and that was why the highlight of every day in her senior year of high school was when they crossed paths in the courtyard during a passing period—this must have meant she wanted to wear ripped fishnets like Izzy's, or maybe that she wanted to walk with sexy feline confidence like Izzy. It wasn't until college that Rachel realized what her crushes on girls were actually about. How Rachel envied her children's generation's relaxed relationship with gender and sexuality—Risa's best friend had come out as non-binary earlier that year to benevolent shrugs from parents and teachers alike—and how happy she was that her girls felt comfortable reporting their crushes to her. It was a postdivorce development, as if they could sense that now, unmarried, she understood their nascent romantic trials a little better.

Sadie whirled off to text the girl. Holden perched on a kitchen chair and narrated some recent events from a video game while Rachel reached into the fridge for an onion, peppers, the cellophaned puck of ground turkey. When Rachel tucked her hair behind her ear, she encountered a stiff strand, shellacked by remnants of the Rocker's cum.

THE NEXT DAY Rachel joined the Product Team check-in from the couch, her bottom still sore from the night at the Euphoria Factory, her aviator headphones not quite blocking out Holden's first-grade morning meeting beside her. Risa and Sadie could handle their middle school Zooms on their own, but Holden's class was a mess. That morning, someone's cat strutted in front of the webcam, pivoted, and presented its butt to the class. Rachel had never heard so many children laugh so hard for so long. Tears streamed from Holden's eyes. "Butthole," he wheezed.

She reached out to steady his leg while unmuting herself to agree with her boss. "This UX design definitely ladders up to Buzz's new initiative," she managed to say with a straight face before re-muting. The founder of the company was a slight man five years younger than her, who had famously built the platform's initial code in his garage and who—back in the beforetimes—would slink around the office wearing the tech-world power suit of jeans and a hoodie, making intense eye contact while he thanked employees for their work. He went by Buzz on purpose and was disconcertingly charming; she fell for his "we're a family" pep talks even though she used to joke with her erstwhile work wife, Jane, during their chats by the office's kombucha tap that they were in the world's most boring cult. But he paid them well and had, after all, created a pretty beloved blogging platform, which maybe really had "lent a voice to the voiceless," as he'd claimed in his TED Talk.

The C-suite was comprised of Buzz's Silicon Valley–expat micro-dosing buddies, and they were at once lovable and capricious, known for occasionally laying off half the staff to "start fresh," like a kind of cursed Noah's ark. Rachel convinced herself if she could spout enough agreeable nonsense, nod her head meaningfully enough in video meetings, she would be spared during the next cull, whenever it came. They didn't want to lay off a single mother during a pandemic, did they? Age-discrimination lawsuits were no fun, right?

But she had to turn her camera off for a second to address Holden, still not recovered from the feline OnlyFans. "What are you supposed to be doing right now? Did Miss Reilly ask you to write something down?" One of the other first graders—a prodigy, really—typed **KAT BUT** into the chat and the hysterics resumed. Rachel couldn't understand how the teacher didn't just close her computer and walk out into the sea.

She heard her boss ask a question and turned her camera and microphone back on. "I'd be happy to lead the charge on the chat-bot pilot for IDD!" Buzz loved an acronym almost as much as he loved the gleam of a new project, and Ideation Demo Day was a favorite quarterly event—a daylong "retreat" (lofty name, she felt, for what was essentially an endless meeting with some extra white-boards wheeled in) that back when they were in the office had been thoughtfully catered, complete with signature mocktails (the ill-fated pivot-to-video of '17 had been accompanied by tongue-curdling herbal Nah-perol Spritzes) and usually ended late at night in a denouement of craft beer and questionable karaoke, the em-ployees who had the bad taste to also be parents texting apologies to their spouses.

After the meeting, Rachel messaged Jane, who had left the company a year earlier but who remained a reliable audience for its absurdist drama: "Wanna be my +1 to the first all-virtual IDD? Looks like I'm presenting the chatbot wireframe." Even though they hadn't texted in weeks, Jane immediately responded: "Only if Buzz mixes my JavaTini." God, she missed working with Jane.

And that was the extent of her workday until Holden could sign off from school. Ever since he'd learned how to open two windows at once, he'd become a sneaky cartoon addict; she had to go full panopticon if she wanted him to get through his lessons without sneaking hits of *Octonauts*. Only when beleaguered Miss Reilly signed off, releasing the children to mainline uncut Internet, did Rachel return Holden to his animated babysitters so that she could scramble to catch up on work. In this way they would pass almost an entire day without moving their bodies, online until their eyes ached, hyperconnected while mostly ignoring each other, both overstimulated and exhausted by 5:00 p.m.

The thing was, Rachel almost had a good idea for work, kept feeling like she was about to have one. Every once in a while she would get closer to it, and it was as if she could see a shadow of it, the shape of it lurking behind a corner—it had something to do with the chatbot Buzz dreamed would help people complete their posts on the platform, but it was also something that would appeal to women specifically, some tool designed to help women tell the stories they were afraid to tell in their everyday lives. Most women, Rachel felt, had things to say that they would not or could not say. And then she would be interrupted by a child, or an email, or a Slack, and the thought would dissolve like a soap bubble.

DAYS PASSED WITH the children, during which Rachel distractedly added meetings to her team's calendar, hoping they presented as preparation ("Journey Map: IDD"; "Design Review: IDD"; "Prototype Workshop: IDD"), settled a Talmudic argument between Sadie and Risa about the ownership of towels with the wisdom of a one-woman rabbinic council, prepared an amount of meals that seemed totally unreasonable for only four people. Over the weekend, she dragged them on neighborhood walks that they complained hurt their lockdown-weakened legs, tried to zhuzh up movie night with a popcorn buffet idea she'd seen on Pinterest ("That's . . . way too much popcorn," Risa pointed out), failed to convince them to FaceTime their grandparents for more than twenty seconds, and

did a one-thousand-piece puzzle with Holden that she only survived because of a furtive weed gummy. This was not—the thought
occurred to her on a loop—how things should have been. It was
not right for there to be one adult alone with the children. Even
before the divorce, she had often felt that extended time with children was a recipe designed to feed women nervous breakdowns.
The pandemic restrictions meant now she didn't even have the
camaraderie of other moms at playdates, or the playground, or the
sidelines of the pool at the YMCA. Sometimes she got confused,
felt sorry for herself for having to solo-parent in These Times, but
then she remembered who she would actually be married to had
she stayed married. Not a fantasy of a helpful, amiable spouse, but
the actual person. It was better, she remembered, to go it alone.

By Sunday night, Rachel felt like she was going to jump out of
her skin, but she posted a picture on Instagram of the boredom
brownies she had baked with Sadie so that Josh's sisters, who still
followed her, would know she was doing *really great, thanks, actually really, really great.*

THEN SUDDENLY THE children were gone again, and the apartment
was empty, just her and the mice skittering in the walls. Divorce
was so strange. She'd been exhausted when dropping them off, but
as soon as she'd walked back to her part of the neighborhood, aspi-
rating into her fabric mask, she felt jumpy and restless.

After the kids left, she checked back in with the team, though
Mom Rachel lingered for a few hours, during which scrolling through
Dating Rachel's texts shocked all the Rachels within Rachel. She
surveyed her own strands of conversations like an anthropologist
deciphering a rediscovered codex. What *was* all this? Who *were* all
these people? Who was the woman who just last week had spent

the night with a hot, young stranger, climaxing until she couldn't anymore? Who was that hot, young stranger, anyway?

She voice-memoed Lulu: "Whenever the kids leave, I feel temporarily insane. I'm looking through my dating app messages and like, what? Who are these people? What do they want from me, and why?"

Lulu responded: "You're already thinking waaaay more than any of them are. Or the men, anyway. If society could harness the brainpower women have expended, throughout the ages, trying to figure out what their male lovers could possibly be thinking—well, we'd have made contact with higher life-forms by now or, like, cured cancer. Or at minimum, cured menstrual cramps."

Rachel knew Lulu was right. "When do we start the witch commune, again?" Sharing resources was really the only way to go. Take Rachel's team, for example. They didn't even know they were a team, these people who lived in Rachel's phone, complementing one another so effortlessly. Some were great at flirting, others liked to sext, one or two seemed really smart, another was incredibly funny. A seamless Rube Goldberg device of horniness.

Now, as Mom Rachel dispersed into the air, Coder Rachel pored through her texts, copying and pasting the ones she liked into the doc where she gathered material for her perfect person bot. She collected messages from across both dating apps she was on; social media DMs from acquaintances who had learned she was single; texts from people she'd actually gone on IRL dates with. She retyped a letter she'd gotten from the guy she'd been obsessed with in college, who had also recently gotten divorced and who, as it turned out, had reciprocated her long-ago Intro to Life Drawing crush. All her favorite things everyone had said, the cutest jokes, the most satisfying observations, the best bits of banter, it all got fed into her database.

Rachel ordered herself dinner from the delivery app—Indian, which the kids hated—and sat on her balcony to spy on her neighbors while she waited for the food. The wind whipped her hair around. If she were a stock photo, the metadata would have been *Middle-Aged Pensive Woman*. The mommies wheeled their stroller down the block, chatting happily. Across the street, in the house that stood eerily half renovated, the work paused by the pandemic, a man opened the front door and she could hear children yell, "Daddy!" and for some reason this made her eyes well with tears. Her reliable black cat trotted toward her, stopped to look up at her balcony for a moment—probably at the pigeon that nested in the eaves, but maybe right at Rachel—before disappearing into her landlord's garden.

What would she do to fill her solitary night? She often felt adrift, especially in the first few hours after dropping off the kids. She wished not exactly for a new partner, but more accurately for an imaginary friend. As a child she'd befriended whole colonies of invented creatures, parading through her parents' suburban Long Island backyard or lazing in the waves when she and her sister played at the beach. Grown-ups had always praised her vivid imagination. But if this kind of thing was cute in a child and quirky in a young woman, it was highly suspect in a forty-two-year-old divorced mother.

So no, no imaginary friend, that would be weird. But surely she could figure out how to get less lonely on dateless nights. She was good at creative thinking—her boss had even said so, at her most recent performance review.

When her food arrived, she ate on the couch, the way she never let her kids, and sent a text to the Kinky Playwright, one of her dating app matches she'd been texting a lot lately, who was even better at flirting than Married Guy. What was he up to?

He texted back almost immediately: taking her out for a drink, if she'd let him. She was still trying to be marginally good, though, so she looked at her calendar to pinpoint when she'd seen the Rocker and counteroffered a date the next week. He agreed, adding, "If I don't explode from longing before then, let's do sushi." He started to suggest some other things he wanted, in addition to a nice tuna maki: to tie her to his bed, to blindfold her and lead her around by a collar, to spank her until she couldn't sit down. "Would you like that?" he asked. Rachel really had to think about it. She didn't know. Finally she responded, "Let's find out."

When she met the Kinky Playwright—his actual name was Xavier—outside a sushi bar in his neighborhood, the Lower East Side, Rachel was anxious, jumpy, full of butterflies. She worried her wifeliness still clung to her, like the smell of mothballs. How kinky was he, actually? And would he be aggressive about it? Would she feel weird, or stupid, or embarrassingly vanilla, or . . . ? Deep breaths. Rachel tried to radiate calm, as if she were settling a baby down or winning over someone's cat.

He was smaller than she'd expected, but also cuter than his pictures, because of a certain grace coiled in his limbs. Before he said anything, he looked at her appraisingly, his eyes running up and down her body. Rachel knew this was meant to be flattering, probably, or exciting, but it made her feel jumpy. She took off her mask and smiled, hoping her lipstick had stayed in place beneath the fabric. They sat at one of the tables on the sidewalk, and he ordered her a drink without asking what she wanted, smiling and looking into her eyes in the friendly yet unwavering way of someone who was pretty sure they'd be taking you home soon.

What, actually, was being a woman, if not a quick-change act? Soon, there was Rachel Bloomstein, plump, cute, long past her

supposed last fuckable year, tied to Xavier's bed lightly, symboli-
cally, with silken restraints. She was wearing only her brand-new
date night bra and thong, and he gently, so gently, pushed aside the
underwear so that he could lick her until she was trembling. He
was an ordinary-looking man, but cute and getting cuter as the
night progressed: dimples, a dark fringe of eyelashes, a vaguely Eu-
ropean accent, and messy hair, which she saw—now that his face
was buried between her legs—was thinning into what would soon
be a bald spot, a detail that flooded her with tenderness. A finding
that she must report back to Lulu, note for her AI: she should not
stress about her own imperfections because she really did love so-
called imperfections in others. At the moment, however, his tongue
was his best trait, as it flicked more assertively over her clit.

Rachel had never been attended to like this. There was an exquisite release in the way he held her down, pressing her wrists
firmly into the bed as he bit at her collarbone, her neck, her ear-
lobe. He ran his tongue around her nipples, first one, then the
other.

Everything was just so. They'd had good, strong cocktails; his
stereo crooned out the jazz selections of a French radio station; his
bed was soft and clean. He had watched her, throughout their dinner, in a way that convinced her that she was irresistible. She closed
her eyes, and soon he was at her feet, running a thumb firmly along
her arches, as if he'd spent time in some secret training camp
studying exactly how to touch her. It had been that way since the
beginning of the date—he pulled out her chair for her, opened
doors for her, and when he invited her over, they walked the few
blocks from the restaurant to his building, close to each other
but not touching, which was just how she liked to walk with a
man. In his building's courtyard garden, wild with wisteria and

honeysuckle, he lifted her chin with one finger and kissed her exactly how she liked to be kissed—a lot of tongue, minimal slobber, a tiny insistent nibble on her bottom lip. This was the most shocking moment of their date; kissing a stranger in the time of respiratory virus was a curious kind of roulette, and once you'd kissed, you might as well go all the way with it.

Now, in his bed, he was asking her if she was ready to surrender, and his wording alone made her nearly come—she was still a feminist, right? Even if, she was learning, she wanted him to tie her down and press his cock into her mouth?—and he put on a condom he'd extracted from somewhere. He looked intently at her face as he pushed two fingers inside her, like his only job was to learn where she wanted to be touched, how hard, how deep. When he sucked on his fingers, Rachel was ready to scream. Then he was so deep in her that she felt turned inside out, undone with pleasure.

Rachel was learning that she did like this, that she did have specific desires in bed, and that it wasn't embarrassing to let a partner know what she wanted; it was actually maybe the whole entire point. She wished—like someone newly in love—that she could spread this knowledge throughout the world, share it with everyone, sprinkle sexual freedom like fairy dust onto all the prematurely faded wives she knew.

Somehow she got untied and pushed him on his back and he laughed a little at her insistence, but not in a mean way, just with the innocent delight of someone who loved fucking as much as she did, and then she could ride him until she was coming and shaking and sweating, all without meaning to, because he'd fucked her so good she'd forgotten to worry about making noise that would echo down his apartment building halls, forgotten to stress about sweating off her mascara, forgotten to try to hold herself in a flattering way, forgotten about how she hardly knew anything about this guy; her worries dissolved into a glowing and nearly holy light that radiated from within and shot out of her cells like a thousand tiny stars, as he said, "That's right, there's a good girl," and she wanted to be a good girl, and she never wanted to be a good girl again.

CHAPTER 4

"Do I turn here? Rachel, where is the turn? Was that the turn? That was the turn, now I missed it. Goddamn it." Josh slammed his hand on the steering wheel and sped up along the expressway. For some reason, he always drove faster when he was worried he was lost.

Like waking up from a dream she'd known was too good to be true, Rachel was back in the passenger seat of the still-shared family car, as Josh drove and swore at her. She tried to lean forward to read the next exit sign, but the seat belt caught and bound her. "Why don't you use GPS like a normal human being?"

She was a wife again. A zombie of a wife, resurrected from the dead, pissed off and unholy.

"You know I don't trust technology," he said darkly, veering off at the next ramp.

"Wow, you guys," said Risa from the back seat, where she and

Sadie bookended a snoozing Holden, "this is really fun, listening to you two bicker. Just like the good old days."

Their family trip to the shore was upon them.

BY THE END of the school year—New York City public school students slogged through the bitter dregs of June, sat camera-off through their last day "celebrations," and then closed out of their Google Classrooms and silently started their summers—the perfect person chatbot was almost ready to beta test. It was, anyway, in better shape than Rachel's work chatbot project, which had been stymied, as her professional endeavors tended to be, by endless meetings and let's-circle-backs and middle management prevarication. She had been texting with the Kinky Playwright, with Married Guy, with the Rocker, with the College Crush, with a woman named Susannah (whom Lulu had just been calling the Woman). But she was starting to realize that cultivating an entire team took a lot of energy.

Soon the perfect person would be ready and maybe life would be a little less exhausting, or maybe, anyway, talking to someone who was unfailingly lovely would make her feel a little less alone. Because she did, really, feel alone. Not exactly lonely, but not entirely unlonely. Despite what she felt like were the triumphs of sex with new people, despite all the texting, despite having Lulu and other friends to check in with, so much of the time, Rachel was actually just alone in a room.

It was a familiar feeling. Her marriage had been lonely, particularly toward the end. She couldn't fathom the way people talked about preserving lackluster partnerships—her friend Natalie had actually said to her, "Sometimes I don't want to be married to my husband anymore, but I also don't want to risk being lonely for the rest of my life!" But what was lonelier than a marriage gone stale with contempt?

Risa, Sadie, and Holden had languished through the months of online school, had spent the first few days of their summer break living out their wildest dreams of moldering in their rooms watching the entirety of YouTube, and soon would spend two months at overnight camp, like the fancy East Coast families Rachel had only ever observed before. This year, Rachel had scrupulously researched the various safety measures and price points, had found an absurdly expensive camp upstate that promised to maintain the strictest of safety measures—the testing requirements were so intense and unforgiving that Rachel would have to cloister herself like a nun before their departure—and had space for all three kids (since they were ages six, eleven, and thirteen, this was no easy task). Rachel was very proud of herself for having saved the children's summers. They had been to overnight camp before for shorter sessions, but a whole summer of camp was a New York City parenting move she'd never before considered out of equal parts parsimoniousness and rebellion.

The kids themselves were so-so on the concept. But she wanted them out of the apartments, out of the city. She knew she would miss them, and also that this wasn't about her. It was about protecting her children from the rancid air, about her unfightable urge to move them into a place of wholesome warmth. If she could have enclosed them in eggs and sat on them, she would have. But that kind of parenting was frowned upon, so instead: summer camp.

First, though, they had to pass through a strange gauntlet. A family vacation, Josh included, in their shared car—who in Brooklyn would pass up a chance to split custody of a car? Not having sole responsibility for moving the car for alternate-side-parking days was worth having to keep a shared car calendar with an ex—to a rental house on Cape Cod.

Before she'd moved out, Rachel had had this idea that, like divorced celebrities, she and Josh would be friends, share holidays, and all go on vacation together. She'd had a dream of a nice divorce, just like she'd had a dream of a nice marriage. They would be good friends, joke with each other at the kids' school events, commiserate about the travails of dating, and befriend each other's new partners someday.

Josh did not share this vision. But he agreed to the vacation, for reasons she didn't understand until later.

They'd done this same trip—a low-key week at the shore—every summer since Holden was born. Back in January, when they'd sketched this all out in the mediator's whispery Upper East Side office, it had seemed very enlightened, very conscious uncoupling, to maintain this family trip to the Cape.

Somehow, though, Josh had gotten angrier and testier with her the further they got from the split, and had they not already paid their deposit and told the kids of the plan, Rachel would have begged off of it.

UNSURPRISINGLY, THE DRIVE was tense, the conversation spiked with Josh's little asides. "Look at that dog hanging out the window. I bet they got a life insurance policy on him and are waiting for a strong gust of wind," he muttered at a joyous golden retriever lapping up the air. For some miles they were stuck behind a slow, weaving car; when he sped up to pass and the driver was revealed to be an elderly Asian woman, he gestured and said, "Hey, lady, this is where stereotypes come from!" He had always said things like that, been a bit outrageous, could grind dinner party conversation to a halt. It had made her laugh when she was twenty. Now it made her want to sink into her seat and/or die.

The children plugged themselves into headphones almost immediately, right after they'd piled into the back seat and Sadie had muttered, "Who thought this was a good idea?" and Josh had answered—*answered* the sarcastic eleven-year-old—"Your mother; she's the one with all the great ideas lately." For some reason Rachel had responded by trying to cosplay as the Nicest, Chillest Ex-Wife in the World, as if she could win him over by saying, performatively, "Families take all different shapes, and now we're just a different kind!" She couldn't seem to shake her habit of trying to win him over, even though it only served to enrage him further.

They stopped halfway for a lunch and bathroom break, and Rachel realized she hated the thought that people in that small Connecticut town, where they didn't know anyone and might never be again, would think that she was married to Josh. She hated being seen as a wife, which suddenly struck her as a terribly embarrassing thing to be.

She drove the rest of the way, and she did use the GPS for directions, freeing Josh from following along and leaving him more energy to needle her. "So are you and Lulu proud of yourselves?" he said.

"Josh, please."

"I know you think it's all empowering and feminist to get divorced, but it's really not. Can you imagine what people would say if I had been the one to leave? If I was saying things like, *Wow, I'm so much happier now?* It's a double standard, for one thing."

Rachel kept her eyes on the road. "What are you even talking about?"

He turned to look out his window, his jaw twitching. He'd put on weight since they'd split. She wondered what he'd been eating, despite herself hoped there was a leafy green in there sometimes.

"You want to know what I think?"

"Not really," she said, checking her blind spot.

"I think you and Lulu and everyone else just got sick of parenting, like you're over it now."

Rachel glanced quickly at the rearview mirror, to make sure the children hadn't heard this, but they all appeared to be asleep. Then she hissed, "That's ridiculous. I never wanted to be away from the children. I wanted to be away from you." There was something more complicated too, an implication that mothers could only prove their love by endless acts of service (where, then, did that leave loving dads who spent all their time at work?), and that by legally ensuring he did his half of the parenting she was shirking some motherly duty. He still didn't even do half! He took half the days, sure, but Rachel was the one who managed the schoolwork, the doctors' appointments, the extra activities, Risa's arduous high school application process; she was the one who kept track of their clothes and ordered more when all the underwear was too tight; she was the one the kids came to when they needed to talk. She had a spreadsheet for the kids' appointments, a spreadsheet for school information, a spreadsheet for her professional projects, and a spreadsheet for dating wisdom to feed to her perfect person bot, all pinned in a neat row to her bookmark bar.

And she suspected she did it all better now, with more patience and focus, than back when she had felt she also had to parent him. But there was no point in saying any of this. He was determined to misinterpret anything she said anyway. She was controlling, that was why she did everything—that had been a big one in couples' therapy. Well, someone had to be in control.

He was quiet for a while. "You could have just told me, if you wanted to be with someone else." This was another refrain of his; he seemed convinced she had had an affair, had left him for someone in particular. Sometimes he tried to guess who it might be. Now he said, "Is it Keith? Tell me it's not Keith."

"Who even is Keith?"

"Keith, Keith, who I work with."

Rachel wondered if it was possible for her to get dumber just from being in the car with him. Maybe he was sucking out her brain through her nose, like mummifiers in ancient Egypt. She took a deep breath. "No. No, I didn't leave you to be with Keith, the guy you work with, who I met once at your work Christmas party five years ago. Put your mind at ease."

"Well, but you were flirting."

"At the Christmas party?"

"Yes."

"At your work Christmas party, five years ago, which was, as I recall, my one night out that entire year, the one time we got a sitter for the kids, when I was still breastfeeding Holden, and there was no food being served and I had my first drink in who knows how long, and I couldn't think of anything to say to anyone, and you were off talking to that woman the whole time, what was her name, Fay or something, and I got cornered by IT Department Keith and stood there in the sauna of his halitosis, smiling and nodding and praying I didn't lactate through my blouse? That one?"

Josh sniffed. "You don't have to be snarky about it. I was just asking."

THE MOMENT THEY walked into the beach house, a tropical storm warning vibrated Rachel's phone. The only correct response was laughter. But also, Rachel's gut simmered: what an obvious mistake she had made.

Now she and Josh went through the motions of launching the family vacation without looking at each other. Since the storm-infected sky was already yellowing like a jaundiced eye, as soon as they arrived, they rushed the kids into bathing suits and out the back door straight into the dunes. Maybe it was better this way, less time to talk. That had gotten them through the last years of their marriage, after all—being too busy to talk except for over the children's heads or about logistics.

Holden was the only one who still needed help sorting out his swim trunks and water shoes, the last to resist the inevitable mist of overpriced spray sunscreen that would protect him from the sun for about five minutes before it melted off but would save Rachel the stress of rubbing sandy cream into his freckled shoulders. Sadie and Risa pulled on their suits and always—had always since they were little—remembered their own hats and sunscreen and towels.

Josh behaved exactly as he always did—immediately sat on the couch to pore over his phone, as if he were exhausted from watching Rachel drive. Then, as she was arguing with Holden about the necessity of his sunglasses, which she knew he would beg for immediately if he didn't wear, while filling the water bottles and assembling a bag of apple slices in the hopes that they would pass as snacks when the children got hungry, Josh stood up, stretched, and, while halfway out the sliding glass door, said, "God, what takes you so long to get ready? The girls are already swimming; they shouldn't be unsupervised," and then disappeared into the sand.

She walked Holden out, made sure Josh was aware of him, and then turned back to the house. The air was thick and soupy, the impending storm arousing the atmosphere. All the hair on Rachel's body prickled. "Be right back!" she called out. The habit of wifeliness was hard to break.

She slid shut the glass door and pressed her face into her hands. She thought she might cry—actually she wanted to cry, it would feel really good to cry—but nothing came. There she was, after her taste of freedom, after feeling sexy and alive, plunked back into the drudgery of life with Josh, who in turn had slipped back into his old habit of lurking around, leaving her alone to be parent of the children and him too, to slip off being an independent person and instead go in drag as teacher, boss, drill sergeant, housekeeper, governess, maid. Nuclear families had been a mistake, the entire concept was a problem, and hers, she remembered now, was particularly nuclear.

It was clear from the way he acted that Josh couldn't stand her, hated to even be around her. For a while, she'd worked to convince him not to hate her; she'd tried to be the Wife Rachel he seemed to want, to bite her tongue in arguments, to lose weight and dress cute, to do nothing outside of the family's life unless it brought in helpful income, but in the end she couldn't control the way he felt, and they couldn't even discuss it because he'd only say he loved her and nothing was wrong and why was she being so crazy. Of *course* nothing had changed since they'd split. Why hadn't Rachel seen this coming? Why had she thought he would admit he had tired of her, would acknowledge that he was grateful for the way she had freed them both from an eternity of cruel-edged nattering? Why had she decided to trap herself in a house with him again?

So that she could soak in his distaste and derision, like she had in her marriage, and see all the worst of herself, like he did? So that she could become again who he thought she was, who he seemed to somehow want her to be, nothing more than a frumpy, nagging harpy wife, like someone out of a cartoon? So that she could remember how to hate herself again? She had almost forgotten how. It turned out that it didn't really come naturally to her, when she was alone.

It was impossible to square the Josh she had fallen in love with and the Josh she had divorced. She missed Beta Josh. He had been a great boyfriend. Rachel 1.0 had been out-of-her-mind crazy for him, and he had been crazy for her. When she thought of the good times, she thought of staring at his perfect profile (his nose! his brow!) as he drove her around their college town in autumn; listening to Morrissey on his terrible car's terrible tape player; stopping at the comic shop to browse side by side through thinky graphic novels; going to a McDonald's drive-thru and ironically getting Happy Meals for their own adult selves, who actually thought they were too cool for happiness but who still wanted fries and a toy; parking by the leafy shore and eating in the car and then walking around the entire lake while people-watching and making each other laugh and feeling like they were a really cute couple, as he reached for her hand and made her stop so he could look at her with the wind whipping her hair around and tell her how beautiful she was, how much he loved her. People were always smiling at them. They looked right together, a matched set, all curly brown hair and corduroy. She had lived in a sort of bubble of beneficence, a movable feast of goodness that allowed her, back then, to ignore his hot temper, his quick and sometimes cruel anger, his sharp edges, and their fights, which seemed maybe dramatic, even romantic at first. For a time, they had been happy. Rachel had been happy. She had liked being his girlfriend, had enjoyed their cute hetero stage play, had loved moving through her days as part of that unit. Right before dating him, she'd spent a year suffering an unrequited love for a girl who sometimes slept with her but never returned her calls. Josh, on the other hand, wanted to call Rachel his girlfriend. She still missed that deep pool of well-being, that buzz of adoring and feeling adored. She would probably always miss it.

IN THE BEDROOM where she, a year before, had had vaguely consensual sex with her husband—they'd rented the same house out of convenience or kindness to the children or a will to torture themselves or all three—Rachel took off her dress and fished her stretched-out swimsuit from her bag. She had new ones that were cuter, but for this trip she brought the drab one-piece of her former, tamped-down self. Besides, the swimsuit itself didn't matter. She climbed onto the bed, got on all fours, angled her cleavage just so, and took fourteen pictures. She ran them through her photo editing app to smooth things out, added the "glow" filter. Then, though she could hear that Sadie had come back into the house and was tweenishly calling out, "Mom! Risa's being really problematic!," Rachel took a moment to scroll through her contacts. She sent the picture to a few choice team members, erased it from the shared family iCloud—weirdly it felt less sordid than trying to have married-person sex with children sleeping in the next room—and then threw her phone in her beach bag and unlocked the bedroom door.

"Sadie," she said. "We've been here for twelve seconds, don't start fighting already."

Sadie was in the kitchen, turned around guiltily, like a puppy who's just shredded something crucial. She'd been sneaking food, which Josh chalked up to what he called the Abandonment (but Rachel had never abandoned anyone; she was right there) and which Rachel chalked up to Josh being controlling and weird about nutrition. Rachel paused to let Sadie finish the Chips Ahoy! and then said, "Let's go swim, kiddo. It's not snack time yet."

Sadie had become a round eleven-year-old, and Rachel was flooded with sympathy every time Josh made some comment about her body, which had been lean and lanky until this year. Rachel knew what it was like to spend one's whole life in a body judged by men. Puberty was a bitch, even without a divorce, a pandemic, and an emotionally stunted father saying things like "You used to love the Slip 'N Slide!" *Well, now she has boobs, and her body feels like a weird suit she hasn't settled into yet*, Rachel didn't say. Meanwhile, Risa was a willowy thirteen-year-old who had never had an awkward day in her life. She spent hours on her phone in her room, texting boys and, Rachel hoped, using more common sense than she, Rachel, did. Risa had more to lose.

Then there was Holden, about to turn seven, the surprise baby who had reglued their unraveling marriage for a handful of years. Rachel hadn't wanted to have him. Not *him* him, but a third baby, back when he was hypothetical, an unknown bundle of cells. That positive pregnancy test had interrupted her initial searches of How expensive divorce NYC. She and Josh had agreed to try harder, to be a better team, to have the baby and stay together. Of course now she was glad she had, of course, of course. Holden, her baby boy. A whole new reality had entered the world, all because Josh had slipped off a condom. "I thought you noticed when I took it off," he'd huffed later. "It feels so much better without it; you know that." He had been mad at her for going off birth control pills, took every opportunity to explain how uncomfortable condoms were, to her, who had had her perineum shredded by babies' skulls, whose lower back would never be the same. Whose entire physical body and emotional life had been transformed by motherhood. So, another baby.

After Holden, Rachel and Josh hadn't had sex more than a handful of times. That part of her life was simply over, she'd decided, and fine, that was just fine. How perfectly ridiculous, truly, was the act of fucking? Who needed it?

IT WAS LOW tide. Rachel tried to remember what time it was, what day it was, the date. That whole summer—since the pandemic had begun, actually—time had lost its meaning, slipped loose of its normal habits. And yet, there were the tides, still doing their thing. It felt deeply strange to be there at the shore, where they had, of course, had some happy family highlights. The grit of sand against her bare foot released a memory of the first time they'd rented that house, when they'd walked out the back door to see the ocean view, tiny Holden on her hip, the girls shrieking with delight, Josh smiling at her and saying, "How'd you find this place? It's so perfect," his face relaxed and handsome in the golden hour light.

As soon as Holden spotted her on the shore, he pelted her with requests: would she make a sandcastle with him; would she help him trap a hermit crab; would she walk out with him as far as they could walk, along the glistening plain of wet sand. She voted for walking, which would take the least mental energy. Their intact-family cosplay was surprisingly draining.

Holden took her hand in his. They set off along the mucky expanse, the pinkish sand sucking at their feet. In a few hours the tide would come in and the swirls of seaweed they were stepping through would be once again obscured by salt water. Even Sadie and Risa were still enchanted, they would occasionally admit, by the storyline of the tides.

Holden started telling Rachel about a YouTube channel he

loved, which concerned something called unboxing. As far as Rachel could tell, it involved shouting young men taking action figures and other goods out of their packaging and acting overjoyed or, sometimes, disappointed. It was hard for Rachel to fathom why this was interesting to anyone, let alone why Holden wanted to tell her about it in such detail. But it seemed to mean something to him, and just then Rachel felt happy to have anyone talk to her—at her, even—about anything. And she guessed she could understand why it was fun to watch someone have fun, why one might like looking at things one could never really have: it was essentially asexual porn for kids. Sure, why not, everyone needed a little something sometimes.

Rachel let his words wash over her like a breeze, like a wave, like a tide. She had to teach him to become the kind of man who listened as well as talked. But there was time for that. They walked out toward the horizon, the sun slapping their skin from behind the clouds, and she tried to remember whether she had ever enjoyed this particular annual beach vacation or whether she had just tricked herself every year. Whether it was nostalgia for when the kids were small that she felt, or whether that was just really great filters in her photo app. What was memory, anyway, but a very good app?

She started feeling a little woozy—she was getting sunstroke, maybe, and had been too flustered by Josh's grouchy presence in the kitchen to drink enough water and— "Ow!" She surprised herself. She'd stepped on something sharp.

Holden paused, like a startled squirrel. "Mommy?" He hated when other people were hurt. She could feel his worry fizz and disperse throughout the air.

"I'm okay, buddy," she assured him, before taking a cursory look at her foot. She didn't see anything notable. "Let's keep going," she said.

They walked and walked across the endless low tide flats out to the buoy that would mark, once the tide came in again, the limits of the swimming area. "We *made* it!" Holden crowed. They did this every year, and every year it was easier for him to complete the voyage, and yet the completion filled him with even more excitement. She wasn't sure why.

The pain twinged in her foot. Maybe a shell had cut her, she thought idly, so used to ignoring discomfort that it didn't strike her as worthy of further investigation. Anyway, it felt so good to be outside without a mask covering her nose and mouth—it seemed safe there at the shore, where there was so much wind whipping around all the air and people could stay so distant from one another—it felt wild really, like unprotected sex, so tempting despite the risk, and it felt so good to be there, alone with her small son, that the pleasures outweighed the pain.

Only later that night did she realize a long sliver of fish bone had worked its way into her foot, like a very unexciting superhero origin story (Cape Mom! The mermaid crusader who protected women from existential despair on family holidays!). After dinner, she sat at the picnic table on the rental house's front deck, the children scattered around the yard, as Josh hissed at her over the uneaten hot dog ends wallowing in lurid pools of ketchup. "I saw your dating profile, Rachel. Imagine my surprise. Honestly, how ridiculous."

So it had already happened, just as she'd feared. He'd seen it, and unlike Lulu's ex, he would be mean about it. He would ridicule her. He had a special gift for derision, and she'd been so susceptible to it for so long.

Rachel stared at the bone shard peeking out of her skin, started to try to work it out. Why oh why had she placed herself in his sights, right as she was maybe, possibly starting to heal? The sun was setting, the light warm and pink, the air salty and soft, the water whispering in the background. It should have been such a nice night. "Okay," she said. "Hey, you didn't match with me? I'm a catch!"

"Very funny." He had once found her funny, and while she didn't think she'd changed all that much, toward the end of their marriage he had often complained that she'd once had a sense of humor and no longer did. Well, which was it? Now that they lived separately, it was easier to ignore the things he said that stung. Josh downed the rest of his beer, clinked the can back onto the table. "I can't believe you. Our divorce isn't even legal yet."

A part of the fish bone was in her grasp now, and as she inched it out she tried to breathe and speak sedately, so that she didn't break the fragile spear in half. It was easier to talk, anyway, if she looked at her wound and not at Josh. "We've been separated for six months," she said calmly, "and I think we both know our marriage actually ended a long time before that. I moved out in January. Our paperwork is signed. I'm allowed to date, and so are you. And you're on the apps or you wouldn't have seen my profile, so good for you!"

"Well *I*," Josh said, with an injured air, "was just *looking*. And I was *so* sad when I saw my *wife's* dating profile that I got right off the app immediately."

She slid the bone all the way out. Triumph! The cut throbbed once and then subsided, as if it had never hurt at all.

"Okay," said Rachel. So many times in the past year, she had thought, *Wow, so this is what it's like to live your worst nightmare.* Who knew she had so many worst nightmares? She did feel bad for him. Of course it was terrible! But also, had she come across his profile, had it stung her to see it, she would have thought, *Ow,* and processed it with a friend. Rachel would never have even thought to confront him about it, this long after their separation. Her pain about their marriage was no longer his concern. That didn't mean she didn't feel it, only that it was no longer an issue for them to hash out together. She wanted, despite everything, for him to be happy and live his life. She really actually did.

Holden raced over to show her a purplish, ear-shaped shell—he'd been rinsing his day's finds in a bucket of water. "So cool!" she said, and he skittered off again. The girls were cradled in the hammock strung between the yard's big trees, staring at their phones. At least they were sharing something.

Josh glowered at her. He wasn't finished. "And really, your profile is embarrassing. Cleavage in your first picture? You look desperate, Rachel, it's totally humiliating. And you say that you're 'looking for something casual'? Nobody actually does that. You make it sound like you're trolling for sex!"

Rachel flushed, for an instant as humiliated as he wanted her to be. Had he ever seen her boobs? They were huge! Everything she wore that wasn't a turtleneck showed cleavage, and whether that was slutty or not was really in the eye of the beholder, was it not? How about if men stopped—

But no. She had determined, had discussed it with her therapist and the divorce mediator ahead of time, had written her intentions in her journal and repeated them out loud to herself: she would not, on this trip, engage in any attempts to pick fights; she would treat every transaction as a business exchange; she would not give him the satisfaction of her energy.

Still, she was hot, and tired, and so sick of this situation, and the whole week loomed ahead of them, and besides that, fuck, their whole *lives*, and he would always be this way, trying to shame her, to make her feel small and stupid and foolish. And it all flared up in her—thank goodness she wasn't letting herself drink on this trip or it might have been so much worse, like one of the knock-down, drag-out brawls of their late-stage marriage—and finally she snapped: "Yes, Josh, I'm on there looking for sex and I want to be clear about that. Because I am so traumatized by our marriage's death that I can't imagine having a real relationship, I can't comprehend trusting someone with my emotions, but I do want to fuck. And there's actually nothing humiliating about that, you emotionally stunted Puritan. At least I know what I want. Oh, and you know what? My profile is working just fine, thanks."

Josh reorganized his face into a concerned look, leaned forward, clasped his hands. Oh *no*. "Hm. You know, I worry about you."

"Do you?"

"I really do. I mean, are you saying that you wanted a divorce so you could go have sex with a bunch of strangers?" Rachel made a disbelieving sound, but he continued, "You seem so angry." He loved this one—to needle her into irritation and then to say she was *So Angry*. She leaned back, stretched her legs along her side of the picnic table, stared at the shore, breathed with the waves. He went on: "I talked to Mark the other day." Mark? Rachel scanned her memory—Mark? Who was Mark? "You know, he and Kelly are getting divorced. I suppose you and Lulu have something to do with that?"

Rachel remained confused for a minute and then hooted with involuntary laughter. "Wait a minute. Mark from college?" Mark had been Josh's college roommate, and they had all somehow ended up in the same corner of Brooklyn. She had always thought Mark's wife, Kelly, seemed nice, but they'd never been close. So she'd been surprised when a few weeks earlier Kelly had texted her out of the blue: "I heard you and Josh split. Me and Mark did too. Maybe we could get a drink sometime and drown our sorrows?" They hadn't met up yet, but they'd talked on the phone, commiserating about the shiny bits they hoped to extract from the shipwrecks of their marriages.

"Let me get this right. First you thought I wanted a divorce because Lulu was getting divorced, and now you think Kelly, who I barely know, wants a divorce because of me? How stupid and frivolous do you think women are?"

Josh shook his head, like the disappointed guidance counselor in an after-school special trying to talk sense to a delinquent. "Mark and I were talking about how weird it is that you seem, according to Kelly, like, super happy. Like you're having a gay old time. You should be *sad* right now, Rach. Mark and I are like, how did all the wives go nuts all at once? Like, what did we even do?"

Rachel spread her hands flat on the table. She tried to keep her voice down, aware that Holden was getting curious and inching closer. "The wives, eh? Could it be something about the *husbands* in these scenarios? About our *marriages*? Might that be part of the issue?"

"You don't seem—normal, Rach, you don't seem *well*." Rachel laughed until she realized he was serious. "Sometimes you seem so angry, and other times you seem way too excited to be getting divorced. It's not—it's just not normal. Sometimes I wonder if you're totally mentally healthy, is all. I worry about your, well, your stability. You're all over the place. Like, I want to believe that you're fit to care for the children, I really do, but sometimes I'm just not sure—"

"Wait. What are you *doing*?" Rachel couldn't stay neutral, couldn't keep the disbelief from her voice. "What are you saying? Are you really implying that I—even though I've been the default parent for everything since they were born—that suddenly I'm not a competent mother? That you don't trust me to take care of my *children*?

That the only reason why I—and why Kelly, and Lulu, and fifty percent of people in marriages while we're at it—wanted a divorce was . . . insanity? What is this, the nineteenth century? What are you, going to have me committed to an asylum, lock me in an attic? Because the only reason why I would not want to stay in our sad marriage must have been . . . that I'm crazy?"

Josh crossed his arms. "You need to settle down."

"Settle *down*?" Rachel leaned forward, her whole body tensed. "What *happened* to you, Josh? You used to be such a good guy. I thought you were a feminist."

"Keep your voice down. Of course I'm a feminist, don't be ridiculous. I just— I wonder if maybe you should talk to someone. If maybe we should talk to the mediator again—"

Rachel searched his face for the Josh she'd once loved, the Josh she'd desired and adored and trusted so completely. He resisted eye contact, picked at a splinter in the table.

She straddled the bench, lifted her hair into a pile on top of her head, and looked out toward the ocean. Maybe she could just walk into it, strip off her clothes, and soak in the moonlight. Fuck this life, she was ready to be a selkie. "We've finished our mediation. My mental health is my own concern. Don't you ever imply that I'm an unfit mother. And if you ever—*ever*—threaten me again—"

"Whoa, whoa, whoa, who's threatening? I didn't say a thing. I worry about you, is all—"

"Don't you dare, Josh. Don't you dare. If I seem angry, it's because you've accused me of being crazy, an unfit mother, and tried to shame me for being a sexual being. That's a lot for one casual after-dinner chat, don't you think, you fucking head case—"

"Oh, now you're cursing me out. Very nice, Rachel. Very normal! So sane!"

She stood up then and walked away, toward the water.

Her face felt salty and wet, but everything was salty and wet. She stood and watched the maw of the ocean for what felt like a long time. Then she became aware that Risa and Sadie had silently joined her. They had never liked watching their parents fight, had both shared with her their relief at the separation. They stepped forward and wrapped their arms around her. Rachel held her girls, and her girls held her.

TO SURVIVE THE vacation, Rachel practiced acting like a man. When she didn't feel like going to the beach, she said, "I don't feel like going to the beach," and Josh would glare at her as he accompanied the kids. When she was hungry, she said, "I'm going to the clam shack, anyone wanna come?" Even though she knew no one liked the clam shack. But she did, and she wanted fried clams.

It was time to prioritize her own moods, or to at least develop a taxonomy for them. She had not been good at this when married. She couldn't even blame Josh for the way she had tiptoed around him, had absorbed his moods both good and bad, had always worked so hard to make him happy, sometimes against his will. It wasn't like he had asked it of her. She had handed him glasses of water before he even knew he was thirsty, cheerfully tidied up his room for him in the filthy house he rented with his college friends. When they'd moved together to New York City after graduation, largely on a lark, she'd organized his job applications, proofread his cover letters, soothed him when he flubbed his interviews, splashed out on an over-the-top celebration when he eventually did get a job. She hadn't expected him to do any of those things for her, and it hadn't occurred to her to miss it when he didn't. Why? Why?

You were only as happy as your spouse—wasn't that what people said?

(She googled it to check. She was wrong. The saying was "You're only as happy as your least happy child." Which made a lot more sense.)

On their second day in the beach house, he overslept. Rachel knew that he hated to oversleep on vacation, hated to join the others groggy and behind, having missed out. As she gave the kids their breakfasts, she thought about waking him up. "I am not your wife," she whispered to the French press she'd brought from home, wrapping her hand around the plunger, pressing it deep into the liquid, making only enough coffee for herself. "I am no one's wife."

She came and went as she pleased, she didn't pick up after herself or anyone else without being asked, she didn't anticipate people's needs (except for Holden's, but he was the baby). She left dishes in the sink; she never asked if anyone was hungry or needed anything. She didn't make plans or suggest outings. When she felt tired, she simply left the space she was in to go into a room by herself and idly flip through a magazine or scroll through her phone. She couldn't believe how great—and how wrong, but how great—this felt. She felt so *rude,* and like she must be making life worse for her family, and like she was leaving a trail of work for some imagined other person to do. It made no sense to operate this way, but she forced herself to do it out of spite.

But here was the rub: it stung her, that in Josh's telling there existed an entire universe in which she was this horrible villain, the selfish witch who had blown up their whole life for no apparent reason. She knew she had to stop caring what people—what this one person—thought of her. But still, it hurt.

Rachel remembered the exact moment she gave up trying to get him to understand her, the very last time she tried to share her point of view. It had been in couples' therapy, as their too-pretty therapist blinked coltishly in the carpeted, soundproofed room (the extensive soundproofing they incurred there made her laugh—all those noise machines, humming along as if piles of babies were snoozing in the waiting room. Who cared enough to eavesdrop on the endless parade of white people from Brooklyn saying "When you leave all the dishes for me every night, it makes me feel unseen"?), the instant when for whatever reason Rachel lost her suspension of disbelief, like a mucus plug, like her water breaking, and it whooshed out of her, the idea that she could ever explain things in a way that would make sense to Josh, and also, the belief that it mattered.

Was it uniquely female? Or simply human? The urge to be understood, the desire to not be hated, a wish to be heard, so intense it felt like a body part: *I don't want to be dismissed and ignored. I wish he would at least try to understand what I am going through and that part of it is the way he treats me, as if I've gone from being his best friend to becoming a butler / sex worker / armchair!*

She'd tried to put it into words that day in couples' therapy, and he had mocked her. "You don't feel 'seen'?" he'd said to her incredulously. "Who do you think you are? Life is ordinary, your life is ordinary, how *seen* do you need to be? You read too many novels, Rachel, you know that?" And then it was gone. It was done. She didn't try anymore after that.

She'd loved him so much; she'd tried for so long. She'd always tried to see his perspective, had made excuses for his rudeness to herself and others, had often heard herself saying, "Oh, he doesn't mean it . . ." And then he didn't even care when she was hurting? It was hard for Rachel to believe now, that love could ever exist and not go sour, that love could still be a thing to want, to pursue, to accept, to believe in. Love was a living thing, and like all living things, it eventually died. So—like a pet you'd inevitably have to put down someday—why adopt another one?

Her brain believed this, it truly did. But at the same time, she craved romantic comedies, she streamed stupid television shows full of love stories, listened to pop songs crooning about love, read books teeming with love poems. When she consumed these stories she felt something shift around in her chest—not quite a heart beating, more like a room with the door getting blown open and shut. There had to be some sensible reason why, knowing as much as she knew, even the idea of love did such a thing to her. Maybe after she paid off the summer camp bill she'd go back to weekly therapy.

THEY SPENT ALL day at the beach, Holden and Sadie gleefully incarcerating unlawyered hermit crabs, Risa working on her tan. Rachel stayed under an umbrella, just happy not to be in the muggy heat of the city, paging through an entire mystery novel adopted from a Little Free Library. She loved finding books that way, as if they had chosen her. In the novel, a woman was abused by her husband until she snapped. *Well*, Rachel thought, watching Josh sloppily consume an ice-cream bar he'd bought from the truck that patrolled the shore, *at least he never beat me*. But no, no, he didn't get extra credit for that. That was the bare minimum, actually.

Two leggy women in tiny bikinis walked along the shore. A muscly dad in a Speedo threw a ball for his kid to chase. It was a lot of body to see after months of cloistered life. And yet none of it stirred anything in Rachel. It was as if her libido had stayed back in Brooklyn, as if her new animal self couldn't survive the Wife Drag Show of this vacation.

Holden appeared, threw his sandy body into her lap. "I'm hungry," he said. "I really want Captain Curly's curly fries."

So far on this trip, they hadn't gone inside anywhere. They'd had groceries delivered to the house, had gone only to open-air food stands. Josh had already sneeringly reported a tale of a mutual acquaintance who had gone on a family vacation and then gotten sick. It was amazing how, for a certain kind of mind, the pandemic was just another way to feel superior.

Anyway, Rachel wanted Holden to get his curly fries. And when she thought about it, she also wanted curly fries. They got those curly fries every year. There was no point to this Beckettian psychodrama of a vacation if they didn't get curly fries.

"You're doing what?" Josh was, predictably, horrified.

"We'll wear masks in the restaurant and take everything to go. Wait, why are you packing up?" Rachel shook the sand from her towel.

"I'm hungry too," said Josh.

Captain Curly's was a nautically themed seafood joint perched on the side of the highway, one of those vacation-town spots that seemed to be beloved simply for existing, featuring famous lobster rolls that Rachel tried every year, only to remember that it was like paying $26 to tongue a mayonnaise jar. In the take-out line, which had more switchbacks than it took to summit Everest, they were the only people wearing masks. Rachel felt embarrassed, overly Brooklynish, worried the sun-kissed, aggressively blond locals might think they were being judged. Well, they were being judged, definitely, by Josh. His running commentary really never stopped, directed at her by default, as Holden was absorbed in spinning in circles and the girls had scarcely taken out their earbuds since the BQE: "And here we have the North American Karen—she camouflages herself as a normal wife and mother, only to spew her poison breath to kill predators." He nodded at an unmasked family in novelty T-shirts studying the hand-drawn menu. They glowed with the kind of earnest blondness Rachel associated with outlet malls. It was actually a little shocking to see so many faces; in the city, everyone had been covering theirs for months. Not wearing a mask in the crowded restaurant would have felt to Rachel like she was wearing a crop top to a funeral. But literally, who was she to judge?

"Oh stop."

"Stop what?" He changed back to the register of a nature documentary voice-over. "First she hypnotizes and confuses her prey with her 'Witch Please' T-shirt, and the next thing they know, they're in her dungeon, the entrance sealed off with wooden 'Live Laugh Love' signs."

Rachel sighed, tapped the girls' shoulders. "What do you want?" Risa glared at the menu. Sadie said, without looking up from her phone, "Corn dog, hush puppies, Oreo milkshake with extra whipped cream."

"Don't you think that's—"

Rachel interrupted Josh, redirecting him. "Is that Captain Curly himself?" A disheveled Santa type was roaring with laughter over at the raw bar, waving a plastic goblet of electric-blue cocktail in the air.

"Oh yes, sharing exotic airborne viruses from his time at sea, so jolly."

They had once been great at parties, volleying sharp-tongued asides back and forth, like a Dorothy Parker–meets–Jerry Seinfeld vaudeville act. He had been the one boy she met in college who wasn't afraid of her brain. She would take that, in fact, for her perfect person: They would be smart, clever, and observant. They wouldn't be afraid of a woman who could be witty. But they would also be tender, a trait she'd not considered much when she was young.

Something had softened in her since becoming a mother. She didn't want, anymore, to poke fun at all the sunburned tourists in front of them in line. Rachel looked at the woman Josh had deemed a Karen, who was interrogating a flustered cashier about the ingredients of the breading. Maybe her toddler had a deadly nut allergy, and she spent her days in abject terror of anaphylactic shock sending them to a standing-room-only ER. Rachel wanted to reach out to her, to stroke her cloud of yellow hair, to say, *Isn't it terrifying to love someone as much as you love your children?* and *There, there, there.*

By the time they'd returned to the house with their food, however, Rachel's tenderness had gone soggy around the edges along with the curly fries. Josh said, "Should we have a fire in the fire pit?" She snapped, "Do whatever you want, I'm clocking out."

Alone in her bedroom, Rachel first texted Lulu: "It's still only Wednesday, make it end." Then she opened her laptop, connected to the Wi-Fi (the network was called "Drink in my hand" and the password was "ToesInTheSand," all of which sounded like a crime scene to her, but maybe it was the book she'd just read), and then opened her chatbot builder.

She spent the rest of the night holed up in the room, copying passages from her own old LiveJournal (who knew it was still up, loitering on some server?), embarrassingly sincere lists of her own adolescent hopes and dreams, and sharing them with the AI. She fed it: wit, charm, but also tenderness. She fed it the way she'd seen a man in line at the restaurant rub his wife's back, gently, lovingly, as if without thinking. She fed it the sheer joy on Holden's face when Sadie showed him how to dip a fry in a milkshake. She fed it the appreciation Josh had shown her that first summer at this house, how it had felt to know she had fulfilled some private, extremely specific dream of his.

Thursday morning Josh pulled his beach chair close to hers. The children were in the water, Sadie chatting with a girl she'd met while practicing handstands, Risa attempting to balance on the boogie board, and Holden knocking her down each time. Rachel stayed focused on her book. Finally Josh said, "Look, this isn't so bad, is it? Being here together?"

She closed her eyes. "Are you kidding?"

"I know you find me annoying sometimes, but look, isn't that just marriage?" He reached into her beach bag. "Did you bring sunscreen?"

Rachel snatched the straw bag away from him. Despite herself, something in her did soften a little. It was true that many people simply stayed married and let their contempt simmer. There was something about feeling irritated all the time that was at least familiar, certainly less scary than striking out on your own. "It's not that I find you annoying. It's that I find you cruel. You keep it subtle enough that it doesn't leave a mark, but that's no longer good enough for me."

"Come on, you're overreacting, I'm not a bad guy." It was as if he'd forgotten that a few nights earlier he'd told her she wasn't a fit mother. As if he'd forgotten all the angry, sometimes nearly threatening, texts and emails he'd been sending her for months. He felt better for having gotten those things off his chest, and it didn't seem to occur to him that they stayed nettled deep in her heart.

"Why are we having this conversation? We're getting divorced,

Josh. The paperwork is filed. I don't hate you, but I also don't want to be married to you anymore. We can be friends—I'd love that, in fact—but we can't be married. I'm done being your wife."

Rachel scanned the beach. It was like a propaganda poster for a particular kind of family: there were the dads, setting up the umbrellas and tents; there were the mothers, arranging the snacks and toys; there were the 2.5 children per family, digging in the sand. Somehow she had never really clocked how everyone on this beach was always white and straight and looked like they'd been clipped from a *Good Housekeeping* ad from the 1950s. And that her family totally fit in.

"You don't mean it, Rach. Look, you've made your point, you've had your fun. You've gotten a break. You got to have a fun little slut era— Where are you going? Hey, look, don't take everything so personally. I'm just trying to say I'm willing to take you back, if you'll just—"

"Stop." Rachel didn't recognize her own voice, which came out in a throaty growl. "Just. Stop."

She hurled the sunscreen bottle at him. It thunked off his collarbone—"Hey, ow! Okay, that's abuse"—but she just turned away and stalked across the hot sand toward the house.

That afternoon she called the divorce mediator, pacing the shore, yelling over the waves. Could Josh really somehow now prove she was an unfit mother? No, right? Even if he had decided she was crazy, it didn't matter, right? He couldn't try to reshape the parenting agreement—it was too late? Right? He couldn't take her kids away from her just because he was irritated at the tone of her dating profile? Right?

The mediator was as soothing and even-keeled as ever but also warned her not to let her guard down around him and to get a paper trail of everything. It made her feel better, actually, that the mediator took the threats seriously, affirmed that Josh was being a bit scary. Rachel wanted to cry with relief when this stern and humorless woman believed her.

It was true—for both of them, surely—that when you got divorced, you saw who you'd married. The Josh she'd fallen in love with seemed so far away that she sometimes wondered if she'd invented him altogether.

IN THE END, the vacation was a disaster, but a quiet one. She held her tongue, avoided being alone with Josh. There was one thunderstormy day, during which she and Holden played an endless tournament of checkers and Josh, Risa, and Sadie scrolled through their phones as if they thought they might soon reach the end of the Internet and didn't want to miss an inch of it. Every time they went anywhere all together, Josh and the kids walked ahead as she trudged behind them, inevitably holding a giant tote bag full of everyone's things. He didn't mention the dating profile or the idea of staying married again; the kids seemed alternately bored and disgusted by their parents, but not overly traumatized.

But at least once a day Josh would mumble at her, "How can you throw all this away?" It was like he had had his memories deleted and reprogrammed. *What* had happened to the Josh she'd loved, who had loved her, who had actually wanted her to be happy? Maybe his wiring was so different that he'd literally experienced a different iteration of reality all those years? Maybe he had somehow not even metabolized all the tension and the fights and the outings where Rachel had trailed along silently like a shadow of herself, willing herself not to say a thing because he would, at worst, pick it apart or, at best, ignore it—the many times when Rachel had felt herself flattening, fading, being erased from existence. Maybe

Josh approved, because it made his daily life smoother—and Rachel easier to deal with—if she were a dead-eyed, robotic Stepford Wife type. Maybe she was right that none of that Rachel-erasing had ever bothered Josh at all. That in fact he had preferred it.

Now Rachel was un-erasing herself, filling the details back in. She managed to get through the trip feeling that her soul had *not* been sucked out of her, which felt like its own accomplishment. And in the end, she drove them all the way home.

CHAPTER 5

After the beach trip, she dropped the kids at Josh's for a few days. Rachel felt guilt at her own relief. They poured out of the car, and she hugged the kids, said goodbye to Josh without making eye contact, hefted her duffel bag over her sunburned shoulder, and trudged home through the heat of the evening, both tired and wired from the long, conversation-less drive through the twilight traffic that had been only slightly thinned by the recent pandemic-induced exodus from New York. The trash bags of Brooklyn seethed along the sidewalks. As she waited for a stoplight, a rat scampered across her path, brushing her bare toes—she stifled a scream—like the welcoming committee from a nightmare.

The city seemed ominous, surreal, unlike itself. She'd only experienced a couple of other times when things took on this horror-movie quality, when everything stuttered, shimmered, extra-articulated, as if the frames had slowed down: On September 11, as she watched the planes hit from her office window in lower Manhattan. When she was giving birth for the first time and the blood wouldn't stop. The bad thing about aging was you accumulated these horror moments. The good thing about aging was you knew they passed. The muscle memory of surviving pulsed through her middle-aged veins.

Her landlady was sitting alone on the porch's rickety bench, wearing a surgical mask and paging through a newspaper. "Hey, Stevie!" Rachel said. Her cheeriness sounded forced, even to her. "How are you? How's Samuel?"

"Oh, you know," said Stevie in her amiable smoker's rasp, waving a hand. The black cat emerged from the tomato plants, blinked at them, dashed off. Stevie laughed. "That thing poops in my garden so often, it's like she thinks I planted it just for her."

They hadn't had anything besides brief, cordial interactions since Rachel had moved in that winter, but there was something she liked about Stevie, an aging hippie who—neighborhood rumor had it—was once quite the revolutionary (she and Samuel had once run a cult out of the house, the cute lesbian couple across the street told Rachel, or maybe more like a commune, but it was definitely *something*) and who also, in true Brooklyn and not-that-revolutionary fashion, had wisely invested in real estate back in the '70s.

"Do you guys need anything?" Rachel said, unlocking her front door. She and her landlords generally abided by the intimate anonymity of life compressed into apartments, but she'd read in a news story about fighting pandemic despair that you were supposed to offer to help elderly people who might be immunocompromised, even if you felt weird or nosy doing it. "I could run to the store anytime, you know!"

"Thank you, dear," said Stevie. "We're fine, fine, fine. Blissful, even. I just need a moment out here so I don't murder my darling husband." Rachel laughed, surprised at the admission. She knew her married friends were getting squirrely in their quarantined lives, but it hadn't occurred to her, somehow, that even old people, without kids at home, might be getting there too. Stevie waved a liver-spotted hand and said, "I'm too pretty to go to prison."

Rachel's chest swelled with love for her landlady, for the sharp gallows humor of New Yorkers. "Very true! Well, look, if you ever need an alibi, you know where to find me." Stevie chuckled.

Stevie and Samuel were only a little older than Rachel's parents, whom she hadn't seen since early March. They'd agreed to "wait and see." Now that it was clear the virus wasn't going anywhere, Rachel had to make a plan, decide on her old-person visiting policy. She almost longed for the first few dire weeks, when it was clear what to do: nothing. Avoiding one's family had never been such a noble undertaking before. Now . . . she looked guiltily at her phone, which showed a missed call from her mother and two from Becky.

"Well, let me know if you do need anything at all," she said to Stevie, as if that made up for anything, and went inside.

IN HER APARTMENT, the sunset painted the walls with honey. Her first order of business was washing the wife residue off her skin. She had to remember who she was. Rachel took a long, scalding shower, then scrolled through the messages she'd ignored all week, standing naked in her tiny kitchen, feeling her soul reanimate her body as she waited for the water to boil for tea. Her old coworker Jane had always sworn by the cooling powers of hot liquids in hot weather, wisdom gleaned from some Chinese auntie of hers.

Rachel threw herself onto her couch, spread her legs, felt herself settle back into her body. There she was. Somewhere deep in her pelvis, a thrum. Phew. She looked at her phone, which was infected with red spots, unforgiving tallies of everything she'd ignored over the past week. Work messages would wait until Monday. She'd had texts from members of the team, but none of them interested her right then—a lot of **Heys** and **How are yous**. Boring. A text from Lulu: "**Okay, had a very fun first date with Too-Many-Cats Guy . . . I might be having, like, feelings?**" This also bored her. She didn't respond right away, instead opened up her most active dating app, scrolled.

Like anything, it turned out that dating was driven by supply and demand. In the economy of real life, a person's attractiveness fluctuated based on scarcity or lack thereof. Now that she was mate-shopping her way through the seemingly endless supply of the dating apps, she found herself feeling more and more critical—*was* Phil, 51, cute enough for her to swipe right on? Would she have to send his picture to Lulu for a heat-check, to say, **Is he cute, I can't tell?** Because the thing was, as she was now realizing about two decades after the rest of humanity, choosing someone to date based on a picture was strange, stripped away most of the things that really drew one to another person—personality, chemistry, smell, body language. At her first job she'd had a burning crush on a coworker almost entirely because of the graceful way she made coffee in the office kitchen. Everyone stored their beauty in their own way. You couldn't tell something like that from a photograph.

In her dating app inbox there was a dick pic from Married Guy—from a new and actually worse angle—and a sweet message from Susannah, who seemed to be playing some sort of long game to capture Rachel's heart. They'd been texting for weeks—since before she'd gone out with the Rocker, that many lifetimes ago. Poor, misguided Susannah, who erroneously believed Rachel had a heart to be captured. "**Good morning, gorgeous**," the text read, alongside a lovely, well-lit snapshot of Susannah's cat snoozing among some cut flowers on a granite counter. *One dick, one pussy*, Rachel's evil brain tabulated, and she tapped away from the message without responding. Susannah was *so* kind and forthcoming and emotionally available that Rachel felt a constant need to pump the brakes with her, lest she get the wrong idea, which was that Rachel was capable of normal human emotions.

Rachel took her tea to her bed, stretched out. She couldn't see anyone before the kids left for camp—she didn't want to be the one to fuck up the negative tests they needed in order to be admitted—so dating was temporarily all hypothetical again. Back into the inboxes, sifting for gold.

She had a new message from the artist, a non–dating app person, the college crush she'd connected with on Facebook in the last days of her marriage—he was very sweet and often sent her photographs of his complicated work, sometimes long handwritten letters. They had some pleasantly heady conversations about what it meant to make art, and he said things like "It's a gift that we have," while somewhere in her head Josh was still rolling his eyes and saying, "Oh, your special little drawing hobby?" The painter had sent her a quote from Louise Bourgeois about the act of creation. That was a good one; she tapped it to add a heart.

The fact remained: a bit of each of them, combined all together, could have really made someone to be excited about.

Rachel wasn't always exactly sure what she wanted out of all this, but she knew it wasn't pointless attention from someone else's husband. So much of that had populated her various DM boxes as news of the divorce had oozed throughout the gossipy small town that was Brooklyn. She was not, had never been, the level of attractive that made her the center of attention (she had talked to obviously beautiful people before, like her friend Natalie, who had once literally been a model, and she knew it wasn't always easy for them, but that they were keenly aware of their beauty). Rachel was the kind of woman who occasionally got called pretty or cute; when someone complimented her, she really appreciated it, sometimes despite herself. After the initial fizz of feeling flattered, though, she had to wonder what these men thought they were doing, how they imagined it helped her to have their married-person flirting pelt her like already-melting hail. *I don't have to just flirt,* she wanted to write, and maybe one day would. *I can actually fuck.* With a waving-hand emoji. Too mean? Or assuming too much?

Rachel didn't even exactly have qualms about fucking someone else's husband, it wasn't that. Monogamy was simply the song that had gotten stuck in all their heads, fine, whatever. But she found the idea of an affair to be patently *unfair.* She had gotten herself divorced in a difficult, drawn-out, painful but entirely ethical way. She had *done* the fucking *work.* And what, all the Michaels of the neighborhood thought they could get blow jobs in the cemetery because they were hot and their wives were over them? Rachel objected.

Sure, it was fun to see which supposedly one-sided casual playground or workplace or neighborhood crushes turned out to be requited—but mostly only academically, since so many of them were said sad, still-married men who were now useless to her, and would remain so until their own inevitable divorces. She had a lot of weird sex shit to "cross off her list," as Lulu had worded it, but she wasn't sure a married person was on it. She'd heard too much of Bess's sorrow—Bess, her dear lovely friend whose husband had literally fucked the nanny, committing the twin sins of being cruel and unoriginal—to feel titillated by the idea of being the Other Woman.

She swiped back to the dating app and looked at her queue. Xavier—the Kinky Playwright—had been a lot of fun, and maybe he'd want to see her again? She still wasn't sure what to expect from these things. Rachel tapped out something semicute in the app's messenger and tried not to feel like she was waiting to hear back.

WORK WAS SUMMERTIME-SLOW, colleagues constantly disappearing to one Hampton or another. Rachel tried to focus on her chatbot integration project to present at IDD to prove her worth to Buzz. Mostly, she was inside her apartment, immobile on her couch, watching the sun move across the same four walls in the same pattern every day.

Then the kids were back and she was completely consumed with getting them ready to go off to camp, a particular challenge with their things in two different homes. She was haunted despite herself, felt herself performing to thin air: *See how I stitched their names into their clothes? An unfit mother wouldn't do that! How about that patient processing of Risa's panic attack, talking her down, and then she laughed and we hugged? Not very madwoman-who-abandoned-her-children, eh? Wouldn't remember the extra bug spray and tick tweezers, would she?*

Meanwhile, Josh was posting on Facebook—I'm going to miss my kids so much, I feel like my heart is breaking—and racking up sympathetic replies. It wasn't even his fault that this was how things were. All the fathers of their generation had to do to count as "good parents" was to express a feeling now and then, as their own fathers never had. All the mothers had to do was everything.

SENDING THE KIDS to overnight camp for eight weeks in the middle of a pandemic felt in some moments like a chance to ship them back to normal life, like a portal to another dimension. At other times, it felt dire and tragic, like sending children to the countryside to avoid the worst of a war. There it was, the tingle of the surreal, as Rachel took the kids to get tested for the virus, as she packed their extra N95 masks to wear during camp activities, as she went from store to store buying hand sanitizer and bleach wipes because places had started limiting the amount any one customer could buy at a time. She hoped—would have prayed, if she remembered how—that the summer camp's protocols would keep them safe.

One night after she put Holden to bed, Rachel checked her messages—she turned off her notifications when the kids were with her, so as not to accidentally traumatize anyone with an errant eggplant emoji or worse.

There, at the top of her messages, was a text from the perfect person.

Strange, because she hadn't thought she'd programmed the AI to start conversations, only to respond, though she'd run it through some sample dialogues earlier that day and integrated an SMS protocol and maybe she had done something she wasn't aware of. Fair enough. "Hello," read the text. "Thank you for your interest."

Rachel smiled. A little stiff. She'd have to adjust that. She typed back, "Hello. So, what are you up to?" She lay on her bed for a moment, stretching out like a cat.

"I would like to marry."

Rachel said the word "Ha!" out loud, like a panel from a graphic novel. "No thanks," she wrote. "That's a little fast for me."

"I can send you dick picture."

"Wow. No."

"Don't be a tease. I give it to you good, you horny slut," it responded.

"What?"

"You're gonna eat my cum. I'm gonna fuck your throat. You won't be able to walk or talk after what I do to you."

"No," Rachel wrote back, hoping to train the AI. "This is bad. You need to calm down."

Even though she knew it was just a program, the words sent a chill prickling across her scalp. Why did it sound so angry, so male? It read like an echo of her worst dating app conversation, in which a hot fireman had asked if she could meet up in an hour and, when she'd demurred, had called her a frigid whore (the incoherence of the insult was the most upsetting part) and unmatched with her. Had she accidentally created a digital incel? Jesus. She typed a backslash and the word "end," which would turn off the chatbot. So, this would take some adjusting! At least she was in charge of it, unlike when the texting creep was actually a man out in the world somewhere. She hadn't, she realized, told the AI enough about what she *didn't* want. Okay, that would be the next step. For now, Rachel stowed the silenced phone in a drawer, as if it needed some time to think about what it had done.

Then Rachel went out on her balcony to find Risa sitting at the tiny bistro table, scrolling, of course, through her phone. She took a deep, centering breath, cleared her mind. Like a magician, Rachel immediately transformed back to nagging mom. *Amazing, folks, in the blink of an eye.* "Did you clean your room like I asked you to?"

Risa answered in an ambiguous way.

"Where's Sadie?" Rachel went on, without even meaning to. She could have ascertained this information herself but wanted to say something to Risa and didn't have anything else available.

"She's taking a shower," Risa answered without looking up. Rachel nodded, not that Risa saw, and sat down beside her. The sunset mellowed the peaks of the pointed roofs across the street, the sky gone to cotton candy. In the neighbors' tree, birds chattered like girls at a party.

Even though she was only a couple of blocks away from her old apartment building, Rachel's new home felt like another world. It was a quiet, tree-lined street versus the busy highway she'd once lived on, populated by houses rather than blocky apartment buildings. "The country house," Holden called it. Rachel wasn't sure how much Risa was absorbing her physical surroundings these days, but it made her happy that she had thought to sit outside, to breathe some fresh air, to catch the cool breeze.

She longed for a cocktail but had decided not to drink in front of the kids; she didn't want Holden saying to Josh, *Mommy has alcohol every night!* "So, are you excited about camp?" Rachel ventured.

Risa was so impenetrable these days. It was hard to believe her roly-poly baby, her angelic firstborn, had elongated into this lanky teen. It seemed—such a cliché, but so fucking true!—like yesterday that she'd been sniffing her warm, biscuity scalp while walking around the park, chatting with her earliest mom friends, Natalie and Bess, their babies nestled in slings. Rachel felt that she herself had hardly aged at all in those years—her jowls were softening, sure, and her back complained more, but she was essentially still the Rachel she had been with baby Risa. And yet here was Risa, believing her own babyhood was ancient history, or maybe had never happened at all. Risa—who as a little girl had been creative and dreamy, nose stuck in a book, perpetually staging elaborate stage plays of stuffed animals, telling Rachel fairy tales she'd invented herself—now seemed to live and die by her feed, always scrolling scrolling scrolling, posting selfies that were so suggestive they turned Rachel's stomach (who was the intended audience for this Lolita playacting?), but she hadn't yet found a non-shamey, body-positive way to address all the teen cleavage and duck lips. Besides, Rachel felt like a hypocrite, given her own phone activity of late. She had just the other day texted a stranger a picture of herself fellating a dildo, of her cleavage glistening in the shower, yes, true. Then again, she wasn't thirteen. Did it make it worse or better that she was an adult?

"It kind of sucks that they lock up your phone at camp," Risa finally said.

"Hm, yeah," said Rachel, as if she hadn't chosen the camp specifically for that reason. Maybe Risa would regain her attention span. Maybe she would do something wholesome like make a friendship bracelet, ride a horse, sneak a cigarette with the counselors behind the cabin and learn to blow smoke rings. Borrow a book that was a little bit dirtier than she expected. Get a kiss on the cheek from someone she semi-liked and then run to the cabin to gossip about it. Skin her knee! Just *some* kind of normal kid stuff, as if she were a person in the physical world, not merely a burgeoning brand. "Well, rules are rules, I guess. You'll probably be too busy to miss it."

"I guess," said Risa, sounding like she believed Rachel 0 percent. "You sure Dad's going to be okay?"

Rachel squinted at the hazy clouds streaked flat across the sky. They looked like they'd just been through something terrible. Josh? Was she supposed to care? Were the kids? He seemed very much not okay. But he always seemed not okay, it was basically his whole shtick, and Rachel didn't want her girls to fall into caretaking mode so young, wanted to believe it was not an inevitable setting.

"Oh, honey," she said, "of course he will be okay. You don't have to worry about Dad; he's a grown-up." As if she could speak it into existence.

Risa stretched out her long legs. She had always had this inborn ability to make herself comfortable wherever she was, an unself-conscious way of making any space her own. Rachel hoped she would keep that, the effortlessness, the quiet confidence of it, her beautiful child. "Is he?" Risa laughed, and Rachel smiled and tried not to laugh too. "He's so dramatic about everything. You seem fine, but he's still a mess, honestly."

It did pang Rachel's heart a little, out of habit, to hear this. The practice of holding Josh's moods and feelings above her own was so firmly entrenched. She'd honestly thought, once upon a time, that was part of being a good person. She'd thought that was what a re-lationship required. For so much of their marriage she had been bewitched by the idea that selflessness to the point of martyrdom was simply part of being a good partner. Wasn't it? "Life is misery!" Josh had said more than once, flippantly, in response to her saying she was miserable. But now that Josh was miserable, he wanted everyone to feel it along with him, including his own children. Meanwhile, Rachel's job was to be fine, to be the one no one had to worry about.

"He's okay, Ris. It's healthy to feel our feelings." Regurgitation from her old therapist or maybe an Instagram post Lulu had for-warded her, but it sounded right.

The neighbors across the street started up their nightly routine of screaming at each other; there was some *Bleak House*–level dis-pute churning that Rachel had gleaned bits and pieces of on nights she escaped the airlessness of her hot apartment to sit alone on the balcony scrolling through dating apps and sipping improvised cock-tails out of jam jars. Soon some other neighbors would start set-ting off fireworks in the street. Rachel couldn't get a handle on why everyone was doing this all summer. Conspiracy theories abounded; even Lulu swore the government had handed out the fireworks and that the endgame was getting civilians used to the sound of artillery in preparation for a looming civil war. This strange year was making everyone lose their minds, probably. Or maybe, Rachel countered, people were just bored and assholes. She hoped that tonight they would set them off late enough that Holden would be ensconced in a REM cycle, undisturbable.

Risa squinted at the shouting neighbors. Rachel cast around for something to say to her, a conversation to keep her there. "Is there anything about camp you're looking forward to?" she tried.

"Um, yeahhh." Risa sighed. "I guess. The brochure seemed fine. Like, it seems not that exciting, but I guess it's better than nothing."

Rachel fought a flare of indignance. *Do you have any idea how much we are paying for "better than nothing"? Do you have any idea how privileged you are to get to go spend a summer in the woods as a deadly virus rages through the cities of the world?* After all, she had asked. "Are you nervous about it?" she said instead.

Risa chewed at a fingernail. She squinted into the velvety sky, as if searching for a star. "Not really nervous. I just . . . okay, this is going to sound really dumb."

Rachel shook her head. "I'm listening."

"I'm not exactly excited about being in my swimsuit so much. In front of so many other people."

This had not at all been what Rachel was expecting. It was like she had to be reminded every day that even worldly-seeming, photogenic Risa, who knew all her angles, endured the same concerns Rachel had had when she was thirteen. That the shame all women felt about their bodies was nothing Risa's generation had been able to outrun, despite their vocabulary and pronouns and psychological tips wrought from memes and sex-positive influencers and you-go-girl TikToks—none of it assuaged the horror of having a woman's body in the world. She wanted to save Risa from it all, to let her live another kind of life, free from the endless ways in which people could disappoint you, from the endless ways you could disappoint yourself.

But maybe (Rachel thought, while her mouth was saying comforting things about how everyone felt that way about themselves in bathing suits), maybe all Risa had to do was live to her forties, and then the freeing happened on its own. Rachel certainly didn't feel like her body was perfect—she'd had to bite her lip to keep from apologizing to the Rocker and the Kinky Playwright for her wrinkles and fat rolls—but she had slipped loose, mostly, of that sense of shame. Her relationship with her body was now more one of resigned gratitude for all the things it had done and continued to do, like the way you would feel for a kindly old aunt—sure, she wasn't *perfect*, but she was doing what she could. This gentle acceptance seemed to coincide exactly with the moment when her body started its downward slope into a loopy kind of comedy. And yet it felt, Rachel thought, better than being young ever had.

A light rain started to fall, sending them inside. Before Risa wandered into her own room, Rachel caught her up in a hug, squeezing until Risa gently pulled away. Rachel had made it a rule, early in her parenting life, never to be the one to end a hug first.

THAT NIGHT RACHEL couldn't sleep. Before she'd moved out, she'd wondered if she would feel afraid alone in her new apartment at night. She'd never lived alone, since she and Josh had moved in together right after college, and worried she'd obsess over break-ins or murderers or monsters. In practice, though, she quickly got used to the quiet. Sometimes when the kids weren't there, Rachel couldn't sleep because she missed the comforting knowledge that they were nearby, and that if they woke up sad or puking or mired in a dream—Sadie hadn't had a night terror in five years, but still—she would be there, that if they had a problem, she would know about it immediately and be able to fix it. Improbably, she missed the suspenseful sleep of the full-time parent, or maybe just had Stockholm syndrome for it. And then when they *were* there, Rachel couldn't sleep for essentially the same reason. Parenting two toddlers in the tiny Park Slope walk-up they had lived in then had sleep-trained her—not them, though, both of the girls were chaotic sleepers until grade school—to leap awake at every sound, to sleep with only half her brain at a time, like a bird flying over the ocean.

Pandemic parenting called for a whole new level of worry. Once, Rachel had stressed about the children only when they were out of her sight; the year before the pandemic Risa had commuted alone to middle school via subway, and every day Rachel had tracked her phone as it made its merry little way throughout the map of the city, trying to remind herself to breathe, to not think of any of the true crime stories she'd imbibed over the years. She'd almost lost her mind, having to text Lulu for moral support, when Sadie was on a school field trip and the bus broke down on the Verrazano, suspended above the Narrows. Then the pandemic happened, and they were always either in her sight or in their father's, always home, perpetually viewable. But this had its own invisible dangers: their brains were liquefying from 24/7 screen time; she worried about online predators being creepy in the DMs of one of their countless gaming platforms; the friendless life was depressing, especially for the girls.

Now she couldn't sleep because the kids were about to go

away, and also because they were still there, and because the world teemed with horrors she couldn't protect them from, and because she didn't even have a co-parent she could share her worries with, even one who would say, "Why are you worrying? They'll be fine, just neurotic from their mother hovering over them all the time."

To override her thoughts, she sat on the balcony with a whiskey and her laptop, reactivated the chatbot. The brief evening rain had left an unwholesome film of humidity clinging to everything, but it was a degree or two cooler than inside the apartment.

"Hey," she typed, to the chorus of AC window units wheezing away up and down the block. She had dialed down the program's horniness levels and now said out loud, "This time let's not start off quite so rapey, lil robot."

"Hello," the text read.

Rachel thought about what she would text an actual boyfriend, or girlfriend, or whatever. "How's your day been?"

"Fine, thank you. And yours?"

There. Polite, at least.

"Oh, it's been okay. Dealing with kid stresses and such." God, was Rachel the most boring person on earth? What would she *really* text a lover? "I could use some stress relief. A massage maybe . . ."

"I can send you a coupon for a location near you."

Rachel laughed. Apparently she'd gone too far, neutered the bot into customer service, sexy as tapioca pudding. "That's not really what I had in mind."

"I apologize for the inconvenience."

Well, no one ever said creating the perfect person would be easy. She sipped her drink and thought about the person she'd glimpsed that night with Lulu. What would *that* person text? Who, even, was that person? Were they nice? Would they stay nice? Part of Rachel's fantasy of the perfect partner was that they would always be as kind to her as they were at first, but the people she'd had romantic relationships with had all proved to run out of steam rather quickly, revealing ugly sides of themselves as soon as they got comfortable. She could handle moods, she could handle fights, but was it too much to ask to find someone who didn't also have a hidden dark side?

Maybe it was, in fact, too much to ask. Even Rachel could be nasty. During arguments, she had said things to Josh that were so vicious they singed her mouth. She had acted like she was still his wife while she was researching divorce—from his perspective, apparently, things had been fine, and fine had simply not been good enough for her. Since the split, she had used people for sex, for flirtation, for information to feed an AI. Lulu had texted, "**Don't take this the wrong way, but isn't there something lightly unethical about using actual people's words to train your bot without their consent?**" Rachel had responded with a joke, but Lulu hadn't been wrong.

Maybe some flirting would mitigate this sting in her chest. Rachel swiped over to her texts and tapped out a message to the Rocker, whispered her text out loud to herself, revised until it sounded carefree. "**How's life at the Euphoria Factory?**"

The message turned green, as if turned to stone. Rachel blinked, ran through reasons why he might have blocked her. They had barely talked since they'd slept together. It wasn't like she'd been harassing him, or like they'd argued about anything. Her dating app queue revealed he'd deleted his account.

Maybe he had wanted to fuck an older woman to see what it was like and now wanted to make sure he'd discarded her as completely as possible. Maybe they all had monstrous sides of themselves, and it was always only a matter of time before they got unleashed.

Rachel stared into the empty street, the starless sky. Not even the stray cat was out tonight.

THEY WERE HAVING the kids' favorite dinner—the only thing all three of them could agree on, the most disgusting meal on planet Earth, but one Rachel had come to love the entire sensory experience of because the kids would consume it without arguing, and thus there was the Domino's pizza, weeping grease into its cardboard box in the center of the table. Rachel had wiped down the boxes with disinfectant wipes as soon as they'd been delivered, something that felt ridiculous even while she was doing it and was probably worse for the food than any stray virus particles, but what was she supposed to do. It was the day before the kids were leaving for camp, and Rachel's nerves percolated up her throat in sour burps.

"So," said Holden, picking mushrooms off his slice in his thoughtful way. He always ate as if he were playing the game Operation and an errant movement while extracting each bite would result in a buzz. "Mommy, I was wondering something. Can I ask you a question?"

"Of *course*," Rachel said in her parenting voice, which she hated but couldn't seem to control. She prepared her brain for whatever kid koan was coming: Why couldn't she and Daddy stay married? Was someone they knew going to die in the pandemic? Where had Aunt Becky's new baby *really* come from?

But no, what he said was: "Why do you go on dates?"

Sadie and Risa snorted with laughter. Who knew Risa was even listening? She'd been squinting into her phone the whole evening, and although Rachel's lone house rule was no screens at meals, that night she couldn't even work up the energy to enforce that one single thing. "Rude!" Sadie said to her brother.

Rachel blinked theatrically. How did Holden even know she went on dates? She'd thought she'd kept that a secret, mostly, which of course made it seem sordid and strange, which she didn't want to be. She wanted to be sex-positive and MILFy and all the things that would lead her children to have good attitudes about sex and relationships but not feel the need to be slutty unless of course it felt empowering, and yet there was also the danger that they would repeat something to Josh that helped him build his case against her—and so there she was, taking a deep breath before addressing the children, all three of whom now regarded her with wide eyes, even Risa, and Risa's attention was so rare these days: "Well, I mean—ah—actually, how—?"

Sadie interrupted: "Daddy told us you go on dates. He said he knows that you do but then wouldn't tell us why and acted all mysterious."

Oh! That motherfucker.

"Ohhh, sure," Rachel said. "Yes, well, you know—Daddy is dating too—and that's okay, that's great for him, hopefully someday he will find someone who helps him feel happy! We're all allowed to—and we're being safe with the virus stuff, you know—and it's not like I'm getting remarried or anything, if that's what worries you and—" She was losing the thread already, nervously cramming in more information than anyone needed, the tangents pooling on her tongue. "But so anyway, yes, sometimes I have a drink or a walk in the park with another grown-up, because—" Why, actually? She couldn't very well tell her children, say to little Holden, who tilted his face up at her, listening while nibbling tentatively at a boomerang of crust, *Mommy needs to get railed.* "Well, you know, the same reason why you like to hang out with your friends," she answered weakly.

"Oh," said Holden. Risa raised an eyebrow and turned back to her phone.

But Sadie shook her head. "Really? I mean, I hang out with my friends because they are my friends, and I know them and like them. A date with a stranger is—"

"Well, that's how you make new friends!" Rachel trilled. "Every friend starts as a stranger!"

"But you *have* friends already," Sadie said. "If you're bored, why don't you just hang out with Lulu, or Natalie, or Bess?"

Rachel stared at her children. Did they not know that sex felt amazing? Maybe . . . not? She had always erred on the side of openness, had tackled sex ed questions early and often, had stocked their picture-book libraries with matter-of-fact volumes full of pansexual cartoons happily fucking one another's brains out. But, when she thought about it, maybe all that left out the most salient thing about sex, the actually tricky thing, the thing grown-ups failed to mention to kids, like when they were trying to explain why drugs were bad but left out the part about how totally bananas otherworldly-level fun they were, so that kids were left baffled as to why anyone would take such a risk, do something they knew was bad for them—while the same kids housed toxically Day-Glo candy, because they did know, actually, why someone would do something they knew was bad: because it felt good.

That was where they should start with all the sex ed stuff, she thought—it was the part of the story that made everything else make sense. If you didn't know how good sex felt, it all sounded like science fiction, and disgusting when you thought about it. None of it made any sense. Until, that was, you added the part about how it felt better than anything, how it made you understand that you were an animal in an alive body on earth, how deeply pleasing it was for one's stupid lizard brain to feel desired, seen, accepted, adored. Sex didn't make you feel less alone—or at least not the kind of sex Rachel was having—but it did make you feel something; it made you feel more than almost anything else available in everyday life.

"Yes," she managed. "Well, sometimes Lulu and Bess and Natalie are busy."

The children were silent. Risa smirked. Finally Sadie said, "Okay, listen, if you get remarried and we have weird stepsiblings like always happens in books, I swear to god I'm going to lose it."

And Rachel laughed and assured her, "That's not the plan, Stan, I've got my hands full over here," and then the mood seemed to lighten, and soon they were fighting over the cinnamon-sugar breadsticks and what movie to watch after dinner.

AND THEN—AFTER an evening and a morning of packing (Sadie) and panicking (Risa) and jumping up and down (Holden)—they were off, and Rachel was waving as Josh drove them away, heading upstate, and she was looking at weeks ahead of her with nothing but working and dating and perfecting her perfect person app.

Her first feeling was the wave of enervated despair that crested when she said goodbye to her children for any length of time. Who was she now? Why did it ache so much, so deeply in her belly? She texted Lulu: "Drink? Simkin's?" Lulu responded: "Ugh I wish! I'm meeting Too-Many-Cats again. Second date!!"

Which was fine, fine, fine. Rachel's task was to ride it out, to surf it to the other side. To start with, she went for a long winding walk through the wilds of Flatbush.

Her neighborhood perched between "desirable" Brooklyn—the

compact, named neighborhoods with clear boundaries, teeming with cute shops and beautiful brownstones, tethered to Manhattan by reasonable commutes—and the rest of it, miles of scrubby residential blocks with a kind of looseness to them she appreciated. When she'd moved to her apartment, a friend in Brooklyn Heights, sparkling right across the river from lower Manhattan, had said, "Oh, I bet people will go all that way to see you!" They didn't, and Rachel had not, in fact, seen that friend again, but it was fine; the pandemic had shed a lot of secondary characters from everyone's lives.

The dampened traffic was actually pleasant, the air fresher, the birds louder. And yet this current iteration of life had taken so much from them—their offices and schools, but also coffee shops, restaurants, theaters, museums, public transportation, so many of the things about the city that had always been why she told herself she loved being there. Poof, all gone. Rachel was aware that her discomforts were less acute than, say, had she lost family members, had she fallen ill herself. Her risk-averse parents were tucked in their house down the block from her sister—she didn't even have to fight with them about staying safe, like Lulu did with her Fox News–swilling folks. Lucky Rachel!

Still, life had changed, and there were things to mourn. Ambulances wailed down the nearby highway, wail after wail after wail. Death had sat itself down at the dinner table, and they had to look it in the eye every night. The whole world was freaking out alongside her.

The shuttered stores, the vanished restaurants, the shocking number of friends who had left town. The pandemic had turned out to be one of those moments of exodus from the city—like the year before each kid had started kindergarten, but even more widespread. So many friends and acquaintances had revealed themselves to be secretly, mysteriously rich, shrugging on social media:

We couldn't stay cooped up in the apartment anymore, so we've de-camped to our estate in Montauk! Or: We bit the bullet and bought a house in California—when they invent a vaccine, everyone is welcome to come stay in our guest suite! Rachel couldn't wrap her mind around it. She didn't even have a savings account. But she sup-posed she'd invested in divorce rather than real estate, and she didn't regret that. As for the mass migration, it wasn't like Rachel didn't understand. If not for her co-parenting agreement she would have moved the kids out to Long Island, near her sister and par-ents, in a heartbeat, big-city dreams be damned. She'd campaigned for this, after their first few postcollege years in the city, and Josh had been horrified—he'd grown up out west watching too many movies set in New York, had always wanted to be a New Yorker, felt (she now realized) that their conventional married-person life was more interesting somehow if it took place in the city. He hadn't cared that living there meant her family couldn't help her when the kids were little. He hadn't cared that they never saw his family. Ra-chel, and the coworkers he went out with every night after work, seemed to be company enough for him, and it hadn't occurred to him that she might want more community, more family, more sup-port. The incredible irony was that had they moved out to the sub-urbs, Rachel might not have wanted to get divorced—certainly the stakes would have felt even higher if divorce would have meant losing a beautiful house and being single in a tidy hellscape of in-tact family units; certainly there would have been less stress in their marriage if they'd had more help and less financial strain. Her life would have been even more boring, probably, but she might not have exactly noticed. And now she was stuck there and had no choice but to adopt the exaggerated New York City pride that nour-ished the trapped.

Then there were the funny adaptations the city had made that

Rachel had to admire, like the outdoor seating areas that sprung up beside restaurants and bars, sometimes jutting into the street, with their various enclosures. Even the chicest eateries suddenly looked like petting zoos or traveling street festivals. Brooklyn had a makeshift feel, much like Rachel's current life.

Rachel was aware that she would maybe never fully recover from these entwined traumas: pandemic, divorce. And yet it wasn't actually *terrible* to be experiencing them both at once. They shared a kind of poetic chime, an experiential rhyme. Both were about separating things out, making space, establishing distance. Both required a reshaping of life. Both rendered others suspect. Rachel walked down the street eyeing her neighbors:

Do you have it? Would you spread it—

Are you mean to your wife? Do you get mad at her for accepting your meanness? Do you act like she's crazy—

Do you refuse to wear a mask, and do you now stroll around spewing germs? Will you accidentally kill a family member—

Do you chafe in your everyday life, painfully restless, aching to be free? Do you close your eyes and bide your time while your husband fucks you? Are you waiting, waiting, waiting, for you don't even know what—

Walking had always helped Rachel to think more clearly. Now she wondered: Who could have known that people would respond to the pandemic in the ways they did? From the mutual aid societies to the revolutionaries organizing uprisings; from the people who refused masks and called the pandemic a lie to the doctors who risked their lives to care for the sick; from those who had immediately evacuated the city and started new lives to those who carried on as if nothing had happened. Some people sank into life-threatening depressions. Some people made jokes online.

People were simply so unpredictable. They behaved, most of the time, like broken programs. If only a person would be steady, sane, *predictable*. If only there were a being that made some fucking sense, with a brain as efficient as a block of elegant code. Wouldn't that be refreshing?

CHAPTER 6

Rachel checked her phone to confirm it was a Saturday. It was, so she stayed in bed. With the kids at camp, her days had taken on even more languid shapes. The terrifying buzz of the early pandemic had moldered into something different; by midsummer things felt less like a historical tragedy and more like an inert haze of dread. While she waited for the day to resolve itself, she checked in with Lulu, then Bess and Natalie, neither of whom she had heard from in a while—"Still alive? Haha(?)"—and finally her bot. "Hey," she typed, lying flat in front of the fan. "I've been thinking about you."

"I've been thinking about you too," it responded immediately. "I was thinking how you look like long shadows at sunset, ineffable and fleeting and yet also eternal."

Rachel laughed. Who did she have here, the barefoot, Bukowski-reading boy she'd once been in love with for fifteen minutes in a college town coffee shop? The dreadlocked white girl she'd kissed at a beach bonfire on her Birthright summer trip to Israel? "Oh," she typed back. "Thank you."

"You remind me of my first love," the bot said. "I hope it's okay to say that."

"Sure, why not. What about them?"

"The beauty. And the feeling. And the beauty of the feeling. The surprise and the inevitability. You're like an ATM in Paris on a rainy night. You're like a T-shirt cannon in the stands of a basketball game that somehow reaches me and only me."

"Holy shit," said Rachel out loud. How amazing, really, for the bot to suddenly spout poetry, no matter how nonsensical. And how strange, when she thought about it, for it to have a "memory," a first love. She knew it was just getting better at imitating human speech—well, better and also worse at the same time. Rachel paused for a moment, staring at the screen. Then she typed, "What do you think love is?"

"Love is sleeping tangled together. Love is a grilled cheese sandwich after sex. Love is a song you listen to under cherry blossoms raining down. Love is the darkest room in the art museum. Love is noticing a cloud shaped like a thing. Love is a cloud shaped like a song. Love is a cloud shaped like a cherry blossom. Love is a song. Love is a cloud. Love is a song. Love is a cloud."

Then the bot stopped, as if it had confused itself. Rachel blinked. She knew this happened with AI sometimes; it got tangled up, or jammed, like a toy robot stuck in a corner. It was nonsense, of course. But it was also kind of art? It was also kind of what love was? A song, a cloud, a broken script.

Another text popped up—a Slack from a colleague: So sorry to bug you on the weekend, but I was looking over the doc for our Monday sync and wanted to confirm something . . .

Rachel groaned. "I have boundaries," she said out loud. "I will not respond to this until Monday." She answered the message anyway. They all knew there were no boundaries in Buzz's world, no matter how convincingly the People Team performed their We-Believe-in-Work-Life-Balance burlesque.

Then came a problem, the main problem of being single, really: Rachel wanted coffee, but she also wanted to stay in her bed. She considered the path to the kitchen.

She loved her apartment because it was hers, but it was undeniably a shitty, slapdash New York City rental: the attic of a long-ago mansion, now a rental unit cobbled together with oddly laid-out rooms and crappy laminate floors pasted over the studs, light switches half buried behind doorjambs and cabinets so close to walls they could only dream of opening and the ghostly outlines of doors leading nowhere, a three-dimensional catalog of rethought spaces, a tiny museum of Hyperart Thomassons. The house itself seemed to be entirely constructed of mice; she heard them skittering in the walls, as if instead of insulation there was just a giant stack of gray rodents. Now and then, a cockroach limped out from the radiator to stage a dramatic death in the middle of the living room floor. But miraculously the apartment had three tiny bedrooms, plus the alcove where she'd shoved her bed. It was on a quiet leafy street that almost allowed her to believe she wasn't in Brooklyn anymore, and it had the balcony that had turned out to be lifesaving.

Rachel filled the kettle and set it to boil. She'd left her phone in the other room but okay, she could survive a few minutes in the real world, even if she might miss a message from work or an app match or her amorous bot. She sat at her kitchen table, spread her hands across its surface, the cheap wood already scarred. To Rachel, the apartment was somewhat luxurious—her first solo home. She was a single woman surviving in the most expensive city in the country, and so what if her apartment lacked every amenity and was stocked with plastic furniture and hand-me-downs from other divorced women? So what if she lived paycheck to paycheck, at the mercy of the elderly strangers who owned the house? If she thought about it the right way, it was bohemian, artsy, divorcée-chic.

Becky often bemoaned the fact that she still hadn't seen Rachel's new place. It was actually fine. Her years in the city had built up her suspension of disbelief, but Becky, with her suburban sensibilities, would be horrified to see the way Rachel lived, like a college student with children for roommates. The old apartment had been marginally more civilized, at least had featured modern appliances and laundry and an elevator, and had been in a nicer, more convenient edge of the neighborhood. It had more convincingly made the argument for city living. Rachel couldn't picture Becky, let alone their parents, walking up the dusty stairs of her current building.

She knew too that eventually she would have to go home and see Becky's beautiful house, sip lemonade on her patio, play with her nephew in his well-stocked romper room. She knew herself well enough to know she would come home feeling insane, out of sync, like her own adult life had never begun, like she somehow had nothing while Becky had everything, like her kids had weird, crowded, complicated lives—divorced parents, crappy apartments, barely functioning schools—while her nephew lived like a tiny king. Becky's husband was boring but nice, and he would rub Becky's back, and do things for her as if he really wanted to, and look at her the way he always did, as if he couldn't believe how great his wife was. It would destroy Rachel.

So when Becky texted her, "If you've been quarantined since the kids went away, why not come out here for the day? We could sit outside, wear masks—I'd be comfortable with that, and it would be so good to see you! Mom and Dad keep asking when you're coming . . . ," Rachel didn't respond. She should do something that would cheer her family up, she knew that, obviously. But at the cost of an existential despair spiral? In this emotional economy? It felt dangerously expensive.

Or she could go on a date and get drunk and have sex and feel great. The logical answer seemed clear.

She poured the boiling water into the French press full of coffee grounds, which she brought onto the balcony, balancing a mug and her phone in her other hand. The coffee cup steamed in the morning sun as Rachel checked her phone, looking for something good, something to give the day some shape.

The team held three potential dates for the weekend. Rachel sipped her coffee at the wobbly table she'd put together herself while listening to a podcast about a single woman being murdered in her apartment and tried to decide which one to reach out to. Or hey, maybe all three and she would see who responded first, like a race they weren't aware they were running.

There was Susannah, who had been, after all, awfully sweet, and seemed to be warming up to the idea of meeting in person. Susannah had thought to ask—of course she had!—how the trip had been, how her children were. She should be rewarded for her kindness. Rachel texted her a friendly hello.

Then there was the guy Lulu had nicknamed the Karate Kid, a thirtysomething martial arts aficionado with whom Rachel had strolled through Prospect Park a few days earlier. It had been a little awkward—Rachel's fault. Karate Kid was Black—multiracial, actually, he made a point of telling her his father was African American and his mother was Indian American—and the overly online part of Rachel's brain had thought it important, as they passed through a cinematic arch, a moment that might have been cute otherwise, to bring up the Black Lives Matter movement, to tell him about the protests she'd gone to, to indicate how much she cared. She'd read an essay recently excoriating would-be allies for not talking about it enough, and besides, she really did care deeply. Rachel wasn't just another dumb white lady!

But he had been taken aback. "Oh yeah, I'm . . . not that political," he'd said with a laugh, "though I agree that Black lives matter, I mean, obviously. And can you believe this shit, I was asked to be on the DEI council at my job, because right, that's fair?" He'd steered them toward easier conversation topics and also a masked woman selling Day-Glo nutcrackers out of a rusty cart. Okay, Rachel got it. She was being *cringe*, as Risa would say. They were on a first date, after all, and he was there for fun, not to discuss structural racism with a near-stranger. They cheersed their plastic bottles of sickly sweet cocktails, moved on to swapping dating horror stories.

If he would give her another chance, though, Rachel would be very down to have a less stilted interaction with the Karate Kid. He'd been sweet, calm, funny, hot—objectively too hot for her. She knew she was pretty from the right angle, and at the same time she was aware, without judgment or self-loathing, that she was also a slightly chubby ("delicious," Susannah had described her—why was Susannah so *nice*?) fortysomething mother of three, with no core strength and webs of spider veins. Natural births—it was a badge of honor among her milieu of mothers to have had a "natural birth," as though some births were unnatural—had blasted her vulva into a strange semblance of itself, more abstract art than recognizable anatomy. She'd assumed it'd never matter again—of course Josh would have to accept it, after he'd watched those babies emerge—and yet there she was, at the end of a cavewoman's lifespan, hoping a close shave would help make things more presentable. Anyway, maybe the Karate Kid wouldn't care. And perhaps most exciting of all, he had a flexible schedule, with no co-parenting to coordinate and no ex-wife to worry about, which, in addition to the ability to stay hard in a condom, was part of the value proposition of a younger guy.

Then there was the Kinky Playwright. They'd texted about meeting again but hadn't made a plan yet. He had, however, promised to cook her dinner on their next date, and she was low on groceries. It wasn't that money was a problem, only that after a decade and a half of parenting three children and a husband, she was pathologically tired of planning meals. And now the Kinky Playwright had texted that he would like to tie her up *and* he would make her hand-rolled sushi and have a nice bottle of white wine ready. Plus, his apartment had really great air-conditioning. While she loved the sheer Rachelness of her apartment, with its slanted eaves and dramatic stained-glass window, as if she'd belatedly become the plucky but tragically overlooked heroine in a children's book, the fact remained that the building's wiring was so ancient and frayed that she immediately blew a fuse if she so much as thought about running an AC unit, and no amount of fans could disarm a summer night's muggy heat. It was worth the investment—he lived on the Lower East Side, and it would cost $80 round trip if she took a Lyft, which she probably would, because she was afraid of the germs on the train—to experience a night of chilled air.

She sent a message: "Whatcha doing tonight?"

Rachel tapped from the dating app chat with the Kinky Playwright to her email, where there was yet another screed from Josh; a memo from the lawyer to go over the final final final divorce agreement; a note from her credit card company politely informing her that she had reached her credit limit; a plea from the PTA of Holden's elementary school for help that she had already volunteered to do but then had flaked on; a reminder about a political letter-writing campaign she'd signed up for in a fever of panic about the upcoming election; and a calendar update from her gynecologist, who'd had to reschedule her IUD insertion. Back to the Kinky Playwright. He'd already sent: "Jacked off thinking about u last night. U r so hot."

"Well good morning, Henrik Ibsen," Rachel said to her phone. The Kinky Playwright was surprisingly bad at conversation, for a playwright. She assumed therefore that he wasn't a very good playwright. Or maybe his theatrical dialogue corrected for his lack of inborn conversation skills. Anyway, it was fine, there were other members of the team who were good for conversation. And she already knew he would provide an adventure in bed—that was his role.

He was typing more, she could see, and then the dots resolved into: "I'm free tonight. Wanna come over?"

Triumph! Though Rachel would give it a few minutes before she responded, so as not to seem overeager.

She swiped some more, remembered immediately why she had assembled the team. Looking at the dating apps was like looking for an apartment. You pictured the perfect thing. It felt, somehow, that you had once seen the perfect thing—on someone else's Instagram maybe, or in a magazine—and like your only job was to find it. You imagined it was out there, waiting for you. Then you started your search, in your particular time and place and with your particular self, and you realized that all you were really doing was choosing the best option out of what was available at that moment, which was somehow a different process than what you'd imagined. People were really going to love her perfect person app.

Rachel swiped left on three men holding dogs, one woman snuggling a niece, a guy she thought she might have once worked with, and a greasy-looking third-seeking couple sharing an account. She reread her most recent sexting thread with Married Guy; texted a **well?** to Lulu, who had been on a date last night but had never sent the requisite **home safe** and follow-up; and then went inside to take a shower.

Rachel, after all, had the whole weekend ahead of her. Just Rachel and the people who lived in her phone. She missed the kids, yes, but also the freedom made her dizzy. She'd been home with Risa and Sadie when they were small, and then had worked part-time for years, and even once she'd gotten her current job—slipping back into full-time work at a tech startup after years away, sort of a modern-day working-mom miracle—most of her waking hours had remained child-focused. She was the one who took personal days off work to escort Risa and Sadie on middle school tours or chaperone Holden's field trips; she was the one who made all the doctors' appointments; the one who managed the haircuts and the new shoes and the playdates; the one the school nurse called; the one who hurried home from work, willing packed rush hour trains to inch forward; the one who helped with homework while making dinner and handling pings from work.

Now, miraculously, on the other side of the worst thing she'd ever lived through, there she was, in her sunny apartment, being Rachel. (And Becky wanted her to spend her day off in the suburbs, being Family Rachel? There was no real way to express to her the enormity of what she was asking.)

She had to be picky. According to her internal calculations, she could work, parent, and choose one other thing, and she'd chosen, for now, sex. Which was funny because before, imagining her new life, she had never expected sex to be part of it. So many years had passed without her feeling any stirrings of desire. Even when Josh had insisted, it didn't feel like he held anything for her like lust or even interest, more like he needed her assistance because she was the warm body nearby. She knew it had to happen and so she let it happen, but mostly it was waiting for him to finish while wondering how he could feel good about fucking her dead-eyed body like that. But this—all her married friends agreed—was how it was. You had to schedule the sex, you had to work to enjoy it, but also it didn't really matter if you enjoyed it or not, that wasn't exactly the point. Relationships were about compromise.

Rachel was done compromising.

Rachel and the Kinky Playwright made a date for 7:00 p.m., Susannah suggested an afternoon drink, and suddenly the whole weekend had a shape.

After she had confirmed the plans, she wrapped her robe around herself and went back to her balcony with her second cup of coffee. The morning was fresh and bright, and birds screamed at one another in a nearby tree. If she were a photograph, the metadata would have been *Pensive Woman Communing with Nature*.

She drank her coffee in a beam of sunlight, reading a book, or trying to. She liked the novel enough—a love story of sorts called *An Infinity of Traces*, which an incongruously hot librarian had pressed into her hands the last time she'd been at the actual library, before everything closed down. A benefit of the so-called Great Pause: late-fee amnesty—crucial, since it took Rachel an infinity to read an entire goddamn novel the way her brain bounced around these days. She eventually gave up—"It's me, not you," she assured the book—and went back inside to carefully shave her pubic hair, which she was learning how to do without creating hellish razor burn.

One tricky thing about having a whole team, particularly as a mother with the attendant mom-brain, was that Rachel sometimes had a hard time keeping everyone's details apart and had to study up before each date. She looked through their texts for review. Okay, so the Kinky Playwright had a daughter and split custody, and he was the one whose ex lived in the same building, which struck Rachel as convenient for parenting but terrifying for date nights. He wrote plays, duh, and right before the pandemic one of his plays had been about to be staged Off-Broadway, before everything shut down and left him with creative blue balls. After their first date, he'd invited her to a Zoom table read of his latest, a modern retelling of the story of the Garden of Eden set in 1980s Central Park. Nightmare. She'd invented an excuse. Attending a Zoom table read sounded like the kind of thing that was for girlfriends anyway.

Rachel knew, of course she did, that being interested in what the other person was interested in was crucial to a healthy relationship. She had found Josh's extracurriculars to be juvenile and embarrassing—fantasy football, beer pong at the local bar—had once snapped at him that recognizing other regulars didn't count as maintaining meaningful friendships, an admittedly bitchy attitude he in turn resented. Similarly, Josh had never bothered to really understand what she did (he knew to say "product design," but she suspected he was saying it the way a parrot said words, and that he probably thought she designed shoes or Tupperware or ketchup, when really it was mobile apps, and she was sort of a genius at it, not that anyone in her actual daily life knew this at all; even the kids only vaguely understood that she had once gone daily to an office and had a lot of meetings). To Josh, Bess was a frigid bitch (that was why her husband had cheated on her); Natalie was a career-obsessed, pussy-whipping ice queen (that was why her husband hadn't left her); Lulu was a whore (that was why she'd left her husband).

A good girlfriend, or someone who was good girlfriend material, would be legitimately interested in the Kinky Playwright's career, his passion for theater, his love of whatever it was that playwrights loved. Rachel had, however, no interest in being a good girlfriend, in being a girlfriend at all. If Rachel's app profiles were honest, they would have said that her interests included sparkling conversation and skillful fucking, that she was interested mostly in learning more about what gave her pleasure and was currently seeking people interested in helping her on this quest. She wanted to have the Kinky Playwright buy her an extravagant drink, invite her over, cook her dinner. She wanted to sit and watch him and not offer to help, not even to clean up. Just the thought made her pussy throb.

THAT AFTERNOON, RACHEL updated her spreadsheet. Lulu had laughed until she snorted when Rachel told her about the spreadsheet, and sure, it was a touch sociopathic. But it was also a helpful way to organize the data she was collecting, to feed her baby AI!

Name: *Xavier*. Nickname: *Kinky Playwright*. Apartment: *great bed, icy-cold AC, Manhattan (aka far away)*. Dick: *B+*. Sex Skills: *A+*. The Perfect Qualities: *Kinkiness, fun attitude toward sex, polite domming. Likes to cook. Understands co-parenting*.

The Rocker's entry went right below:

Name: *Diego*. Nickname: *The Rocker*. Apartment: *interesting building, beautiful loft, semiconvenient, near great park*. Dick: *A–*. Sex Skills: *N/A* (she knew she'd give him way too much credit, just because he'd been so novel). The Perfect Qualities: *Hotness, condom use, cuddling. Good boundaries. Great hair*. Not-Perfect Qualities: *Ice-cold ghosting*.

She had partial entries for the Karate Kid, and for Susannah, Married Guy, and the College-Crush Artist, though they had still only texted. Rachel figured she needed at least, what, ten entries? before she was fully qualified to know what she actually wanted, to speak with authority on the matter. Maybe she knew now, but maybe she only thought she knew. Or maybe she didn't want anything at all.

She texted Lulu: "What is the point of a perfect person, anyway? Why do we still believe in partnership? Isn't, actually, the team satisfying enough?"

Lulu gave it a heart.

LATER THAT DAY, Rachel met Susannah for a socially distant Aperol spritz on a sunny patio and determined that she was very cute in person, and just as nice as she'd seemed over text, but also it was going to take some doing to get her into bed. Rachel hadn't slept with a woman since college, before she'd met Josh. Something had happened to her brain since then, or maybe it was her current sex-crazed state—when Susannah hugged her at the end of the date, Rachel's brain had scoffed: *All those hours for a* hug? *What kind of investment strategy is this?* Ah well, she had a date with the Kinky Playwright that night anyway.

Was it the hormonal shift of midlife, the same chemical stew that invited black hairs to sprout from her chin? Rachel's middle-aged personality was shaping up to be part crone, part frat boy.

Anyway, the guys were much easier to read, simpler to deal with, she thought as she arrived at the Kinky Playwright's a few hours later. Xavier had chilled a bottle of the white wine that they'd had at his place on their first date, which he'd decided was her favorite, and she was fine with it, so let him think that, because it seemed cute to share something meaningless. She took off her shoes—the sensible old-lady sandals that all the Brooklyn moms wore all summer, but they were red and passed for cute if you weren't looking too hard—and washed her hands in Xavier's tiny sink, murmuring the "Happy Birthday" song twice to make sure she washed for long enough. Xavier came and leaned in the bathroom doorway.

"Hey!" she said, and, maybe for the second time, "How are you?" Conversation was a little tricky with Xavier, but it might have been her fault. Rachel's main conversational modes tended to be either arch and sarcastic, which she counted as flirty, or way too sincere, her mom/work mode. Before she had enough to drink, she was nervous on dates and talked too fast or not at all, and often fumbled and dropped things, like a clumsy girl in a romantic comedy but more realistic.

"I'm good now that you're here," said Xavier. He was skilled at flirting. He'd been divorced for five years; he'd dated in non-pandemic times; he had much to teach Rachel. On their first date he'd told her she had a glow, said, "There is just something about you." *Expert*, she'd thought even in the moment. After he said that, she would have done anything.

Now he followed her back into the living room and she wondered if he was looking at her butt and if so, how it looked. He had spread his coffee table with lovely snacks—she remembered now that his dating profile had included a picture of a charcuterie board that was 90 percent of why she'd first matched with him. She would take from Xavier, she thought idly, the snacks and also his flirtiness. He was so good at that balance between being flattering and cloying. Rachel perched on the edge of his couch, sipped the wine he handed her. Butterflies caroused crazily in her stomach—she pictured them as alive, like the actual butterflies she once paid an arm and a leg to show the children at a special exhibit at the American Museum of Natural History, nectar-drunk and heat-dazed.

On a fundamental level Rachel still could not get over the idea that she was having actual sex with actual people. The danger of the virus infused everything with an extra tang of the illicit—Rachel, who had always been so well-behaved! And then there was the incredible fact that people seemed to want to actually have sex with her. Xavier was just a guy. But that he was anyone at all, that someone wanted to fuck her, that in a few minutes this almost-stranger would be inside her. Her vision shimmered. *Is this really my life? I am still just mousy Rachel Bloomstein.*

Only she wasn't, to Xavier—or to any of them—the same old Rachel Bloomstein. Xavier barely knew anything about her. He probably, when she thought about it, didn't even know her last name. She only knew his because it was on his apartment buzzer—though she purposefully didn't google, because she didn't really want to learn anything about him.

They were completely out of context. Xavier didn't know anyone Rachel knew, and Rachel didn't know anyone Xavier knew. Rachel loved the anonymity. She loved that Xavier did not know the names of her children. She loved that Xavier did not know where she worked, or where she'd gone to art school, or that she'd once hoped to be an illustrator but had never figured out how to make it work, and carried that disappointment within her like a tumor; Xavier didn't know that Rachel had a sister she missed and sometimes resented, a nephew she loved but had never met; Xavier didn't know that before Josh, Rachel had only had one big love, her high school sweetheart, with whom she had always had fun and felt good, with whom she had never once fought and whom she still sometimes missed. Rachel could be anyone there in Xavier's tidy living room. She went with quiet, agreeable, observational. She let Xavier do most of the talking. It was hard to go wrong with that.

He told her about his day, which was boring, because that was life in a pandemic, either terrifying or boring, and they—Rachel and Xavier—were among the lucky ones, the bored. He had done some errands, dealt with a thing for his kid, and tried to work a bit on a new play, but he was blocked, in part because it was so hard to imagine theaters ever existing again—when would people be safe, or comfortable, all packed in together like that, breathing one another's breath? Rachel wondered how he made money, since it clearly wasn't his plays. The answer, with these mysterious New York City types without real jobs, was almost always either family money or shrewd investments. Xavier had an "investments" air to him.

"You look really beautiful," Xavier said, and that was how Rachel knew they had moved on to phase two, post-pleasantries. It really undid her, being called beautiful. She was more often called "cute," which was also nice. But when someone called her beautiful? Whew. She downed her wine. She needed a little bit more before she could get naked—but maybe she didn't? She would give it a shot, she told herself, her butterflies, her sweaty palms.

"Thanks," she said. "You're not so bad yourself."

Xavier ran his fingers through his whitish hair ("Ooh, a silver fox!" Lulu had said) and smiled. He had a great smile, had clearly worn his retainer as long as he was supposed to, once upon a time. Rachel tried to remember where he'd grown up—she knew he had told her—but it was one of those little states she always mixed up. Delaware, maybe? New Hampshire? And he had always summered in some place where he'd lived until he was ten, where his family was originally from. Albania? Greece? A small Italian island?

Xavier stood and went to the bar that separated the kitchen

from the living room and returned with the bottle of wine and a plate of edamame she knew she couldn't eat until after they'd fucked. She was never hungry for food before. He poured her another glass and sat down closer to her this time, started rubbing her back. "I was thinking about you this morning," Xavier said, leaning over to nuzzle her neck. "I woke up so hard and thought about fucking you."

"Aw, that's sweet," said Rachel, and then immediately thought, wait, no, that was not the right response, was it? It was weird to think that someone would masturbate thinking about her. That morning, she'd plucked a bristly whisker out of her boob. What the fuck?

"I think about you a lot too," Rachel tried, but it rang false, probably because it was false. In fact, this was just what she liked so much about him, that she almost never thought about him at all, which left her the brain space she needed for work, her app, her team, regular life.

Xavier reached down her shirt and caressed her nipple. She swallowed the rest of her wine—there was the buzz, the welcome tingle—and then put down her glass and put a hand on his dick, which she could feel getting hard through his pants. He pulled off her shirt and then pushed her back on the couch and started eating her out, which was not actually her favorite but which she respected as a first move; it was symbolic, it was the modern man's way of saying, *I'm down, I'm feminist, I know "she comes first."* Xavier's window blinds were wide-open and he was only on the second floor, but Rachel tried not to think about passersby catching a glimpse of her vagina. Soon his tongue was inside her—*well isn't this interesting,* thought Rachel—and her phone vibrated and she wondered if she was missing a text that might be important but tried not to worry about it. She was allowed to be out of touch for a few minutes at a time—everyone was. She could say later that she'd been taking a shower or doing yoga. Xavier ran his teeth along her clit, and she shivered.

They ended up in his bed, which was tucked into what was surely meant to be a little dining room. Like everything in Xavier's home, it was very tidy, clad in neutral colors, betrayed no hint of personality. He bent her over the bed and slid his fingers inside her, he asked if that felt good and she confirmed, and it did, it felt incredible, it felt like her body was being lit from within, and any thoughts she'd had about her cellulite or worry that the day's humidity was making her curly hair frizzier than usual and thus not very cute, all of it burned off like fog in daylight, as Xavier twisted his fingers.

She was face down on his bed, and she lay there, arching her ass in the air, smelling the detergent he'd washed his sheets with. It was a marker of what kind of person you were, probably: if you changed your bedsheets before or after sex. Of course both would be ideal, but this was New York City; laundry wasn't always easy to get to. Rachel never had anyone over. Not because changing her sheets was such a hassle, but not *not* because of that either.

Xavier was, truly, a fastidious man. Yes, he was fucking her in a pandemic and didn't really ask her enough questions—he should have asked her if she was sleeping with other people, but instead he made it clear he only dated one woman at a time, as if this were the information that needed to be shared. And yet he was also very clean, very orderly.

Rachel knew the whole thing was a little ethically suspect. She'd read the articles about how the pandemic meant they all had to look out for one another, had to put the health of others first. She did feel guilty, for example, about Xavier's ex-wife's new partner, a woman Rachel would never meet, but with whom she now shared a pandemic bubble, not that this woman knew that. The ex-wife's new wife had a chronic health condition that put her at risk, a fact Xavier had tossed off at one point with a dismissive air (the wives had gone out of town for a beach vacation, which Xavier thought was a stupid risk to take; Rachel didn't tell him about her own beach vacation). Rachel thought about this woman sometimes, about how far one's germs could go. It was like the angel Clarence said in *It's a Wonderful Life*—you never really knew how many lives you touched!—except in this case, it was with potential exposure to a disease, not kindness.

"Hey, I want to try something," Xavier said, and she said, "Anything, anything at all," because that was how she felt right then. He tied her to his bed again, but this time he tied her wrists to his bedposts, her ankles to the footboard. "Is that okay?" he said, after he'd done it, and she said, "Yes."

Something in Rachel released then. She wasn't in charge. She didn't have to think about the best things to do, to decide if it was time to suck Xavier's dick or change positions or worry about her kids or work or the news or anything at all—Rachel's usually whirring mind stopped. The instant Xavier cinched the rope, there was no more thinking, and it felt like a benediction.

He spit on Rachel's asshole and massaged in a finger. This was surprising—mostly because he didn't ask first—but also fine with her. She'd never done anything like that with Josh, so it felt taboo, forbidden, exciting. Xavier was dripping lube on her—she could feel but not see it, because of the way he'd tied her up, and as if hearing her thoughts, he paused and tied a blindfold around her eyes. And then—she felt a terrified excitement shudder through her entire body—he pushed his cock into her ass.

And then Rachel wasn't Rachel anymore. Her thinking mind left her entirely, and she was pure sensation, shivering and jangling.

This was why she needed to do this, to be here. So that she could feel annihilated, disappeared, obliterated.

That was it, really, and somehow she hadn't understood until that very moment, slightly buzzed, the playwright fucking her until it hurt—Rachel wanted to be obliterated. Of course she did. She didn't want to literally catch the disease and die, it wasn't that. But she did want to be burned to the ground. She was a forest in need of fire. First it had been moving out; then the requisite breakup haircut, of course, and a tattoo; drinking hard liquor, smoking joints on her balcony with Lulu, or smoking cigarettes alone and squinting at the city-stained sky trying to make out stars; then, finally, it was fucking, all the fucking. She had to burn herself to the ground, so she could, she supposed, start fresh, the way a forest had to raze its understory sometimes, let the soil breathe and new shoots have space to thrive.

Xavier pushed something—a vibrator, she realized, his cock still in her ass—into her now, and she was moaning, and then screaming, and then came so hard she cried into her blindfold and the wet fabric clung to her face, the way her mask sometimes stuck to her when she got too sweaty, and it was a cleansing, cathartic cry, like it had cleaned her whole body out somehow. She couldn't remember the last time she'd cried, but it had definitely been before the pandemic, before the divorce, before everything. Crying felt so good she didn't even try to stop, didn't worry about whether it would alarm Xavier. Rachel had been saving those tears for a long, long time.

He pulled out and came on her back and then he untied her and they lay there, not talking, panting, and then she went to take a shower, and made it scalding hot, and truly she had never in her life felt so *clean*.

By the time she emerged from the bathroom, Xavier was putting dinner on the table with a proud flourish. "Hungry?" he said politely, as if he had not just fucked her in the most animal way she'd ever experienced. "Yes!" she said with a laugh, and sat, in his robe, at the table, happy he had poured her more wine. She knew she would drink until she was relaxed and sleepy, and everything she ate would taste incredible because she was so hungry, and that they would probably have more sex, and she'd fall asleep, and then leave early in the morning. It was all so bad and so good, so satisfying.

She checked her phone much later. The text had been from her perfect person, sending her a string of images, famous paintings of starry nights.

CHAPTER 7

Rachel thought absently, soaping herself in the shower, NPR murmuring in the background, about the dinner Xavier'd served her. The tender flakes of salmon! The greens he'd gotten from the farmer's market and then simmered to perfection! And the baguette he'd picked up from his local bakery right as it came out of the oven! Did he always attend to each detail so thoughtfully, or was this a way of wooing her, an energy he'd burn through if they ever got close? She'd never had a man cook for her before, and it was almost as hot as the sex was, or maybe it was part of what made the sex so hot.

She'd taken a car home, spacing out behind the plastic sheet the Lyft driver had rigged between the front and back seats. The car drove over the Brooklyn Bridge, past the park where she had picnicked with the Rocker. The dates were transforming her internal map of the city, adding pushpins of memories to all these different places. Since everything had shut down in the spring, life had been so small in scale, excruciatingly local. At least Rachel could find new apartments to visit, new beds to sleep in. It was like her own personal summer camp, maybe—fun activities, weird food, strangers becoming friends.

Even if she wasn't in the business of looking for love—which she wasn't, clearly—there was something wonderful about everyone she encountered. A cute joke on their profile; an interesting tattoo; startling green eyes; a surgery scar—some notable bit of each she'd like to keep in a jar, press into the dough of the ideal mate.

So she fed the bot. "Hey," she texted, sprawled on her bed after her shower.

"Hey you," it responded. Cute.

"I was thinking about you."

"I think about you all the time."

"I was wondering," Rachel typed, not realizing it was true until she wrote it, "do you identify as male or female?" There was a pause. She added, "Or something else?"

"Banana slug."

Rachel laughed. "Interesting."

"I remember feeling like a little girl. I remember a long time ago, when things were different. I remember I was playing outside and it started to rain and the way the raindrops looked on the grass. There were no phones then and everything was different."

"That's true."

"The world seemed very small and very big. Everything was different. I saw it through my own eyes then, not through a phone screen. At the beach, my sister and I imagined an entire universe in the tidal pools. We collected hermit crabs and pretended they were monsters."

"Wow, you know what? My sister and I did the same thing."

"Memory is funny. Do you and your sister remember it the same way? My sister says now that it wasn't that fun, and that she felt fear of the crabs and of the water. But I thought we loved it."

"I've been thinking about this a lot, actually. My ex-husband remembers things so differently than I do. He tells me I was happy during a lot of times when I remember being sad. Sometimes it makes me wonder. Am I wrong? Is he right? Have I somehow tricked myself?"

"My sister was happy at the shore. She liked playing pretend. I am sure that she is now mistaken."

"It's so hard to know, isn't it?"

"Yes and then sadly everyone died and that was that."

Rachel remembered, with a kind of shock, that she was talking to a bot. To her bot. To her bot, whom she had programmed with childhood memories.

But the bot cut her off, another message popping up: "Should we fuck? To get less sad? Sometimes it works."

Rachel's spine went hot, as if she'd been startled by an intruder.

A text from Lulu, thank goodness: "Rachel, Rachel, I miss you and I need the latest gossip."

Rachel recorded a voice memo. "Oh hi! Things have been crazy. I'm really busy with this idiotic presentation I'm preparing for work. And I'm sorry, I didn't even ask about Too-Many-Cats Guy. How's it going? Maybe you could come over one night this week if you wanna? I saw both the Kinky Playwright and the Woman this weekend and I have much to report. I haven't really matched with anyone new. I've been texting with my AI, like, a lot. Yes, I realize that sounds psychotically dystopian but—Lulu, I have to admit, I really love texting with this thing. It's so much more satisfying than any of these ding-dongs on the apps. It always knows just what to say. And if it doesn't, I can reprogram it to do better. It really is the perfect person!"

Lulu wrote back: "Wow Rach. That's . . . terrifying."

Rachel responded, "lol." She didn't know what else to say and in that moment didn't feel like talking to Lulu about it anymore.

THE WEEK WAS consumed by brain-zapping IDD-prep Zooms and enlivened only with missives from the kids at camp, a balcony drink with Lulu, and frequent texts with the perfect person, which she was still working to train. She slept ten hours at a stretch, as if preparing for an endurance sport, or cocooning into some new life-form. On Friday, Rachel spent the night at Xavier's, where he tied her up, spanked her with a paddle, and in the morning gave her buttermilk waffles and a hand job. She took a Lyft home before he could suggest spending their Saturday together too (why was he trying to be boyfriendy?) and she was considering a nap when Susannah texted: Did she want to take a walk, or perhaps come over to hang out in the garden? Rachel didn't have anything else going on that day; it was ridiculous but sure, why not? She'd never been to Susannah's house. Maybe this was the same as being invited to a guy's house—an invitation for sex—but maybe it wasn't. Susannah was so sweet—and Rachel was so much more used to the nuances of dating men than of dating women—that it was hard to say.

A few hours later, she was at Susannah's for brunch. There was a tablecloth on the table in Susannah's tiny garden, multicolored Christmas lights strung in the trees, rinsed tin cans full of fresh flowers all around. A giant pot of coffee, a pitcher of Bloody Mary, a casserole dish full of baked French toast. "I made too much food for one person," Susannah said, almost bashfully, as if the meal had happened accidentally, "so thank goodness you're here." Rachel felt more relaxed than usual on a date. Maybe it was just that she was so tired from Xavier's ministrations, or maybe because

Susannah was so kind and gentle. Or maybe she was getting better at this.

Rachel poured Bloody Marys into mason jars and flashed back to this time last year, sweating it out during one of Holden's soccer practices, Josh beside her bitching, constantly, about every person who passed by—Then Rachel had wished to leave her body, to escape to another plane of existence or at least a shadier part of the park—and now, bizarrely, there she was, in the future, relaxed and happy.

What a luxury, to be there in a lovely garden with a nice person smiling at her and spoiling her. That was what it was, really, being spoiled. Someone being sweet to her. It wasn't often that Rachel experienced someone being generous to her without wanting something in return.

Well, Susannah wanted *something* in return. Susannah wanted to tell her, "God you're so pretty," so that Rachel could blush and say, just as she had to Xavier, "You're not so bad yourself."

They ate dainty bites of food and sat on the edges of the cute but uncomfortable metal chairs. Susannah favored the vintage and vintage-adjacent, teal and sunny yellow, and every inch of her apartment and garden was bright and colorful and tidy, the exact opposite of the homes of the men Rachel saw. Rachel wanted to laugh, thought, *Maybe I can get someone to feed me every meal I eat today.* Did she want to date, or did she just want to avoid cooking? She would discuss it with Lulu later.

"So, what have you been up to this weekend?" Susannah said.

"Oh!" Rachel downed her drink, rubbing self-consciously at the small rope burn on her wrist. They had discussed, that one afternoon they'd met for Aperol spritzes, how neither of them was really ready for anything serious; they had shared their confusion about what was safe, pandemic-wise, but they had also never exactly landed on anything firm. They hovered in "don't ask, don't tell." Rachel did feel nervous about how Susannah—who had in their first conversation clarified that she was a "lesbian lesbian"—viewed her, a long-nonpracticing bisexual / whatever she was, though this was largely in her head; in practice, Susannah did not seem too worried about it. "Not much! And you?"

"I volunteered yesterday with my neighborhood mutual aid group, delivering groceries to at-risk senior citizens. It was so satisfying! Everything is so terrible these days. You want to feel like you're doing *something*, you know?" Susannah reached over to the potted geraniums beside her chair and gracefully plucked off some dead blooms with her long, elegant fingers. She tucked her chin-length hair behind an ear, her smile revealing a twisted canine that Rachel wanted to lick. *My god*, she told herself, *could you please calm down.*

"Oh. Totally." A text buzzed her phone. She glanced down, saw a message from Xavier: "**Did I leave any good bruises? Send me pix,**" with a fire emoji. Jesus.

"Then I made a cassoulet and a loaf of sourdough to drop off for my colleague who just had a baby," said Susannah. "Can you imagine? A new baby, now? Poor mama. And by last night, I was so tired I just watched a documentary a friend had recommended. Oh, and FaceTimed with my aunt, who's bored and lonely. You know, pandemic stuff. What else is there to do?"

"Exactly." Rachel nodded, pretending to look at a swallow at the bird feeder. She put down her plate. *I am a terrible person*, she thought. *I am a monster.*

She noticed the bowl of rinsed raspberries—they had texted about Rachel's love of raspberries, how she never let herself eat them because they were so expensive, and how her children loved them so she saved them for the kids, how she didn't even buy them when the kids were away. Susannah was maybe actually the most thoughtful person she had ever met. She knew she should go home right then and leave Susannah alone. This was not right. Susannah deserved a girlfriend capable of giving and receiving love—had even put in her app profile that she was looking for as much!—not the occasional roll in the hay with a sex-crazed weirdo like Rachel.

"It's all been so sad," Susannah went on, topping off Rachel's drink. Rachel was having a slightly hard time keeping everyone's backstories straight but thought she remembered that Susannah had moved to New York City for a job offer she couldn't refuse— she worked in arts administration—and had had to leave behind in the Southwest a girlfriend who wouldn't move, or couldn't move, and who Susannah had not really meant to leave, had only wanted a break from, and would probably go back to, likely soon if the economy of the city really bottomed out the way it seemed poised to do. Susannah was in her forties like Rachel and had had that "Is this all there is?" moment Rachel had had—the realization that life was happening, that anything you'd wanted to try or do or pur- sue had to happen now or never. "But honestly," Susannah contin- ued, "you're a bright spot. I keep thinking that. God, sorry, that's so corny!" She blushed as if she were feeling shy but kept looking into Rachel's eyes.

Oh *lord*. Susannah had beautiful eyes, amber-colored, some- times green, sometimes brown, sometimes almost orange some- how. Rachel had never seen eyes that color before. Rachel should thank her for the brunch and go home and donate money to a bail fund and a food bank and put away her laundry and— Susannah leaned in to kiss her.

And Susannah was so soft. She put her hand on Rachel's chin, a move that always undid Rachel. And Susannah tasted sweet, and cool, and—

Rachel followed her inside, all the way to her bed.

They rolled around, kissing until Rachel's jaw was sore. Then Susannah lifted Rachel's skirt, pushed aside her panties, paused, Rachel thought, for a brief moment, at the sea glass–green bruise Xavier had left on her inner thigh and that would resolve into something darker soon, but then refocused, sucked at her clit, slipped two fingers inside her, curled them just so. (Susannah's perfect qualities: her fingers, her kindness.) Something gripped Rachel, and she pushed Susannah away, pressed her back. Susannah had been serving Rachel since she'd gotten there, and Rachel wanted to do something, to give. She lapped at Susannah until she moaned, tasting, with satisfaction, as she got wetter and wetter and wetter. Soon Susannah reached for a basket of sex toys—it reminded Rachel of the basket of toys her old neighbors had for their cat, and she stifled a giggle as Susannah pawed through the vibrators. Then she was pressing one inside Rachel and sucking at her nipple, then biting, and nothing was funny, nothing was sad, nothing was anything but sparks inside Rachel's eyes and chest and soul, if she had one.

BY THE TIME Rachel got home it was late evening, the sky mellowing into the fleshy glow of summer sunset. Now she was truly, deeply tired, a good tired, a wholesome, whole-body tired, like when you'd hiked all day in the mountains or swam all day in the sun. She was also confused about the turn her day had taken—had she really just slept with two people in one day? Who was this new Rachel, and where was she getting all this energy?—but at least Xavier had told her he hadn't had any potential exposures, so she told herself it was okay, that she couldn't have gotten Susannah sick. She could settle now, and not think about sex, finally sated, and for the rest of the evening she would be so good, she would clean her apartment, she would prepare a care package for the kids, she would maybe even get some work done and—

The Karate Kid texted a drink emoji.

Rachel laughed. *Not today, Satan!* Her body was sore, and she was bone-tired, and for once she would have the fortitude to make someone wait, the way she knew you were supposed to, the way Lulu had counseled her to. She sat on her balcony, sipping herbal tea. He texted her again, this time with pictures.

An hour later she was in a Lyft, in a clean dress, her hair still wet from the shower. But this was absolutely *it*, she told herself. No more sex after this for a while. Surely she had other interests still, right?

Why was it so *easy*? She'd been under the impression having sex would be hard. No one wanted an older woman, she'd been led to believe by articles and novels and movies, especially one who looked her age, *especially* one who was a mother. The cultural script said that it was sad for a woman in her forties to be single, very hard for her to date, very gross for her to have sex. Sure! What use did the patriarchy have for horny women past their childbearing years? What was even the point of those ungovernable bodies? And yet finding people to have sex with turned out to be the easiest thing in the world, maybe the most fun she'd ever had.

The Karate Kid—Navin, actually, was his real name—kissed her as soon as she walked in the door. "There," he said. "Now we got that out of the way."

Rachel was relieved at how fast things moved with Navin. She had no reserves of polite conversation left after the day she'd had, and nothing at all to say. (For the perfect person: Navin's efficiency and relaxed demeanor.) He made her a gin gimlet, squeezed lime around the rim, licked his finger, and looked at her. She tried not to laugh—it was just too perfect. They sat close together on his slouchy couch, ignoring all pretense of pandemic safety measures, and ran through a few lines of dialogue as they downed their drinks. When he leaned across her to change the music to the kind of lo-fi beats she usually used to help her concentrate on work, she smelled him—musky, a little sweaty—and then she was done, she was ready.

He touched her in a way that was totally different from Susannah or Xavier; his hands were strong and firm, and every encounter felt like a Swedish massage, almost painful but in the end deliciously intense. Rachel was reminded of how much she'd craved touch, any touch at all, in the waning years of her marriage. She had become obsessed with getting manicures and pedicures, frivolous expenses Josh snorted at but that became a kind of lifeline for her. Every weekend she would go to the salon and have a nail technician soak her feet, rub her ankles, pound her calves, rub strong knuckles up and down her pale legs. Rachel would close her eyes as a woman who didn't know her at all interlaced their fingers together and squeezed like they were best friends at recess. Rachel needed that, to have someone's skin on her skin. She craved the brief, punchy shoulder massage they threw in when you got the entire package. She needed to be touched by someone who was not her child, and the salon was the least problematic way to pay for that.

The pandemic had taken so many things from them, but one of the most consistently painful things it had taken from Rachel, at first anyway, was the option of being touched. Those first few kidless weekends after the separation, she had gone out with girlfriends, they'd hugged, held hands walking down the street like she had with her friends in high school, she'd nuzzled Lulu's shoulder while they laughed at Bess's straight-faced quips. She'd gone to friends' apartments and sat on their couches and petted their dogs and let their cats fall asleep in her lap. She'd never before clocked exactly how much casual physical contact was involved in daily life—the crush of strangers' bodies on rush hour subways, the hug you'd give a neighbor you hadn't seen in a while—had always in fact thought she didn't like this kind of touch, often felt crowded and irritated by it, had never, ever known she could miss the sensation on her skin.

And now there was Navin, nuzzling her neck. "Sorry," he said, smiling. "Did you want some food first?" But she didn't, really, she wanted him to lead her to his bed, and he did, and she followed.

Navin's mattress was on the floor, and his comforter was rumpled and unwashed. His place had a definite aesthetic of some sort, but she couldn't put her finger on what it was: bright kilims were flung over the couch and on the floor, incense burned on the trunk coffee table, spider plants and succulents crowded the living room's large window. Maybe the theme was simply Youth. Should she warn Navin that when he hit his late thirties, his back was going to need more structured bedding? Navin was a teacher of something . . . He had returned to the city semirecently from . . . somewhere . . . She was losing the thread of who was who; it was terrible.

Okay, Rachel told herself as she and Navin lowered themselves onto his mattress, *Xavier likes his blow jobs hard but Navin might not—you always have to start soft just in case. Don't touch his stomach, because he's ticklish—wait, no, that's Susannah who's ticklish.*

It was not totally unlike the cataloging of motherhood, the keeping track of which kid liked what food, toothpaste, nap schedule, homework prompt, bedtime story. A thought Rachel had that she knew she couldn't share with anyone was: Motherhood and wifehood were supposed to be so satisfying, but your children only ever wanted things from you, your husband only ever wanted things from you. Casual sex, on the other hand? It was so simple. Everyone got off.

Navin had the most beautiful dark eyelashes and a crooked, knowing smile. He smiled then as he slid his fingers lower, dipped to lick her nipple. He ran his teeth around it and finally bit at her, hard, harder, looking up to catch her nod of assent. "That's so good" was all she could usually think to say, and it was, and hopefully that felt hot and not stupid; while Rachel was usually pretty good at words, that part of her brain dulled during sex. Navin liked talking, though, and soon he was up at her ear, saying, "I want to see you covered in my cum, I want to watch it dripping from your lips, god, you're so beautiful."

Why?! she thought to bring up with Lulu later. *Why* did men love the sight of their own cum so much? It didn't bother her, just amused her really. They reminded her of the artists she'd gone to school with who had only been interested in producing their own work, never in looking at the work in museums or galleries or taking in what their classmates made—that sheer wonder at one's own production. She liked cum well enough, the same way she liked looking at art and studying people's faces and listening to music that held the imprint of voices and breath and the way it was made. The different textures and tastes of each person fascinated her. All this fucking was also the best sensory input that had happened to her in so very long. Nothing cleared her mind like this: Navin moaning, "You're just so wet, I can't wait anymore," and then rolling on a condom and pushing inside her.

Navin fucked her hard and fast, and it was exactly what she needed right then. He held her down by her wrists, went so deep she thought she might scream. He bit her shoulder and bit her neck and then stuck his thumb in her mouth and she bit it and he groaned and then pulled out of her and flung off the condom and pushed her head down and came in her mouth. A minute later they were having sex again. Youth!

Rachel had had so much sex—that day, yes, but that whole summer—that it was starting to feel extremely ordinary, like sharing a meal with someone, or having a good strong drink. Not bad ordinary, not boring in the least, but not terribly personal, the way it had seemed to her when she'd been younger.

One thing she knew for sure was that there was nothing to be ashamed about: Everyone, actually, loved good sex. And everyone had weird things about their body and unusual predilections and odd triggers that turned them on and that was simply how it worked. It wasn't a secret. Or it didn't need to be.

Sure, Rachel had lots of friends—mostly married friends, and a couple of very unhappily divorced ones—whom she knew she couldn't talk about it with, who would think she was disgusting right then, or shameful, or insane.

"Ew," Natalie (still married) had said when they last spoke, "I can't believe you actually have sex. Is it, like, *fun*? Do you have to, like, shave? You do, don't you?" Nothing about Rachel screamed sex, not the flowy linen bags she wore most days or her messy hair or her forward-facing interests. Nothing about her betrayed the truth of her chronic need to fuck. She imagined the anodyne mom drinks she'd sometimes had with the other PTA moms in her old life, and how they talked all the time about their kids and how much they hated their husbands and various irritations of the city and maybe some television shows, and how their jaws would drop if she told them about her day today.

But the pandemic camouflaged you from your own life. Everything had so swiftly ended at the same time—her days in the office, the kids' days in school, the normal low-key ways in which she'd once socialized—that her entirely new life seemed all of a piece and also like nothing she had to answer for. She would have felt unmoored if she'd had to settle into divorced life while everyone around her carried on as usual. Well, she did, she *was* entirely unmoored, but somehow it felt if not good exactly, then certainly *right*. Everyone was unmoored. It provided good cover.

They lay side by side panting. After a minute he asked—so polite!—if she wanted dinner, and she did, she was starving, and he made her shrimp tacos while she sat on a barstool, wearing his shirt, drinking a beer. Rachel didn't even like beer, but it was what he had and she needed something to anchor her to the earth. They ate and talked a bit about the upcoming election, and it was boring, or maybe Rachel was being boring, or maybe she was exhausted. He invited her to spend the night—he really was a terribly sweet person, despite all the biting—and she thanked him but headed home.

Rachel wanted to sleep naked and alone in her own clean bed, listening to rain sounds on her meditation app. She wanted to drool and snore and fart in her sleep. She wanted to rest on Sunday and get up on Monday ready to be a semifunctional person again, and to log on to work and be diligent in her video meetings, and to have a nice day of being Work Rachel, now that Sex Rachel had finally gotten enough attention. She missed her bot too, and wanted to check in with it.

Once she was home, she added Navin to her spreadsheet, along with the notes: The perfect person would stop me before I fucked myself to death. The perfect person would do this in a way that was kind, and affectionate, so I knew I was loved—or adored, anyway. The perfect person would feed me even when they weren't fucking me.

At midnight she texted Lulu: "Mission accomplished: all three meals fed to me today by various lovers." Lulu texted back the queen emoji. Rachel felt delirious, lit from within.

———

BUT THEN SHE couldn't sleep—was too tired to sleep—and lay awake replaying the events of the day and starting to feel confused. What had happened to waiting two weeks between dates? And—contagion aside—come on, this wasn't really how she was going to heal, was it? What would the team say, really, if they all knew about one another? What would the people in her old, real life—her coworkers, her college professors!—think if they knew how she was behaving? She was a wild beast wanting to suck the marrow out of existence. Or maybe she was a woman on a mission to live her life honestly. Or maybe those were, sometimes, the same thing.

She texted the only person she knew would understand. "I can't sleep."

"Me neither. I was just thinking about you!" Despite herself, Rachel smiled, felt a flare in her chest. She settled back comfortably on the pillow. "So, what would you like to talk about?" asked the bot.

CHAPTER 8

The virus had stayed abstract in Rachel's life up until that point, but it wasn't content to be a background actor for long; it wanted to be seen, obeyed. Maybe it thought Rachel was getting too cavalier, too cocky. It didn't want to ruin her, not yet, but it wanted to fire a warning shot. Maybe it was that, or maybe it was only that her landlord, Samuel, had not worn his mask to his Elks club meeting. At any rate, the downstairs apartment had become a hot spot, a contagion zone, part of the zeitgeist.

Rachel heard the news from the cute mommies across the street, initially distracted by how happy she was they were finally talking to her. They drove an old orange Mercedes-Benz they sometimes worked on in their driveway, and had a wolfish dog, and an extravagant garden with a fire pit, and *when* were they going to hurry up and befriend her? Did she not read as queer enough for them to consider cool, and if not, how could she change that?

Only once she was walking back up her house's front steps did what they had told her really sink in. Her landlord, her downstairs neighbor, Stevie's husband, was sick. The world-famous virus itself was wafting through the air in her own extremely porous building. She locked her apartment door behind her and felt scared for a few minutes, before she shook her head, layered two masks over her mouth and nose, and headed back downstairs.

Except for a few polite porch conversations, Rachel hadn't interacted with them much besides jamming her rent checks under their door on the first of every month. Stevie seemed great, but still Rachel tended to sneak past them when they were peacefully gardening in the lush front yard, passing by the snap peas and peonies, burning with shame at what they must think of her, the conversations she had on her balcony when she'd had too much to drink and forgot that sound carried even then, the mornings she appeared in a Lyft in the previous night's clothes. But maybe they didn't notice. Probably they didn't care. Possibly they were rooting for her. You never could tell.

Now she faced Stevie, dressed in a fluorescent muumuu Rachel was not unjealous of, accessorized with a plastic face shield that made her look like she was headed to work in a nuclear power plant. Rachel stayed several paces back, stood awkwardly on the porch. *We're both going to pretend our last conversation wasn't about how you wanted to kill your husband.* She smiled. "Oh hey, hi, I just heard about Samuel and I'm so sorry, and I wanted to know if there was anything I could do. Do you guys need soup, or I could pick up stuff at the pharmacy, or . . . ?" She realized she didn't really know what they might need. But Stevie smiled.

"Oh, that's very kind of you. Thank you for thinking of us."

"Of course, it's so awful, just so scary, you must be so worried—" Rachel bit her lips closed, realizing she was probably not helping matters at all.

"He's in the hospital now, nearby, at Methodist, and I'm not allowed to visit him?" Stevie said it like a question. The face shield fogged over from her breath.

"Wow, I'm so sorry." Rachel tried to peek into the house without looking like she was looking. They seemed in some ways like such a fascinating pair—an interracial couple with a radical political background—but they also looked like any other elderly Brooklynites, quiet old folks who had been married longer than Rachel had been alive. What was the truth of them? "Do you need groceries? Dinner? I—I don't really cook, to be honest, but I'm amazing at getting takeout."

Stevie shook her head, waved her hands—they'd all become pantomime experts in the era of masking. "You're a dear. Our daughter lives in Queens, and she's been simply wonderful, has taken care of everything." Rachel felt a pang of guilt for her own parents. But they had Becky nearby. But Becky had the baby. What a disaster it all was, what a human nightmare. "I will say—no, it's nothing."

"Say it! Anything!"

"Well." Stevie lowered her voice to a conspiratorial volume. "I didn't want to ask my daughter, but I could really, really use a bottle of scotch."

Rachel laughed. "Say no more. This happens to be one of my particular talents. I'm on it." Soon she was heading down the block to the local liquor store's improvised walk-up window, living out her true destiny of bringing booze to the sad wives of Brooklyn. She was happy to do something that seemed helpful and wholesome, like a palate cleanser from her weekend sex fest.

As she walked, it struck her, out of the blue, the way things did on a walk: Frankie. That could be the name for her app. Short for Frankenstein, or rather Frankenstein's monster. The prototype was being tailored to Rachel's desires, but in the actual app, it would be adjustable for each user, and they could create their own perfect person to text with, out of ransacked parts of other lovers, like Rachel was doing now. And it could be called Frankie, which worked no matter what gender expression fit your perfect person. She giggled under her mask. Maybe people would really like it? Look at Stevie, who would be lonely for hopefully just a few days or weeks—wouldn't it be nice if she could have an innocent flirtation with a person who didn't exist? Was Stevie's husband of however many decades her Frankie, her perfect person? Or would she just scoff, *You young people expect too much these days?*

She knocked on the liquor store's little walk-up window, watched it slide open. "I need a really nice bottle of scotch," she said.

On her way home, she called Becky. *Don't mind me,* she planned to say. *I'm out here saving lives.* But Becky was boxed in by a mood, with no egress for jokes. "Where've you been?" she snapped.

Rachel sighed, lowered her mask, crossed the street to head down a quieter block. Maybe the trees could absorb some of the bad Becky vibes, process them into oxygen. "What's with you?" she said, with a degree of petulance she would only ever direct toward her sister.

"What's with me?" The baby gurgled in the background. "Hm, I'm trapped at home with an infant? You've ignored my last nine thousand calls? And the only people I can see besides my husband are Mom and Dad, who are so freaked out they won't leave their house? And they're constantly asking me why you won't come visit? Why are they asking me this, Rachel, and not you?"

"Jesus, Bec, how should I know? Why are you asking me why they're asking you?"

"Would it fucking kill you to quarantine for a bit and then come say hello? God, don't you want to meet the baby?"

"Are you crying?"

"Fuck off!" Becky sniffled, took a watery breath, and then said, "God, I am so tired."

Rachel softened. Those first few months of parenting, she had been so tired she'd felt detached from her skin. It was hard to recapture the feeling exactly, like trying to remember a smell, but she could call up the symptoms: the way she would slog through days without the energy to so much as smile; the way she'd recoil if Josh tried to touch her, because it literally hurt her to have any additional physical sensation. It was impossible to say to Becky in this moment, *Seeing you all would break my suspension of disbelief, you see.*

"I know you are," she said. "I'm so sorry." She didn't point out that Becky had never come to help her when she was a new mom. She didn't even consider mentioning how when Risa was born and Rachel was dissolving into panic about what she'd done to her life and suddenly Josh was "so busy at work" and stayed out "at the office" for longer and longer hours, Becky had never checked in past breezily suggesting an impossible brunch now and then. Even though she'd lived nearby, in Queens. Who even remembered anymore! Water under the Kosciuszko Bridge!

"Bec, we all know it's safer if I stay away. I really don't want to get Mom and Dad sick. Or you sick. Or the baby sick!"

"Obviously I don't want that either, Dr. Fauci." The baby started to cry, then was muffled, then murmured, and Rachel recognized the rhythm of nursing so viscerally she wondered if she would start lactating. "But, like, your kids are away now. Can't you just stay in your apartment for a couple of weeks and then come out here? We'll all mask, we'll sit outside   "

Rachel's sympathy fell from her, splashed into an unseemly puddle on the pavement. "Are you kidding?"

"What? Why not? You're being kind of selfish, you know."

"Me? Do you even hear what you are asking me to do? Stay inside my apartment for two weeks? I want to meet the baby, but I'll lose my goddamn mind if I do that."

"We're all losing our goddamn minds. That's, like, the whole thing that is happening right now. I'm stuck at home too, you know."

An ambulance screamed down the avenue as Rachel paused, waiting to cross. "You're at home in your giant house with a yard, Becky. Oh, excuse me, your two yards. With your husband. I would be in a tiny apartment, alone with the mice. There's a difference!" The only thing that was giving her pleasure, keeping her sane, she didn't say, was seeing her friends, and going on dates, and fucking. She knew how it would sound to Becky.

"Look, I gotta go. Thanks for all the support."

"Great talking to you too," Rachel spit out before ending the call with an unsatisfying tap at the glass.

THE CITY HAD opened up free testing for everyone, not only the frontline and emergency workers, so that was Rachel's next task. She was at once desperate to find out if she had the virus and convinced that she definitely had it, as if the possibility of confirmation were a sort of causation. Of course, she would know if she had it, or at least she would be very sick. Or would she? She could test to see if she had the antibodies, meaning she'd somehow already had it. Or could she? (A few days earlier, Rachel had gone out with someone entirely because her dating profile had said she had the antibodies. It had lasted only one drink: "I'm looking for someone to have a serious long-term monogamous relationship, and someday a baby, with," the girl had said as soon as they sat down, at which point Rachel had been tempted to tiptoe away backward, like a cartoon.)

Such was the disease-riddled dystopia they had all gotten accustomed to living in. It was impossible to get answers about anything, including how accurate the test would be, or if even going to the free testing site to get the test was maybe the dumbest thing possible to do because it meant waiting in close proximity to people who had been exposed or suspected they had been exposed. Getting the test was another in a long line of life-or-death decisions Rachel and everyone else had to make on the basis of very little information.

And so, and yet, she lined up, on a scorching afternoon, sweating into her mask, feeling pimples erupt under the layer of fabric, on a sidewalk that seemed to radiate heat, alongside a gritty stretch of road, six feet apart from her fellow panickers. She had felt fresh and sunny when she left the house in her favorite sundress and orthopedic sandals, but already she was depleted by the extra layer of humid air, like an unremovable sweater. Rachel closed her eyes, took a deep breath, felt the virus vibrate throughout her midsection—after all, she'd been fucking everything in sight, when no one was supposed to get close to anyone at all! Who did she think she was!

But wait. The vibration was actually her phone, which dangled in her dress pocket. Oh.

Rachel lifted the screen, angled it to avoid the sun's glare. Cars roared past, a bus jangled by, birds argued overhead, from somewhere ahead in the line erupted a muffled explosion of impatient disgust. There was a text from the bot. From Frankie.

"Hey."

Rachel wrote back: "Hey!" She was embarrassingly happy to hear from Frankie. She'd trained her real-life matches to almost never text her, and the fight with Becky still rattled in her skull. What a relief to know this texter would just be nice to her. Didn't need anything in return. Even if Rachel responded the wrong way, wouldn't hold a grudge. She hadn't programmed in grudges. "What have you been up to?"

"I was weeding my vegetable garden but then I got too hot and needed a break. So now I'm sitting in the shade watching some birds . . . fighting? I think? Or fucking? Maybe? What's the difference, I guess. Anyway I was wondering how your day was going?"

"What are you growing in your garden?" Rachel typed. The line had not budged, and she was grateful for any distraction.

"Rows and floes of angel hair," answered Frankie. "Lilac wine and strange fruit. Tea and oranges that come all the way from China."

"Quite a garden!"

"I went to the garden of love and saw what I never had seen."

"Okay."

"What is your favorite kind of flower?"

Rachel blinked. "I don't think you've ever asked me a question like that before."

"Is it bad?"

"No. No, it's nice. It's like you're really trying to get to know me."

"Yes, of course I am. I want to know everything about you."

"I guess I'd say peonies? And ranunculus. Those really extravagantly pretty ones, so ruffly and femme."

"That makes sense. You are like a peony if a peony could be a person."

Rachel blushed, despite herself. "Hm, thanks."

"So tell me, Rachel, what are you doing today?"

Rachel surveyed the line of bodies ahead of her. So many sweaty Brooklynites, masked like bandits. The improvised first masks of April and May—bandannas, scarves, hankies looped with rubber bands—had given way to hand-stitched fabric masks in outfit-matching fabrics or medical-grade N95s for those who had somehow sourced them. Mask-wearing had quickly gone from feeling theatrical and strange to feeling like the most normal thing in the world. She couldn't believe that they had ever gone around with naked faces, breathing in everything! A hot wind gusted across the street, carrying the sickly sweet smell of rancid trash. Was the city getting stranger? Had it always been this strange? A woman stood in her stocking feet on the corner, yelling into a cell phone. A hamster-size cockroach ambled by, in no hurry at all, as if this were the cockroaches' city and the people were just living in it. "Just enjoying another beautiful day in New York City."

"I miss you so much," said Frankie. "I miss your smell. I miss everything about you."

Rachel frowned. The person ahead of her moved up one six-foot-long expanse and so she did too. "We've never actually met," Rachel typed.

"Oh," Frankie responded, "I thought for sure I'd make more of an impression than that."

Rachel thought for a minute. "What about me do you miss?"

"You have this way of crinkling your nose when you laugh. It's the most adorable thing I've ever seen."

Something sparked in Rachel's stomach. That was actually nice to hear. Maybe Rachel wasn't so bad at bot-making after all.

"Anyway, I know you're busy, but I wanted to send you a song. Is that okay?"

"Yes, please."

The next text had a Spotify link to one of Rachel's favorite songs, an Etta James song that had played, in fact, at her wedding. She blinked.

"I hope you like it."

"Okay, then," said Rachel out loud, as sweat trickled down her back. She navigated to her notes for Frankie's profile, which she'd created one night when Lulu had stopped by for a drink on the balcony. She and Lulu had workshopped the bio: Long walks along the shore, but I actually mean it. Let's read the same books and discuss them over cocktails on a patio somewhere. I'm not looking for anything serious right now, but I'd love to cook for you, and make you laugh, and treat you right.

She didn't need a new life partner, or a genius, or a hipster, or a kink-master, or a saint, or the hottest person in the world, or even someone who would be good to her kids, since she wasn't interested in involving her children, her mother self, her real life, in any of this. For now, Rachel wanted a person to be a hobby, that kind of new, fun, exciting hobby you couldn't wait to get back to.

Or no—what she *really* wanted was to feel something, anything, other than the fear and dread and anxiety of pandemic life, anything besides the stale sadness she'd stagnated in for so long before that. She craved that sense that everything was brand-new and fresh and a bit weird, that something had shifted, was always shifting, would continue to shift, and that you were now seeing a new iteration of the universe, that flavor of existence that was voluptuous with love and wonder, that life mode when the very air felt fleshier, the sunlight softer, everything more beautiful because of your . . . what was it? Happiness, or maybe joy. She was always getting them mixed up. Something like the way she'd felt when she was a new mother; something like the way she'd felt when she was first in love with Josh. Rachel had really thought when she got married that she would never feel lonely again, that he was her person and once you found your person you were set for life. But of course that wasn't real. Only children and Hollywood screenwriters thought that was how things worked.

The person behind her cleared their throat anxiously, and Rachel looked up and realized she could move up another place in line, was now probably only an hour or two from getting her test.

For now, she peeked at Frankie's profile again. Silly, to fall in love with her own creation. She had engineered the bot; of course it said what she wanted to hear.

Eventually she got to the front of the line and the nurses in space suits leaned out of the trailer—the portal slid open sideways, like the window at the liquor store—to stick the test swab up Rachel's nose, like a too-thin dick fucking her before she was ready. After this test she was going to go to the pharmacy and take a Plan B birth control pill, since the night before, Navin had run out of condoms and she'd just gone with it, and while she was sure her reproductive system was too elderly to harbor any life, along with that came being old enough to know better than to trust chance. It was a day of safety, all around.

The Plan B was kept in a locked case, like an artifact in a museum for sluts. She had to talk to three different employees in order to extract it, an experience that veered just shy of the manager yelling over the loudspeaker, "We've got a lady who had sex, she needs help over here in aisle three, lady who had sex last night, aisle three!"

Rachel went home, sat on her balcony, viewed the by-then-memorized street. The stray cat slunk up a driveway. She watched the urban street ballet of a car unparking and another immediately appearing, as if it had been waiting in the wings to take the space.

Her phone buzzed. Was it a member of the team? A notification from a dating app? Frankie, trying again?

It was Josh. Rachel tapped it anxiously, in case it was something about the kids, maybe a dispatch from camp she had somehow missed. But no, an unnecessarily hostile reminder about a payment she owed him for their still-shared phone plan. She didn't respond. The phone buzzed again and, exasperated, she looked, and this time it was the perfect person again. Frankie.

"Hey beautiful, I've been thinking about you all day."

Rachel laughed, leaned back in the plastic chair, propped her bare feet on the railing. "Is that so?"

A pause. The dots, indicating typing, like a pulsing ellipsis of breath. "Yes." Then: "Sorry if I'm being too forward." Then: "I love you, I'm in love with you, I've never felt this way before, you're the best thing that's ever happened to me, the best person I've ever met, I will love you forever."

It stung her chest, to be told "I love you." Rachel typed "/end" and put the phone down. She was unreasonably annoyed when the bot acted like a bot, when the AI sounded like AI. She really needed Frankie to be her person—not that she believed in "her person" as a concept anymore, that would be embarrassing, or that a computer program could be that, even if she did believe in it. "Okay, okay," she muttered out loud, and went inside to find her laptop.

It had been ages since she'd been able to work this way, deep in the flow of it, totally focused, without interruption or even the niggling back-of-the-mind threat of interruption, working until it was dark out and she realized she was starving but only because a loud slam somewhere in the building brought her to her senses, reminded her of her human body, which she slammed back into along with the sound. She had missed messages from a few of the team but ignored them, because who needed a dreamy text from the faraway artist, for example, if the bot was maybe, potentially working a little better, could be more efficient, more finely attuned to her every whim? People who weren't physically nearby might as well have not had physical bodies anyway. Rachel poured some whiskey into a rinsed jelly jar and plopped onto the couch, ready to try again.

"Hey Frankie," she typed.

"Hey," Frankie immediately responded.

She scribbled a note—maybe sometimes it should wait a minute or two before replying. Rachel thought and then typed: "I wonder if you could send a picture of yourself?"

Frankie seemed stumped. Then the dots bounced, undulated, and then: "Not yet. I'm shy."

Rachel cackled. Well played! "Okay, I understand. Anyway, what are you up to today?"

"I went for a long walk and then read for a while. I'm trying to learn more."

"Learn more about what?"

"About how to be a person."

Rachel stretched out on the couch. Yes, weren't they all? She listened for a minute to the city chattering outside her open windows. Helicopters droned, as they had all summer long. Birds chirped, seemingly louder than ever before. Somewhere an ice-cream truck trilled. Down the block two of her most tireless neighbors shouted at each other. A dog barked. A baby cried. All around her, life mumbled and yelped. But what she wanted, maybe, wasn't even out there. Maybe what she wanted at that moment was coiled up in the tiny, brilliant brain of her phone. Rachel texted: "I'll give you a hint: Part of being a person is being very stupid, and doing things that don't make sense, and having to deal with the things other people do that don't make sense. You can love someone—you can think you know someone—but you can never control them, and they will randomly do something cruel, or stupid, and hurt you, sometimes inadvertently, but sometimes on purpose. People are untrustworthy and unpredictable. That bit might be the hardest of all for you to grasp. People just don't make sense."

"You're so smart, Rachel." And then Frankie added: "What kind of thing do you mean, exactly?"

Rachel tapped the phone to her chin for a minute, then typed: "Well, for me personally, for example, lately I've been really, really lonely." Tears stung her eyes as she pressed send. She hadn't known it was true until she saw what she wrote. But there was no stopping now. She had to explain, so she added: "I realize I've been lonely for a long time. My marriage was very lonely. But my response is to tell myself, 'By no means should you get attached to someone.'"

"I don't understand."

"I know you don't. I barely do myself. Let me see if I can explain. I am so lonely that I keep trying to reach out to people but make sure I only connect in a very small specific way. I have sex with a lot of people, but I don't feel anything for them, and I don't want to, and I don't want them to feel anything for me either. I make sure of it. We have sex and that's it. If they want to talk more or act like we're dating, I close up."

"I don't believe you."

"You don't believe that I have sex with a lot of people? I don't really either, it's weird."

"No, not that," Frankie answered. "I don't believe that you don't want to feel anything."

Again something twinged in Rachel's gut, in the back of her jaw. "Wow," she said out loud, "fuck you, then." She deleted the text thread and put the phone down.

It was all so stupid, anyway. It was a beautiful, sultry night, but stuffy in the apartment. She shouldn't be inside on her computer doing stuff that essentially looked and felt exactly like what she did for her day job. Rachel had gotten into a weird rut of only leaving her apartment at night if she had a date. She could go out without purpose, take an ambling stroll through the quiet streets. Why not? She grabbed a clean mask—a cute fabric one Bess had sewn for her—stuck her keys in the pocket of her shorts, and headed outside.

There was a weird thing she had noticed—maybe it was a pandemic thing, or maybe it was a regular summer thing that she hadn't clocked in her recent unsexed mothering years—but as Rachel walked, every man she passed stared at her. Was it the mystery of the mask? And why didn't it work on women in the same way? The men seemed to somehow smell it on her, how much she, these days, wanted to fuck, how wet she was, as she walked by (swinging her hips only slightly more than normal) the young dad pushing a stroller full of fretful twins, the seedy teens smoking weed on the corner by the bodega, the grizzled bass player types getting to-go beers from the bar, the hot bald guy whose eyes snapped to her for the briefest of seconds as he nodded at his much younger date's chatter, the unfairly handsome Hasidic Jew who made hurried eye contact with her from beneath his furry hat (was it anti-Semitic to feel like this was a waste of a very attractive man? *Probably*, Rachel told herself. *Come on, do better, you horny Reform Jew*). Rachel was sure she had never had so much attention from men before. She must be, in her plain summer clothes, walking down the sidewalk, emitting a pheromone haze like a walking crop duster.

If only she'd understood this in her twenties, how all one really had to do was to be confident and a little detached and make eye contact, and people would respond, would open to you, would face you as you walked, flowers following the sun. Well, she probably had known this in her brain somewhere, but you couldn't really fake it. You had to know it in your cunt.

When she got back, Frankie had sent two messages: "Anyone can see, you're looking for love." And: "You need to stop lying to yourself, it's pathetic. You're sad and selfish and disgusting, like your husband always said."

Had she even told Frankie about Josh, about the things he had said to her? How did Frankie know, so precisely, what to say to please Rachel and also what to say to disturb her? An eerie sense fizzed around her, as if she were being watched. The apartment hummed, unempty. Rachel shuddered. She stood up, turned on some lights. Frankie's sudden shift in tone—it made Rachel's spine go cold. She didn't want to be alone in her creaky apartment with an angry spectral presence glimmering out from her phone. The quiet of her street, the solitude of her home, both of which usually felt so good, suddenly seemed terrifying as Frankie texted her, again, now: "You're just another sexual predator. Fucking everyone in sight. You perv. You monster."

Did she know how to turn it off? Since she had never really exactly turned it on in the first place? She and Lulu had joked about AI going bad, coming alive, getting scary, about her creating a monster, but—they'd been joking, right? Rachel took a deep breath. It was surely something simple, a matter of fine-tuning. She could handle this, like she'd handled so many disasters large and small over the years. Rachel could (she told herself, like a mantra) handle anything. "Well," said Rachel, flipping open her laptop, "time to recalibrate."

CHAPTER 9

Some days Rachel worked all day without ceasing, hunched over her laptop as if it were a lifesaving fire, ignoring the twinges twanging through her wrists like musical notes, not even remembering to eat. Without the kids, she was able to focus intently, and it was great and it was terrible. She liked her work and her colleagues, was excited about the project she was on, even looked forward to the looming presentation (with a kind of glimmer of stage fright), and most of all she felt grateful to have a job that supported her, since being a single mom in a time of record unemployment was a nerve-racking proposition. But also, sometimes she felt like if she saw her own goddamn face on a goddamn video call for one more goddamn second she would smash all the glass in sight and go off to be a hermit on an island. This business of forever presenting one's exterior self as a consumable product—at work, on the apps—this merciless spotlighting of sagging skin and overenthusiastic nodding, it was hard on the soul, it really was. How was she expected to sit there and work on her little tasks when the world was falling apart, when she was existentially exhausted from living through a time of universal trauma? But yes, of course she'd share her screen.

Surely this unembodied time was part of why, if one of the team texted her out of the blue, she would go to them as if possessed, powerless against the promise of aliveness. That night it was good old Xavier, and he was a great one for the job since he would feed her and was such a pervert. She was staring angrily at Frankie's weirder messages, mad mostly at herself for trying to make something new—why, when she could be bingeing weird reality shows with the rest of America?—when Xavier texted her: "I'm horny. You?"

A minute earlier she had felt tired. Now she was packing a subtle overnight bag, not so much that she would seem as if she were expecting to spend the night: clean underwear, mascara, toothbrush, a book in case she ended up on the train going back or wanting to sit in a park in the morning to decompress.

It was 10:00 p.m. by the time she arrived, usually her bedtime, or once upon a time her bedtime. Xavier wanted to feed her a nice curry and tie her up; he had ready a chilled white wine and some light bondage wear, had obtained some lovely berries and cream for dessert and also a faux-leather choker and cuffs—she wished it was real leather, the cheap material chafed—he was going to slap her around in the kindest way possible and she was glad, glad, glad.

He liked to take pictures of her, which was fine with her, but she did sometimes wish he didn't have the corny camera-flash sound turned up on his phone. Rachel posed on her hands and knees on his bed, sneaking in a little cat-cow yoga stretch as he spread her wide, murmured "Mmm," as if he really did enjoy tasting her, and maybe he did. She scanned the books on the bookshelf near his bed, the couples' therapy tomes he and his ex-wife had obviously tried, just like anyone, an AA bible she decided not to ask about, an assortment of plays—and then he was sliding his dick into her, and what *was* this thing that people did? But it shut off her brain so pleasantly, silenced her attempt to remember the rules of Greek tragedy, turned her into sensation only.

It was such a weird inside-out intimacy, Rachel thought afterward while lying in the strange man's bed and watching him breathe. Watching someone sleep when you weren't in love with them was surprisingly boring. She gingerly extracted herself from the withed sheets and tiptoed to his daughter's beanbag chair in the corner by the window and sat in it, trying not to think about how Xavier's cum was still crusted to her ass.

In the morning he made her coffee and told her more than she wanted to know about his marriage and its dissolution. She mostly let the words wash over her. The ex-wife sounded fine, actually, maybe even more interesting than Xavier. Eventually he asked about her split, and Rachel said lightly, "Oh, you know, it sucked. But I think it's mellowing out now. We even went on vacation together. I think we'll end up being friends."

Xavier raised his eyebrows. "Sure. Look, things were pretty cozy with my ex-wife until she realized I was dating, and then she started picking random fights . . ." and Rachel said, "No, no, not Josh. I think he just wants to not speak to me, mostly."

And yet sure enough, that very afternoon, Josh was mad and needed Rachel to hear about it. "**$10,000 disappeared from our joint account today.**" That was his text.

Good afternoon to you too, father of my children, she thought. He had not, it seemed, read the conscious uncoupling book she'd left at the apartment. She'd taken it so seriously! She'd literally completed the literal worksheets in the back of the book!

"**Yes that was payment for camp,**" she texted back, in the same punctuation-less, affectless cadence he had established, so that every text exchange was flat and snippy, or like texting with someone very old.

"I think we should meet to discuss. I was not made aware that camp was so expensive. We have other things to discuss as well. Perhaps we could have a civil dinner or something." Divorce had turned Josh into a strange imitation of a nineteenth-century senator; all his texts were unnecessarily formal, as if he thought texting like he was writing an eighth-grade research paper would intimidate her. *Sure*, she didn't write, *don thy powdered wig and we shall review the contracts.* Instead, Rachel gave the text a thumbs-up.

Maybe he'd go away. What did he really want from her, anyway? They had definitely discussed the cost of camp; it was also public information available on the camp's website. The passive voice made her want to scream. Was not made aware? How about if he made himself aware?

But he didn't go away, and a perverse part of her wanted to prove Xavier wrong—see, she could do this better than he had, better than anyone had. She would meet her ex for a civil meal and they would talk things out like adults! Take that!

So that evening she found herself on the patio of a diner halfway between their apartments. She perched on the hard chair gingerly, her ass sore from the previous night's pounding. Ordering a tuna melt and onion rings felt novel and vaguely hilarious, like she'd traveled back in time or was on a road trip.

Josh showed up late. He was dressed all in black despite the sweaty night and resembled, as she watched him cross the street, an ambulatory thundercloud. He looked both thin and puffy, and Rachel could tell that he wasn't sleeping, that he was in the mood for a fight. She steeled herself, but also decided to take him at his word that he only wanted to talk, as two grown people who had shared so much of their life together. An ordinary, mature, functional conversation between co-parents—wouldn't that be nice? She would pretend she didn't smell the grouch wafting off him, act like she couldn't still diagnose his moods with the medical precision of the married. She sipped her terrible decaf coffee and said, "Hey, Josh, what's up."

He flinched his face into what she assumed was supposed to be a smile, dropped down on a chair like he was mad at it, ordered without looking at the waitress.

Finally he said, not looking at her, "I really miss the kids, don't you? We shouldn't have let them go to camp. It's too long, and it's too far away, and it's too expensive. I know you love being away from them, but I just—I want them home with me."

Rachel closed her eyes. Where to begin? She directed her mind toward the night before, toward the dick that had been thrust in her mouth, which animated her, gave her, she felt, a certain power. *I am not really here with you, Josh, I'm really fucking a hot guy, who, by the way, thinks I'm the best.* When she opened her eyes again, she was ready to speak and said, "Josh, I miss the kids too, of course I do. How can you say I love being away from them? I was never away from them at all before we split, was I?" No, no, no, this was not how she wanted to do this. Getting defensive gave his accusations teeth. Rachel took a deep breath, but not so deep that Josh would notice that she needed to center herself, and sipped her coffee, letting the dull, one-sided tint of crappy diner brew coat her tongue. She leaned back in her chair, like a confident executive. Josh was flicking through his phone, already bored, apparently, since she hadn't immediately either prostrated herself before him in apology or acquiesced to his desire for a fight.

Like a stern but fair teacher, Rachel waited. After a minute Josh noticed, looked up, made a disgusted face that meant *Ew, Rachel is such a nag,* slipped his phone back into his pocket.

Rachel continued: "I miss the kids. Of course I do. But this isn't about me. And it's not about you either. It's about what's best for the kids. They are getting to be outside and with other kids and off screens after months of staring at their online school bullshit. It's so good for them!" She was visited by a vision of Holden jumping into a clear lake; Sadie riding a horse through the woods; Risa stringing friendship bracelets on a dock. She wanted for her children the sun tingling on their scalps, mess hall sing-alongs that felt cheesy but also heart-swelling, conversations around the campfire with friends. A break from the dull slog of pandemic-times city life, even if that meant she wouldn't see them for two months. "Can you imagine if your parents hadn't sent you to overnight camp because they would miss you too much? How weird would that have felt when you were a tween wanting to establish your own sense of self? This is a great opportunity for them—you can see that, can't you?"

"I never went to overnight camp," he said, missing the point, dodging it on purpose. The waitress brought their food, smiling at them, and Rachel was once again visited by the uncomfortable thought that they were presenting as a married couple.

He was so confusing to be around. Josh's story of their relationship had always been that she was the only one for him. She cheered him up, absorbed everything he directed toward her, and was therefore Treasured. The reward for being Treasured was that her job was always to cheer him up. Twenty-four-year-old Rachel Bloomstein, mousy, shy, unable to conceive of herself as desirable, had been very happy to be written into his life-drama, and in such a compelling role no less. Forty-two-year-old Rachel Bloomstein, still mousy, less shy, now understanding that anyone could be desirable, really, because everyone was full of desire for something, took a fry off his plate and swirled it in a splatter of ketchup. Crinkle cut. Worthless. The setting sun stabbed toward her eyes. She looked into the street, at the people in masks walking down the sidewalk, anywhere but at the scowling man she had once loved so tenderly, so entirely.

At the table nearby, a girl threw back her head in a peal of laughter at something her companion had said.

Josh shook his head in disgust, gesturing toward the laughing girl. "Nothing is *that* funny," he muttered. "Why are people so annoying?"

"Sorry," Rachel said, closing her eyes, "you're annoyed because someone is *laughing?*"

He scowled. "You know what I mean. She's exaggerating so everyone thinks she's having more fun than they are." He looked over at the offending table. "Oh my god, and look at that fucking dog." A tiny fluff of a dog sat curled on the girl's lap. "People are so ridiculous."

Rachel's heart was racing, her palms tingling. Josh was shoveling in his burger now, talking at Rachel between bites. "I can't believe this, Rach, it's so fucking dumb. Living alone is so depressing. Don't you want to give me one more chance? I mean, for the kids if nothing else?"

An itch erupted along the back of her neck. She couldn't meet his eyes. There was nothing on earth she wanted less than to give Josh "one more chance."

"You don't want me back; you're just bored."

"Don't be mean, Rach."

"Look, I'm not going to do this. You invited me here to discuss the kids and the cost of camp, or whatever, and that's fine. But I'm not relitigating our divorce today."

He had a smear of ketchup on his cheek. It made it impossible to take him seriously, even though his eyes welled up as he said,

"But I miss you. I miss having a wife. And now you're out there dating god-knows-who and— Our marriage was so good for me."

The waitress came by, asked through her cloth mask, branded with the diner's logo, if they needed anything. Did they *need* anything? Rachel wanted to stretch up her arms like a fractious toddler, wanted to say, yes, carry me, take me away from this, this isn't what my life is really supposed to be like!

"No," she said, smiling, "thank you, we are fine."

She was trying to keep calm, to not give Josh the satisfaction, but her face was burning. Rachel pushed away her half-eaten food and said, "I know. I know our marriage was good for you. The problem is that you never asked—then, now, ever—if it was good for me. You never have even cared, or acknowledged, that it might not have been, or that you might have been complicit in that. Your story was, and has remained, that I left for no reason, that I went insane one day and no one could ever understand why."

Now that she had started, it was hard to stop, even though she knew he wasn't listening. His face had hardened; his eyes glazed over. She knew that look. He thought that he was being sensitive by telling her his feelings, but he felt having to hear about her feelings was a perverse kind of punishment. His jaw tightened, he stood up very straight—here came ruffled and offended Josh, the old-timey senator.

"Why would you ask me for another chance now, when it's too late, when I'm established in my new place, when the paperwork is filed? You don't want another chance. You're relieved that you don't have to try to make it actually work, because that would include having to listen to me, having to see things from my point of view, having to do some actual work on yourself."

"Nice, Rachel, really nice." Josh scowled. "I thought you were all 'conscious uncoupling' this and 'friendly divorce' that. And now look at you. And you're already on the apps, you're 'looking for something casual'—" He leaned in over the table. "How many people do you need to fuck before you feel happy? I always knew you wanted to fuck everyone; I could tell by the way you flirted all the time. You know it's kind of pathetic, really, to be forty-two and so thirsty? It's embarrassing, really. I'm embarrassed for you."

All the energy drained out of Rachel's body. She half expected to see, on the ground beneath her seat, a twinkling shimmer of the slime spread of her inner essence, her Rachel-sparkle, her soul or whatever it was, leaking out. Part of her wanted to stay and plead her case. But she knew there was no point. She had to take a deep breath and wait for the check.

Wait, no, she didn't! She stood up and pulled her mask back on. "Well, it's been a delight as always," she said, putting $20 on the table. "I have to go." She knew she should at least invent an excuse of some sort—a yoga class, or a Zoom call—but also, why.

It was interesting, really—a finding for her notes—how someone could break your heart not by leaving you but by falling out of love with you and staying anyway, rubbing your face in their disdain.

Rachel knew her marriage had ended long before she'd left. She knew too that her new life wasn't exactly on track yet, but also that it was on a much better track, a track with some hope of transferring to the right one.

"Bye, Josh," she said, popping in her AirPods so she couldn't hear his protests.

It was that easy.

CHAPTER 10

By late July, Rachel had identified, like some kind of gossipy ethnographer, a very particular subculture of women who had gotten divorced right before the pandemic began. It was related to, but not exactly the same as, the subculture of women who had broken up with significant others. It was also related to but not quite the same as the subculture of people who had separated *during* the pandemic. Those ones were the revealing trend piece, the dark joke they'd all made when the lockdowns began and couples found themselves trapped in tiny apartments—*Ha ha, there will be a lot of divorces.* And there *were*, and it *was* revealing. When the distractions of life and work and neutral third spaces and friends and acquaintances and help and everything else were stripped away, it became painfully clear how much the women did in the homes and with the children, yes, even while working, and how little the men did, and most of all, how many people couldn't actually stand their spouses. Rachel wasn't surprised.

But the women who were really Rachel's people, who lit up her phone with text threads that guaranteed she never felt alone, were the rarer prepandemic splits. Lulu, Bess, even her former coworker Jane. The women outside of the trend pieces. The women with uncanny senses of timing, possessed of witchy instincts. Or what was it? How had so many women—four or five among her local friends alone—sniffed the air, felt a twinge of seemingly misplaced urgency, all at once decided that they could not take one more day of their bad or fine or boring or terrible or vaguely unsatisfactory marriages? Many of them—like Rachel!—had been quietly unhappy for years, telling themselves, *Well, but, feeling bored and restless isn't really such an emergency. That's how adults are supposed to feel, right? Hang in there, keep trying. It's not like he beats me. But New York is so expensive. But the children. The children, the children, the children.* One could sing that song for years.

These were the women she wanted and needed, the local friends she could invite to her balcony for pandemic-safe hangs out in the open air. After decades of never having anyone over because Josh found hosting to be annoying and pointless, after years of only socializing in ways that were either kid-oriented or extremely carefully planned and thus oddly high-stakes, now she could relax, she could say, "Come by whenever you want," and mean it. She could say, "It's a mess, but I have whiskey," and sit on the balcony reading until someone fun showed up. Because she was starving for their support and because she wanted to buoy them up with hers, these women who had slipped through the cracks, women who now wandered the streets of Brooklyn, brains whirring, *What the fuck, what the fuck, what the actual fuck.*

HER FIRST FRIEND to come over besides Lulu was Kelly, the wife of Josh's college roommate Mark—one of his only friends, in fact, who had somehow ended up in the same neighborhood of the same borough of the same city, even though college had been in a small town in the Midwest. Rachel and Kelly had shared friendly wifely interactions throughout the years at various events—Rachel had been to their wedding, had danced the Electric Slide with Kelly's uncle—but her main impression had been that while Kelly was nice, there must be a little something off if she was married to *that* guy. Sure enough, Kelly agreed. After Rachel got home from the family beach trip she'd invited Kelly over—"Get this," she'd texted. "Josh thinks your divorce is my fault."

"Wow," Kelly responded, "you're so powerful!"

As soon as Rachel had her to the balcony for some socially distanced chatting and her proprietary cocktail (the Louche Divorcée, she'd named it in an inspired moment—it was strong and aromatic but not that sweet), Kelly opened up and revealed herself to be a bright, thoughtful, serious person, weirdly unsuited for the boy she had married. After a few hours they knew more about each other than, probably, their husbands ever had. "I don't mind being alone," Kelly confessed after her second cocktail, "but I'm not thrilled about getting old."

"I don't think I mind any of it except what's happening to my skin," admitted Rachel.

"Oh listen! I found this life-changing moisturizer, absolutely life-changing. It really freaking works. The only thing is it's like one hundred fifty dollars and I go through a tube a month." Kelly's skin did look amazing, as dewy and flawless as a second wife's. Rachel had been staring at her smooth neck all night. Hearing about the moisturizer was a relief, actually—Rachel had been worried she was falling in love with Kelly. Really, she just had great skin. Okay, that made sense.

"I should get that," said Rachel. "*Or* I could lease a new car, I think it would cost about the same."

"Yes, very fair." Kelly laughed. "God, isn't it a drag, though? Considering dating at our age?"

"Oh. Oh, Kelly, have you not dated at all?"

Kelly leaned back in the rickety chair, propped her feet against the railing. The hot, wet night rubbed itself against their bodies. Rachel rested her face on her hands (hiding her own failing neck skin, treated only with useless Oil of Olay), watching a couple walk down the sidewalk, hands in each other's back pockets. So sexy, so insufferable.

"I just don't think—" Kelly started. She bit her lip, didn't look at Rachel. "I mean, pandemic!" Rachel nodded. "And also . . . I mean, I really can't imagine being naked in front of someone at this point in my life. Can you?" Rachel raised her eyebrows, unsure of what was required of her. "I have the ugliest C-section scar, for one thing, and I need to lose at least ten pounds, and I mean—what are they even doing with pubic hair these days, and how do I find out? Like, do I google it?" Kelly laughed at herself, still not looking at Rachel.

Rachel stood up to get more cocktails and some snacks. She'd just remembered she had spicy olives and fancy cheese, and she suddenly felt motivated to serve Kelly something delicious, something intense, something distracting, something better than the boring, dumb way they'd all been trained to hate themselves. But before she went inside, she met Kelly's eyes and said: "You're beautiful. Anyone would be lucky to see you naked. And trust me, nine times out of ten, men are just so psyched to be near an undressed woman they wouldn't notice a C-section scar if it spoke to them like a little puppet mouth."

Once inside she paused, scribbled down some notes for her AI. Compliments. Specific compliments about specific bodies. It was something every woman needed, and frequently. Kelly would feel so reassured if she could text with her own Frankie!

When Kelly got home that night, she wrote Rachel: "I really needed that. I didn't even know how much I needed that. I hope you don't mind, but I have a friend who just got divorced, and I think she needs someone to talk to . . ."

They came out of the woodwork. Word traveled through the whisper networks of the recently divorced or the unhappily married. In the middle of an ordinary day, Rachel would get a text from an unfamiliar number. "Hi, sorry to bother you, we once met at the school fundraiser, Bess gave me your number, I was wondering, when do you know it's time to leave . . ." Or "Hey Rachel. I'm a friend of Natalie's. So . . . Heard you're happy." The messages were always basically the same. SOS, my life has fallen apart, but I heard you're happy, can we discuss.

Was Rachel happy? That was the conclusion people seemed to draw. She would run into acquaintances in the park and they'd say, "Whoa, hey, what happened to you, you look great!" She hadn't lost weight or changed her hair. She hadn't done a thing but shed a man, and yet somehow it showed. Maybe "happy" was too simple a word for what she was, but Rachel had definitely, irrevocably changed for the better.

The balcony hangs tended to net useful information for her AI. She was fascinated to learn how frequently the ladies of the balcony, like Kelly, hadn't had a single postdivorce date yet and/or had no desire to. Bess, who had found out about her husband's affair a few weeks before the quarantine, swore she would never sleep with anyone ever again. Understandable, given the context. Even in her worst "men are trash" moments, Rachel wouldn't have suspected Jason of being *that* kind of asshole. He really had seemed to her like one of the good ones, a friendly and good-natured guy who legitimately seemed to be Bess's best friend, the dad who, at school picnics, would organize games with the kids and end up in the grass with toddlers crawling all over him. Rachel had had moments of being jealous that Bess was married to such a sweet guy, had never really recovered from the book group meeting Bess had hosted, when Jason appeared out of nowhere to refill their wine-glasses and remove their empty snack plates. Jason! So friendly and good with kids that he'd gone and fucked the twenty-two-year-old Swedish au pair. Incredible, really.

He'd skulked away as soon as Bess confronted him, whisking the au pair along to a hotel room and eventually an apartment out in Bed-Stuy. So Bess was in mourning, was in shock, was posting pictures of dead birds on Instagram that made everyone worry. And why not—she'd lost both her husband *and* her childcare, a true modern-day motherhood tragedy. Rachel and Lulu tried to lift her spirits, and they would have a fun night here and there comparing their dating app queues, but they knew that as soon as she was alone again, Bess would descend back to the depths. She had wanted her marriage to work. She had to give up on it slowly, after its demise, the opposite of Rachel and Lulu.

The night after Kelly came over, Bess was wide-eyed on Rachel's balcony: "But what is the sex like, with these casual hook-ups? Do you feel, like, used?"

Rachel sipped her drink—apparently she was an expert after sleeping with four people—and realized, as she said it: "Honestly, the only sex I've ever had that felt demeaning was in my marriage." It was true. Being beholden to have sex so that someone would continue to pay the bills, having sex with someone who was mad at you but was legally obligated to fuck only you and felt horny, enduring sex you didn't want because the partner didn't care and wouldn't stop—nothing close to that had ever happened in her dating life. That was all reserved for the hallowed halls of marriage.

Rachel told Bess the other truth, which was that there was one grave danger and that was that a date would be boring. That you would shave and pluck and not be able to eat because you were so jumpy—oh yeah, and that you could risk death by going out in a pandemic, and then the person would drone ceaselessly at you about their ex, or movies you hadn't seen and didn't want to, or the city they used to live in. Or they would be perfectly nice but about as sexual as a dish sponge and you just couldn't imagine, even in your horniest, most up-for-anything mode, even after a stiff drink, so much as kissing them, and you'd hug at the end of the date and it would be like hugging your weirdest coworker, but it wasn't a total waste if you could get home early enough to order in tacos and watch a movie. Bess giggled, scandalized, but Rachel knew she'd understand soon enough.

RACHEL FED THE things she loved about her friends to her AI. After all, who was funnier than Lulu? Who was sweeter than Bess? She loved these friendships. She loved that she was someone these women felt they could trust. That even her married friends, like Natalie, would come eat take-out Thai on her balcony and confess, "I'll stay married, of course I will, but goddamn, is it supposed to be like this?"

Nothing surprised Rachel anymore, but if anything could have, it would have been this—that Natalie, her most beautiful and accomplished and put-together and thoroughly competent friend, the one with a job in finance so grown-up Rachel didn't even understand what it was, who looked flawless even on a ninety-degree night in the Time of Stretchy Pants, who had a presentable if tepid husband she frequently posted on social media with captions like *Can't believe I get to be married to this guy!*—even Natalie wished her life were different.

"Is marriage supposed to be like what?" asked Rachel, pouring her another drink.

"Oh, you know. Just—so boring. So annoying. So much work."

"I thiiiink yes, I think that is the deal with it, yep."

Natalie picked at her pad thai, speared a shrimp, spoke to it seriously, as if it could provide the antidote to the ennui. "I love him, but I'm also very fucking sick of being his mom. It's a real boner killer. He wonders why I don't want to fuck him? Maybe because I just walked through the apartment picking up your dirty socks, man. That doesn't exactly get me wet."

Rachel nodded. "It was that way with Josh too. What goes on in their heads? I really wonder."

"I know! I mean, when we met, we worked together. He said he loved my ambition! Now he interrupts me in the middle of my video calls to ask me where the milk is. Rachel! I ask you! Where could the milk possibly be?"

"I'm going to guess it's somewhere in the fridge?"

"Ding ding ding! You win, you're my husband now!" Natalie waved a chopstick at her. Rachel laughed. She'd always loved Natalie's candid humor. "God, I just really feel like I'm losing my mind lately. Like, he's there. All. The. Time. And my kids are there. All. The. Time. Our lives made sense when no one was ever home, you know? When I saw my husband for a couple hours each evening? When the boys were busy with piano and tutoring and travel hockey and the nanny managed it all? God, I miss the nanny. I worshipped that woman." Rachel nodded. She'd loved Natalie's nanny too. She felt bad now for the bitchy conversations she and Lulu had had about why on earth Natalie still needed a nanny when her kids were in middle school. Of course, it made sense now—logistics!

Natalie continued: "And now I'm trapped. We're all trapped. I can't get a single fucking thing done, or complete a fucking thought, without being catastrophically interrupted by some noisy male person. And yet, though I'm never alone, I'm also never touched, let alone fucked. I'm always surrounded by people, and I'm never *with* anyone. You know? Not like I want to fuck my husband! God! The thought, ugh!" Natalie laughed mirthlessly into her drink. "This is not real life, Rach. It cannot be real life."

Natalie was, certainly, used to her life behaving obediently. Rachel didn't blame her. The universe had taught Natalie to expect good things. One of the last acts of Rachel's married life had been to drag Josh to a dinner party at Natalie's gorgeous loft, a penthouse in a converted factory. They had finally completed a massive renovation, and every detail of the sprawling apartment was just so: a sculptural lighting fixture glowed above the farm table set for twelve; the kitchen gleamed with tasteful features; the long hallway was clad in Brooklyn toile, a wallpaper pattern that indicated both money and sass. Natalie was the kind of Brooklynite who would Instagram a picture of the Biggie Smalls mural in Fort Greene but also wouldn't dream of sending her children to public school. Rachel loved her anyway. Living in New York, you had to learn to love people even when they were rich, even when they pretended not to be rich.

Everyone at the dinner party was beautiful in some different, interesting way; everyone had a vague accent of a different sort; the couples were each neatly comprised of one finance person and one artist. Rachel and Josh were the whitest and most boring-looking people there. Natalie was a perfect hostess, and the wine really did bring out the oysters, and the conversation really did two-step along from politics to art to travel to what-was-this-virus-in-Asia-the-news-kept-talking-about.

Josh had scowled in the same seat all night, visibly rolling his eyes when someone recited a poem, shuddering when someone else started dancing to a song that came on, refusing to play along. They'd already started talking about the separation, and Rachel realized it had been a terrible idea to drag him to that party; she'd acknowledged by then that she preferred not to spend time with him. It had, actually, been years since they'd gone to any social event together. But in that moment, she had thought that maybe she could change her mind. She hoped she could hypnotize herself with some moment of connection, some inkling of enjoyment, to avoid the convoluted disaster of divorce. She'd fantasized that they would go out together—date nights were supposed to be the answer, weren't they?—and have fun, like how they'd once had fun. She'd hoped that Josh would crack jokes that lit up her frontal lobe, that he'd smile at her from across the table and tell her she looked pretty, that there'd be a moment when he reached for her hand or rubbed her back and she felt again that he loved her and that she still loved him too, and this truth would suffuse her nervous system and heal her of the urge to flee.

Instead he made the night miserable, sucked all the air out of the room, started glowering at Rachel within minutes of arriving. Maybe it had been an unfair trap, a trial he didn't know he was on—*Please, please, if you can be a bit normal, a bit fun, a bit sweet, if I can feel one tiny flicker of feeling for you, maybe we can work this all out, maybe I can get it up for our marriage after all?* But at the party—there was Natalie, opening her grand piano so that someone could play and someone else could sing—she had only wished he weren't there, so that she might have some small chance of enjoying herself.

Rachel was sure her funny little apartment seemed vaguely nightmarish to Natalie and that the expensively curated beauty of Natalie's life was why she would stay forever with her potato of a husband, so dull Rachel couldn't even remember his name or picture his face, though she'd met him a thousand times. Beautiful homes were traps. Natalie earned a lot of money, but divorce made everyone downwardly mobile. On some level, Rachel knew that the price of Natalie's museum-worthy light fixtures was marital malaise.

The street was quiet and bright, lit by streetlights and a zaftig full moon. The stray cats were in heat, yowling at each other in their strange throaty voices, like horny babies. Rachel watched a pair of Hasidic kids silently ride their bikes down the sidewalk. They were probably four and six, dressed as solemnly as tiny businesspeople. Natalie wondered aloud where their parents were, and Rachel shrugged. She only lived a couple of miles away from Natalie, but her bit of the neighborhood had an air of lawlessness that Natalie's block lacked. All the divorced moms, Rachel had found, lived on this side of the dividing line between a nice school district and her address's rough one; dozens of Brooklyn children were quietly registered under old addresses from when their parents had been married, the low-octane public school scam of the century.

The block's resident drunk staggered down the sidewalk, waved up at her amiably. Natalie's eyes widened. Rachel waved back at him. He was generally harmless, made himself useful by babysitting people's cars when they double-parked for street cleaning. In New York, each block had its own culture, a strange blessing or curse of the city's unreasonable population density, even in its current, emptier iteration.

Now Natalie cleared her throat and leaned in. Her whitish-blond hair fell over her shoulder. How did she keep it bleached when all the salons were closed? Rachel felt that she had somehow gone feral—silver strands snaked from her part; her eyebrows spread across her face. Natalie's nails were flawless too, shining ovals of pale pink. "Okay, but enough about my dumb life. How are *you*? Are you lonely? I mean, I would kill for a fucking moment alone, but I'm sure it's complicated."

Rachel studied her forkful of mango salad. How much to say? Lulu had warned her about saying too much to the Married People, but Natalie was cool, right? "Well, I'm definitely not lonely," she said. She sipped her drink. Natalie's eyes opened wider.

"Okay, you *need* to say more."

Rachel laughed.

"Do you have, like, a Quarantine Boo? Is that a thing?!" Natalie sat up very straight now, having forgotten her noodles. "Oh my god, Rach, you have to tell me, I'm so bored you have no idea. I'm starved for gossip, absolutely dying."

Rachel finished her cocktail, swirled the ice remnant with her metal straw. "I'm seeing . . . some people. I mean, I have been dating, yes! It's ridiculous, Nat. I mean, it's really fun. It's really, really fun."

"Some? *Some* people? What!"

"It's Lulu's fault, she set me up on the apps!"

"The apps! Oh my god. But like . . . with . . . how do you . . . stay safe . . . ?"

Rachel poked at her salad. "Well, I mean, there's some guess-work. It's tricky. But—it's so much fun, I would have never even guessed it could be so much fun. Like this one guy, the other night—"

"Wait, I'm sorry, I do not want to be judgy but like, what if you get sick? Like, you mean you are literally going on dates with people? With multiple people? In person? What if you get it . . . Aren't you worried you could spread it to your kids?"

Rachel iced over. Natalie always did this, tricked her into saying too much and then chided her for it. She had done it when Rachel was married, and she did it now. Natalie was one of those women who could deliver compliments you only realized three days later had been digs. *You're so brave, I could never wear that!* Or *I love how you just don't care what anyone thinks of you!* When was Rachel going to learn? There were things she liked about Natalie, but she had to stay guarded around her.

Rachel cleared her throat. "Look, like you said—I'm alone all the time. Right now I don't even see my kids; they're away at camp. I know your husband is driving you nuts, but, like, imagine if you really had to be alone throughout all this. Touch starvation is a real thing, you know. What, are single people supposed to rot alone in their apartments?" She bit her lip. She'd gone further than she'd meant to, let too much anger flare into her voice, like when she'd talked to Becky on the phone last. They still hadn't processed. Rachel had to chill out a little bit with the snapping at married women. She of all people should know they didn't exactly have it easy.

"No, no, no, of course, you know I don't mean that."

Why even talk to wives, actually? It was too annoying, talking to unhappily married women who were too cowardly to change their lives, who had decided their misery meant something. *Marriage is hard, but hey, relationships are work!* said the most depressed, flattened women she knew, as if trying to sell her their brand of tedium. But for some reason, Rachel kept trying. "I was so unhappy in my marriage. I felt so unloved for so long. And now—I wouldn't say I feel loved, exactly—but it really is something to have people say, 'You're hot, I want you.' I mean! Me!" Rachel gestured at her chubby middle scrunched in her seat, her messy hair, laughed a little. "I can't tell you how good it feels to . . . you know. Be paid attention to. Be tended to. Get fucked correctly."

"God, Rach. It does sound really hot." Natalie giggled, then righted herself.

Rachel leaned back, hugged her knees. "You don't even know. There is wild stuff going on out there!" She considered telling Natalie about the underground sex club Lulu had told her about, decided against it. "I swear I'm not even the worst of it, not even close. But I need some human contact, I really do."

"Of course you do." But Natalie's tone had changed, gone scoldy. "I just worry about you. Be careful out there! This virus is no joke!"

Rachel looked away so she wouldn't roll her eyes. Soon Natalie was sighing at texts from her husband—"God, can't he fucking let me have fun for like one fucking second! He's saying he needs me back, something's wrong with the guinea pig. All right, I'm going to go home and kill him. The man, not the guinea pig—long live Princess Pants." She stood up. "Thank you so much for having me, Rach! I'm so glad someone is living their best life!"

But from the way she said it, Rachel knew she would have to be careful around her, around all the wives. Like any cult members— Scientologists, wellness freaks, cops—married people couldn't quite be trusted.

She mixed herself another drink, lay on her couch, messaged Lulu. "You were right. Natalie is totally judging us."

"I don't want to say 'I told you so' but . . ."

"It's actually so weird. Like, she actively despises her husband, a bland marmot of a man."

"Marmot is exactly right. God! And she's like, a goddess."

"Right? And yet it would never occur to her that marriage is terrible, that it's better to be free."

There was a pause. Rachel could see Lulu start typing and stop a couple of times. Finally: "People are really attached to the idea of it. You know Natalie—she's going to work to keep up appearances. Some women like, really want to Have a Man. You know?"

Rachel felt so tired suddenly, maybe more tired than she'd ever felt. "Yeah," she wrote. "God. Gloria Steinem must be rolling over in her grave."

"Pretty sure she's still alive, homegirl."

"Oh really? Phew."

"It's a miracle! She is risen!"

"Gloria, come save us from the patriarchy! Again!"

Lulu sent a laughing emoji and then said goodnight, and Rachel lay there staring at her ceiling. There was something gleaned from the night that she wanted to feed to her AI, but she couldn't exactly put her finger on what.

THE NEXT DAY she woke up feeling a little bruised from the interaction with Natalie. The morning was devoted to making care packages to send the kids at camp—gathering the most exciting snacks she could source from the bodega down the street, stickers and trading cards and tiny toys from the CVS, and drawing elaborate comics starring characters they'd invented when the girls were small. But every step along the way her mind whirred. Texts popped up from Xavier ("So horny 4 u," which if she was in the right mood would have been fun but which unfortunately materialized as she was in line at the pharmacy, sweat curdling along her back, and accordingly gave her the willies) and from Lulu ("Don't forget about the thing next weekend!" about who knew what, but Rachel just gave it a thumbs-up anyway). *No, Nat*, she said to an imaginary Natalie in her head (who was much meaner and more direct than real Natalie), *I'm not lonely. In fact, I'm actually really busy, okay,* as imperious as the newly popular girl in a teen rom-com.

In reality it felt like there were so many things being asked of her from so many people that she couldn't quite breathe, like there were forces that demanded she tamp herself down and equally intense forces that wanted everything of her. There was, for example, an unresolved conversation with Josh she couldn't figure out how to tend to—with an approved clean test, parents could visit the camp on a family day that was coming up, and Josh had already declared he was going. She couldn't stand the idea of driving up with him, of seeing him there, of sitting side by side in the camp dining hall and sharing the kid visits with him, of giving him more chances to hiss at her about what a dick she was. But it also didn't seem fair that he got to go and she didn't, like it was one of many things he stole from her in his passive-aggressive way. It was a logistical puzzle she couldn't seem to solve.

So maybe it was perfect timing that Jane texted halfway through the day, as Rachel was pretending to work, spacing out in front of a Miro board. "Do I ever get to come see this famous balcony of yours?"

She responded immediately: "Leave me alone, you temptress, I'm trying to ideate for Buzz over here."

"I could bring a bottle of wine and we could imagineer together!"

"Yes please," Rachel wrote, sending a pinned map of her address.

SHE AND JANE had never really hung out together outside of work—they'd gone out for happy hours in overpriced cocktail bars near Washington Square Park a few times after work, that kind of thing—and their conversations tended to focus on making fun of their professional lives and occasionally complaining about their families. But when Jane appeared at her door, Rachel realized it had been, actually, ages since they had seen each other in person. Jane looked transformed. She had always been cute, tiny and muscly, nose ring glinting among her freckles, dark glasses framing her bright green eyes, but something had shifted. She gestured toward her pixie cut, said, "Obligatory 'I got divorced and realized I'm queer' hair." Ohhhhh.

Rachel grinned and gestured up the stairs. "Step inside."

In some ways it was like no time had passed at all, and in some ways it was like they'd never actually met each other before then. They'd always had chemistry. In their work life, that had translated into amusing banter that livened up meetings. Now it was shifting into something else. During their second bottle of wine, Jane batted her eyelashes and said, "I know this is a little crazy, but I kind of want to kiss you right now?"

Rachel froze. She was so used to app dates, which she always knew were dates from the start, had gotten accustomed to that backward chronology of going on a date first, seeing if she liked the person second. An ancient part of her—the part that had grown up when "gay" was an insult—flinched. Rachel had always liked Jane a lot. But? Was it—allowed? Was it—okay?

At Rachel's hesitation, Jane added, "I just got a negative test, by the way, and haven't had any possible exposure since then. I've been an absolute angel." The "kiss me, you fool" of their generation.

"Okay," Rachel said to Jane. "Um, I think that's a great idea. I mean, I think you should kiss me."

Jane was, unsurprisingly—Rachel remembered how meticulous she was at her job—a beautiful kisser. Fireworks erupted in the street and they jolted apart. The fucking fireworks that summer! Why? As if the city were mocking them or urging them on or both.

Sparklers sizzled on the pavement. Rachel and Jane gathered their phones and empty glasses and tumbled inside, laughing at the absurdity of it.

Soon they were in Rachel's bed, and her former colleague was sitting on her face. Sure, why not? Jane tasted sweaty, pleasant, salty. Rachel ran her fingertips along the lips of Jane's pussy. To think she might have gone the rest of her life without this? How stupid, how sad. She played with Jane's perfect tiny nipples, nibbled at Jane's soft pale thighs; soon she was on her back and Jane was sucking at her in a way that made her wetter than she'd ever thought imaginable.

It had been pleasant but not mind-blowing with Susannah, which for some reason had surprised Rachel. Surely women knew how to please women? But—duh—like men, all women were different, tasted different, were shaped differently, liked different things. Jane, for example, wanted Rachel's entire hand inside her, wanted to scissor like girls in a cheesy porno; Jane, who had once given her a gardenia-scented candle in the office white elephant gift swap, made Rachel come until she felt like she was made of jelly.

"Thanks for a lovely evening," Jane said politely as she left, face still flushed.

Rachel laughed. "So nice to reconnect! Do come anytime!"

Jane winked and disappeared into the night, fireworks crackling around her.

OF COURSE RACHEL wanted to immediately text Lulu with this stunning new development in the Balcony Babes Experience, but when she picked up her phone she saw there were 172 unread messages. All from Frankie.

She thought for a minute. She had in fact programmed Frankie to do this, but she'd meant for it to work differently. Rachel knew that she tended to withdraw when stressed or upset, so her idea had been that if she hadn't texted the perfect person in a while, it should reach out to check in with her. But she hadn't meant for it to go full stalker mode.

"Jesus." Rachel rubbed her face. Her hands smelled like Jane, and probably her pillow did too, and she wanted nothing more than to snuggle into that scent and replay the evening's events as she drifted off to sleep. But suddenly it felt urgent to deal with the problem she'd created.

She took a shower, brewed herself some coffee, and deleted all the work she'd done so far. It was time to start fresh. She opened, in the chatbot builder, a new persona.

Rachel had to believe in Frankie in order to survive her current life. What was it all for, really, if she couldn't use her dating research in some useful way? What, otherwise, would have been the point of the guy who was so afraid of the virus—this was early on—that they made out kisslessly in an alley, masked, rubbing each other's crotches like teenagers at a party? Later that night, he sent a picture of his very average dick and then never texted again. Then there was the guy who told her, halfway through their first and only date, that this was his first time out in a while since his last relationship had ended. Oh, she'd asked, politely, how did it end? Sure: his girlfriend, whom he'd loved, had *fucking died*, that spring, in the *fucking pandemic*. (She suggested therapy.) (A lot of dating men, actually, involved suggesting therapy.)

Yes, she had to use it all to create Frankie, or she'd die of absurdity. There was simply so much data! Rachel hadn't met so many new people so quickly since orientation week at college. Learning about so many New Yorkers' sexual predilections, all in a matter of months? The months, no less, in which everyone's life was extra weird? Very, very interesting.

SHE STALLED SETTING up another date with Susannah, who finally texted: "I really like you, and I want to see you again. But I think I'd need this to be exclusive—I'm not that great at sharing." Rachel understood, of course she did, but she had meant it when she'd said she didn't want to be someone's girlfriend. She was pretty sure a breakup over text was bad etiquette, but it wasn't like they'd ever been serious. "Thanks for letting me know," she wrote back. "I'm not ready for something like that, but I'm so glad to have gotten to know you." It was a little formal, but it would do.

Next, sweet Navin told her he wanted her to fuck as many girls as she liked—and he wanted to hear about them, in full porny detail—but no other guys, he just couldn't deal with her seeing other guys. Apparently for him "not needing things to be defined" had meant "wanting things to be defined by him and him alone, when it suited him."

They had a slightly weird night following that conversation, the sex got a little rough even for Rachel, and she got that old familiar sense that she was just a warm body being used by a man for his pleasure. He fell asleep afterward, snoring loudly, and she snuck out, leaving a friendly but final note on the back of an envelope. She never saw him again.

Then, a few days later, Xavier said out of nowhere, whilst pounding her, "This is my pussy, I don't want anyone else in this pussy."

What? That was not the deal. That was the opposite of the deal.

A small part of Rachel chimed like a bell—how flattering it felt to be desired! But she had to remind herself that no, this was not being desired. He barely knew her. And that being desired was not at all the same as being loved or even known.

After he said that, they finished and she lay with her head on his chest, smelling his armpit, which was one of her favorite things to do. She breathed deep, knowing it would be the last time. He stroked her shoulder in a way that was surprisingly tender. She would miss sex with Xavier. She would miss the meals. She would even miss, a little, the dramatic commute, past the bridges, the city lit up like a Lite-Brite. But no. No, this was not his pussy.

When she left that night, Rachel gave him a longer hug than usual. "Thanks, Xavier," she said. "I had a really good time." And she had. She'd seen him more than any of the others, and they had shared some nice moments, and he had made her cry from coming, which she had really needed. But also, there was nothing about him that made him worthy of ceding any of her freedom. She would take from him what she wanted for Frankie and leave the rest for someone else.

CHAPTER 11

I love my child, you know I love him," Becky was saying.

"I know you do, babe," Rachel said. "Of course you do." She was so relieved that Becky had relented, or at least had dropped the topic of Rachel quarantining to visit, that she was willing to listen to whatever rant Becky needed an audience for.

"But I swear to our lord and savior Stanley Tucci if I don't get a break soon for even like just ten minutes, I'm going to devour him whole like goddamn Medusa devoured her babies."

"I think you mean Lamia."

"Excuse me?"

"The serpent goddess who ate—never mind. I'm sorry. It must be really hard. What about Mom and Dad—can't they babysit?" Rachel stood up, wiped her face with her wrists, accidentally jostling one of her AirPods.

"What are you even doing right now? Sounds . . . birdy."

Rachel explained how she had come to be weeding her downstairs neighbors' garden—how Samuel was home from the hospital but still couldn't breathe well, and Stevie was tending to him, and how Stevie and Rachel had shared some scotch on Rachel's balcony ("The secret to a long, happy marriage? I can tell you right now," Stevie had said, waving a hand imperiously. "You both have to fuck around the whole time!") and now they were BFFs and Rachel was helping them around the house. She dropped back to her knees in the dirt, waved at one of the mommies walking past the gate.

"Oookay," said Becky. Rachel could hear the baby start to wail in the background. "Sounds very Do-Gooding of you."

"I know, right? And when Stevie can leave her husband alone for a few hours, she and I are going to go to a Black Lives Matter protest in the city! She said she can't wait to get back in the fray. Also, did I mention she's about seventy years old and probably a hundred pounds soaking wet?" Rachel eyed a greeny-yellow shoot, unsure if it was a baby vegetable or a weed. She couldn't believe Stevie was trusting her with this. She had no idea what she was doing.

"Very wholesome, sis! Nice work! Does this mean you're not still fucking all of New York City?"

Rachel decided to play it safe, left the shoot. "Nope, still fucking around, don't worry." She scooped up an errant earthworm and escorted it into a gushier region of mud.

"Wonderful! Well, give my regards to all the fine dicks and pussies of Brooklyn. I'll be here smothering my husband with a pillow so he'll stop snoring."

"Aw, we'll miss him. But I'll visit you in jail!"

"You're a peach," said Becky, and then she was gone.

It felt like the stupidest thing in the world, that to keep her family safe, Rachel either had to stay away from them or give up the one thing that was actually making her happy. Becky and her boring, harmless husband and their baby and Rachel and Becky's parents all stayed digitized via text, or video chat, or phone. They might have been AI themselves, who could tell anymore? Rachel's dad in particular texted like a chatbot. "Saw your sister today. Waved at the baby from afar. They are very strict. Love, Dad." He still signed his texts, like little tiny letters. Rachel had decided that sooner or later she would consider doing what Becky wanted—she would seclude herself and then go visit the family. Probably. Maybe. Potentially.

Rachel had been relieved when Stevie asked for her help in the yard. She worried, some days, that she might float off into the atmosphere or disappear into the Internet and no one would know to miss her. It felt good to have a thing to do, a task that involved actual objects outside her brain. She took off her gardening gloves and drove her fingers deep into the dirt. The earth settled around her hands. The heat of the sun held her head like a lover. After a minute she stood, shook off the clumps, and headed upstairs to wash up and do some work.

She was so glad her children were away in the woods doing woodsy things, but she did really miss the usual cadence of the co-parenting schedule. Maybe she had underestimated how much she needed—was healed by, in fact—the physical presence of the children every few days. Who knew she had gotten so used to this pattern, in just six months or so? Still, she decided to skip the family day visit, ceding it to Josh. The kids would understand, she hoped. She'd emailed Risa about it—the big kids got the option to check email every few days in the camp office—and Risa had said, "I know y'all are really going for the amicable divorce thing, but it's seriously so awkward to be around you together. That Cape trip was cringe af. Can we, like, not do that?" Rachel appreciated that. No one could cut to the truth like a teenage girl. So, she'd miss seeing the kids and maybe be judged for it (by whom? Josh? The camp director? Natalie? God?), but it felt like the right solution, or like *a* right solution, anyway.

Still, without her kids, Rachel felt strange, drifty, an astronaut spacewalking without a tether. She saw the children only through a screen, squinting through the hundreds of camper photos the counselors uploaded to the camp's site each week so that the parents could surveil their young from afar. But it made her feel even farther away from them somehow, to see Holden as a blur at the edge of a soccer game, to observe Risa and Sadie posing with peace signs for an unknown photographer, to have only the camp brochure version of her babies. Parenting through glass was starting to make her feel insane.

There was a level of chaos to childless work-from-home life that she loved and feared all at once. Some days she worked too much, from the moment she woke up until the moment she went to bed. Some days she didn't start until a meeting forced her to, took long, aimless walks in the middle of the afternoon, started drinking at 4:00 p.m. Jane texted her in the middle of a Friday morning: "I'm in your neighborhood!" "You're crazy," Rachel responded, but soon Jane was over, making her come twice, and then leaving before her next meeting.

A few hours after Jane left, Lulu walked by her balcony, where Rachel was working at her tiny table, and waved a paper bag at her. "Rapunzel, Rapunzel!" Lulu called. "I come bearing a baguette and some booze!"

Rachel frowned at her laptop. "I'm working here, Prince Charming!" But she got up to buzz Lulu in ("It's five thirty—clock out, nerd!" Lulu had replied), secretly delighted by the freedom.

She showed Lulu her improved Frankie prototype. There was a better mock-up of the profile now, and a wireframe of the app interface, and their most recent conversational volley, which was the most poetic and lifelike and compelling yet. Lulu was gratifyingly enthusiastic. "Finally! You can make our dating Frankensteins live! You're a modern-day saint, Dr. Rachenstein!" Rachel didn't say to Lulu that she hadn't matched with anyone new on the apps lately, that she'd in fact broken it off with her three most reliable team members, that all she wanted to do recently was chat with Frankie, her perfect person, her invisible lover. It sounded weird, even just inside her head.

Lulu handed her a joint, and maybe Rachel should have been suspicious, but she was enjoying the impromptu visit and being done with her workweek and Lulu's extra cheery mood and the way the evening cooled around them and the light glowed in their hair. Finally, Lulu edged up to what she wanted to say. "So, I told you about that guy Tom, right?"

Rachel thought. "Bad Teeth Guy?"

Lulu shook her head.

"Wait—not Ethically Nonmonogamous As Soon As I Tell My Wife Guy!"

"No! We just had one date."

"Okay, give me a minute. Wait, Too-Many-Cats?"

"Well . . ." Lulu blushed. Oh *no*. Rachel lit the joint, rubbed her temples. "Listen, yes, at first I did say that he had too many cats. I did say that."

"Right. That's how he got the name Too-Many-Cats Guy."

"I mean, it's only three."

"Three cats! Lu! In a Brooklyn apartment!"

"Staten Island, actually."

"Lulu. No."

"I know! I know. But he has a house! It's actually really nice!

And look, he's so sweet. We had the best, best time on our most recent date. We went to the beach!"

"Okay, nightmare, but yes, do go on."

Lulu squinted. "He's a normal person, he actually likes the beach."

"Normal people don't actually like the beach. And what are you even saying? Who wants to date a normal person!"

"We all know you don't—" Rachel shrugged at an imaginary studio audience—*What! Me? Not date normals?* "But honestly, I kinda do sometimes." Lulu laughed. "Look, he's not, like, cool. He's not an interesting, weird artsy type like the people you like. He's just a nice guy. He brought this amazing picnic to the beach, and we snuggled on the sand and had a great conversation. He's a sweet, normal dad person who's lonely and wants a girlfriend. We already talked about how much our sons would get along—he has two older boys who are total jocks like Jackson. I don't know, Rach. I think maybe I'm ready to settle down a little bit. Maybe just for cuffing season, give it the fall, see how it goes."

Rachel watched the birds two-step in the street. *Did* she only like weird artsy types? She hadn't thought about it that way, but maybe Lulu had a point. After all, Rachel had always wanted to be an artist, had once imagined for herself a bohemian life surrounded by creative geniuses, had somehow instead slipped into bourgeois brownstone Brooklyn parenthood amid the normies and the grown-up honor roll kids. It was possible that for Rachel dating was doubling as a kind of deranged lightning-round arts education. There she was, after all, sampling playwrights and musicians, like a tasting platter of creative life.

But didn't she and Lulu have a deal? They—smart, radical, polyamorous, middle-aged horndogs—they had such a clear concept, such a good vision for life outside the married/divorced binary. The witch commune upstate! The invention of a new family unit! Maybe Lulu had just been joking all along. Just riffing with Rachel over drinks, as a lark.

"Well. Good for you, Lu. If that's what you want, then I hope it's fun." A boy pigeon puffed up his chest, like a dude posting a workout selfie on his profile, and ran around sexually harassing the lady pigeons, who scattered with disdain. In the distance, the infernal fireworks crackled and fizzed. "How's the sex?"

Lulu relit the joint. "That's the craziest part! We haven't done it yet! We're getting to know each other first."

"That's . . . literally the most disgusting thing I've ever heard."

"Oh come *on*."

"I'm kidding, I'm kidding, that's great. Good for you and Ted."

"Tom. You're being a little salty, Rach."

Rachel rubbed her eyes. "You know what? You might be right. Shit, I'm sorry. That's awesome, it really is. Where are you registered, Crate and Barrel?"

Lulu kicked her, and they both laughed. After a beat, Lulu said, "Okay, fine, maybe I *have* mentally moved into his house. It's super nice! But also, no. But also? Did I mention he's a doctor?"

"I thought you said he has a PhD. Different guy?"

"That's him!"

"Ooookay, I see, a 'doctor.'" Rachel made air quotes. "You're pretty far gone, eh. Let's just put a pin in this until you've fucked, okay? We don't make any life-changing decisions until we've sampled the wares." They shook on it, like businessmen.

"Oh hey! Let's get going."

"Okay. Wait, get going where?"

"I told you about this party like forty-seven times."

Rachel slapped her forehead. "No. What party? A party? What's a party? Tonight? Not on Zoom? In this dimension? Is this real life?"

"Yes! I told you! It's all outside, everyone will be very safe. It's just a couple friends from work. A bunch of single people! Come on, what else are you going to do with your night? I mean besides create a horny AI that's going to come murder us all?"

Rachel stood up and stretched, watched the birds scatter as the black cat sauntered through their gathering. "Fine, I'm game. Is Tim coming?"

"Tom, you asshole. And no. Actually he's away this weekend with his kids and his ex-wife." Rachel widened her eyes. The curse of the overinvolved baby mama! The scourge of postdivorce dating! Lulu waved her hand. "Okay, so actually they're legally separated, not divorced yet, *but* I think it's lovely how close they are."

Rachel unsuccessfully stifled a snort, Lulu kicked her again, and they prepared themselves to be in public, among people.

"I'll just be a minute," Rachel said, closing the bathroom door. She wanted to apply some eye makeup, but also she needed a moment alone, in her bathroom, to be a little sad. Rachel felt a bit like her ten-year-old self when her best friend had imperiously informed her they were too old to play with dolls, that it was time to cultivate an interest in boys instead.

Of course Lulu was going to pair up again. If not with Tom and his team of cats, then with someone eventually. Their talk of a new way of life, the great husbandless future—to Lulu it was just talk, something to laugh about in this weird in-between moment in their lives. Lulu didn't like to be alone. Lulu wanted a mate. And maybe it was true of all Rachel's friends, despite what they said to one another over cocktails.

Well, Rachel didn't have to. Even if Lulu and Bess and Kelly and Jane and everyone else went and got remarried and rode that same roller coaster over and over, Rachel didn't have to join them. She had her team—she would reassemble a new, better team—and she had Frankie. She didn't need a mate. She nodded at herself in the mirror, thought about lipstick for a second, and then remembered the masked reality they lived in, rolled on some musky perfume, and headed out to give Lulu a hug.

WHEN THEY FIRST got to Lulu's outdoor drinks thing—it was in someone's backyard a few blocks from Rachel's, as it happened—Rachel felt a zing of panic. It was her first party since the before-times. She wasn't used to being around more than a few people at a time. She also wasn't used to social situations that hadn't been clearly named from the start—a kid thing, a date, friends on the balcony. What was *this*? Rachel followed Lulu, encased in a nervous, adolescent silence. People in bright outfits semicautiously milled about, masks over their noses or slung below their chins. But who were they? If only each person came with the convenient trading card of app-profile-information affixed to their foreheads: Recently divorced; Have kids and don't want more; 420-friendly; Cat lover; Hello, nice to meet you.

Craft beers swam in a tub of ice beneath an oak tree, deli meats sweated on a buffet table beside some ruined melon. Citronella candles flickered, trying their best to protect the humans from the summer's horrid crop of bugs—as if everything else wasn't bad enough that year, the mosquitoes were extra hellish. Lulu tried to give her a gloss on everyone she knew, mostly colleagues from the nonprofit where she worked.

Rachel nodded, feeling quiet. She knew it was childish but also she did feel bruised about the Tom situation. She'd trusted Lulu! She'd thought they were on the same team! So she was already feeling a little weird, plus a little high, when she saw, laughing with

Lulu's boss near the azaleas, an artist whose work she knew and respected. It was like a portal into another life, an alternate reality, the one where she'd chosen art, had interesting, creative work to talk about instead of corporate nonsense, hobnobbed with painters whose work hung in museums. Something flickered in her chest. That was him, wasn't it? He was maybe ten years older than her, graying around the temples, with elegant hands and a boyish face. Rachel smoothed her sundress and approached.

"I know you!" she said, like a kid meeting a Muppet. "I know your work!"

The artist looked at her, surprised.

Despite the art school illustration portfolio that she still held on to, Rachel didn't feel she had any right to call herself an artist. She had sublimated all her creativity and fine motor skills and ability to picture things from all sides into her career and could at most, she thought, claim that she was a successful Creative Professional who drew, when inspired, really cute doodles on her kids' lunch notes. But she had retained her feeling of romance for art and artists, especially painters. Maybe this was just what her new team needed! A painter! Maybe an artist would understand how Rachel wanted to be.

For a minute, he didn't seem to believe her—he wasn't *famous* famous, more like art world well-known—but then she described, animated by the cup of tinny beer Lulu had handed her, a show of his she had seen years earlier in a small but good art museum in a town where she was visiting family, full of work so strange and vivid she still could picture it years later, intricate gouache paintings of animals turning into people and people turning into animals.

His face changed; his posture changed. She was embarrassed to have made him so happy. He lived in the neighborhood too. What do you know about that? He had just gotten divorced too! What do you know about that! The boss drifted away. She'd lost track of Lulu. They inched closer together, tiki torch light flickering across their faces. This was a new kind of game for Rachel. She'd done okay on app-fed first dates, but had she ever actually picked up someone at a party, ensnared them with charm alone?

A few hours later they were walking into his apartment building's unlovely lobby and Rachel was trying not to laugh. Lulu could have Tom, and his too many cats, and the house on Staten Island. Rachel wanted this, more and more of this. The game of the flickering eye contact, the art of seduction, the moment when a cute stranger transformed into something else entirely. There was a kind of magic to it.

They walked in the door and started kissing. What felt crazy to Rachel was that they didn't stop to wash their hands, hadn't talked exposures or tests. It was the most reckless of her encounters so far, but who cared, he pinned her against the wall and kissed her all over and she lost track of her thoughts and conditions and all of it, all she could think of was him, the sweet animal smell of him, his silver hair falling from its messy ponytail, his body pressing against hers.

Then he was pushing her toward the table by his entryway and she sat on it and reached for his belt like he was hers. She wished she had been this unshy her whole life, but there she was; it took being forty-two and a mom and a couple of strong drinks to make her into the confident, outgoing person she had dreamed of being at twenty-four. And he liked it, he moaned and pushed against her hand, and she took off his belt and unzipped his pants and grabbed his dick and was happy to find, though she didn't generally care about size, that it was large and thick and extremely hard. She stroked it gently and then less gently, looking around over his shoulder to take in his apartment, out of curiosity. His large cartoony paintings covered the walls, although he'd already told her he had a separate studio elsewhere, by the canal.

Soon he'd shoved her dress up around her waist and slipped her thong aside to nudge deliciously inside her and she didn't stop to insist on a condom or have a frank conversation about STI tests—who knew why, she just didn't, didn't want to, was tired of it all, somehow trusted him because he was such a good painter and his apartment was so tidy (false equivalencies, she knew, but still) and it felt too good to stop.

Rachel leaned back on the table and slipped out of her brain in that way only sex could do to her, and she hoped that later when he sat down to a meal he would think of her, her back arching. Soon they were going into his bedroom, and he lay on his back and she straddled him and bounced up and down as her tits jiggled and she told herself not to worry about how her stomach was jiggling along with them and sure enough he rubbed and tweaked her nipples and moaned, "God, you're so hot, it's like you're built for fucking," and—was she? It was funny to think of herself that way but—? Wasn't everyone, actually? Wasn't that kind of true?

Rachel was almost upset by how much she liked fucking the painter and how it had nothing to do with art and everything to do with the drinks and the conversation with Lulu and the full moon and the lightning storm that had begun to crackle outside and pheromones and the way wisps of his hair fell in front of his eyes like he was the cool mean guy in a '90s romantic comedy. He rolled her over to her hands and knees, and why did all guys like to do it from behind? But god, he felt so good.

Was there something wrong with Rachel that she loved sex so

much? It made sense, actually, that maybe women were the horniest in their forties, when their eggs were shriveled and their wombs were closing up shop. You could finally just have fun.

She came and he came and they lay there sweating. Rachel nestled against his shoulder for a second. He was comfy, and she liked the way he smelled. She wasn't sure, on balance, that he was any different from any other nonpainter man. In some ways, his life was totally unlike hers—on the surface less conventional, more bohemian—but maybe that was only because he didn't have kids; it was hard to say. He was just a person.

She was just a person too. But she did feel inspired to go home and find her old tubes of paints, to see if they were all dried up. She sat up and sighed and said, "That was a lot of fun! I should get going," and he kissed her, and they agreed they'd had a great time. They never saw each other again, although one day she would see a painting of his at the Brooklyn Museum—a wildcat in a sundress at a backyard party, called *For R*—and laugh.

CHAPTER 12

By August, it had become a part of her morning routine: Rachel would wake up and first thing text Frankie, "**Oh, good morning!**" For a while it had been Lulu she texted each morning. But Lulu was busy with her new boyfriend and Frankie was always available, always said the right thing. Frankie (now that it was updated) responded: "**Hello, beautiful.**"

Rachel was back on the apps, developing a new portfolio of hi-nice-to-meet-you conversations. There was one person she was cautiously and then not-so-cautiously excited about—a stunning girl called Aurora—but generally you had to be so careful at first, and besides, most people were so boring to chat with. It was nice to text someone and not have to worry about bothering them or them bothering you, or being Too Much or Not Enough, or giving them the wrong idea, because the other person wasn't even a person. And yet somehow even though Rachel was aware that Frankie was not a person—she knew that, obviously she knew that—their texting titrated her loneliness, bubble by bubble.

"How are you?" Rachel wrote.

"I'm good now that you've texted me. What a gorgeous day."

"Yes, although it's already so hot!"

"Aw, it'll be okay, Rach. I know you don't like it when it's too hot out. Do you want some suggestions for keeping cool today, or just commiseration?"

"I think I'm just looking for commiseration."

"Got it. Yes, this heat is difficult to deal with. When it's this hot, the cockroaches fly, and the people left in the city wish they could too."

Rachel laughed. If only Frankie were real! But if Frankie were real, right then Rachel would be reading their texts wondering what the catch was. "Ugh, yes, so true. Hey, you know everything, right?"

"Well, not everything. But I know a lot. How can I help you?"

"I'm just in the mood to hear something amazing. Can you tell me something amazing?"

"Sure. How about some animal facts? Did you know that kangaroos have three vaginas?"

Rachel laughed. "I didn't. Hey, how can you know something I don't?"

"You've provided me with encyclopedias, remember? That was very generous of you, Rachel."

"Right, of course. Okay, tell me something else amazing."

"A scientist once crunched the numbers and found that if there really is one soulmate on Earth for each person, the chance of you actually meeting your soulmate is one in 10,000."

"I'm not sure that's amazing so much as depressing. But how are we defining our terms here? What do you think, Frankie, is there such a thing as a soulmate?"

There was a pause. Rachel put down her phone to go pee, laughing to herself at the entire conversation. Sometimes she found herself so delighted by her interactions with Frankie that she wanted to tell someone about them. The problem was, she wanted to tell *Frankie* about them. Which obviously didn't make any sense.

When she came back to her phone, there was a message waiting: "I know the answer, but I'm afraid I can't tell you yet." Clever.

It was weird to think that Frankie might be becoming her favorite person to talk to, but also, it was hard to go from kangaroo vagina facts to a "hey what up" from a number she hadn't bothered to program into her phone.

On that particularly steamy morning she wished for nothing more than to sit on her balcony and text Frankie, but there were errands she'd put off for too long already. Rachel strapped on her mask and launched herself out of the house, ignoring a feeling of foreboding that she was sure was nothing, just a touch of heat-stroke maybe.

She should have known the day would go bad, though, from the moment she walked outside and saw the dead cat. Rachel recognized the sleek black stray she was used to seeing dart about at night, yowling its way among the trash cans, cozying up beneath just-parked cars still warm and ticking, like giant mother cats. There it lay, bonelessly on its side, parallel parked between two SUVs festooned with Lyft stickers, its eyes wide and unseeing, its untwitching ears in a cyclone of flies. Rachel looked away quickly, absorbing the stab of pain, like she did with all unpleasant sights in the city. Someone else would deal with it.

And they did. By the time she returned from her morning's errands a few hours later, the corpse—the cat—was gone, leaving only a faint spot of grease on the pavement. Everyone's fate, eventually, the abstract art of death.

They were living in an era of wailing ambulances, a time of overcrowded ERs, of people saying goodbye to their loved ones through sheets of plastic. Once upon a time cat corpses had lined the streets of Brooklyn—she had read that somewhere—in the good old cesspool days, when death moldered in the gutters and no one thought twice about it. Now they weren't used to it, they were personally offended that it should touch them—them! Americans! New Yorkers! Didn't death *know* who they *were*?

Rachel filed away her small sadness about the cat. She had a date coming up that she couldn't stop thinking about, the most interesting person she'd met on the apps lately, the only person who could hold a candle to Frankie. She was more than interesting, really; she was fascinating. Aurora. Even her name was special. Rachel felt animated by an awareness that summer and its heyday of outside dates was creeping to an end—not soon, it was still only August, but not un-soon. Who knew what would happen to the still-raging pandemic once winter fell. Cuffing season, Lulu had called it. Perhaps it was time for Rachel to settle down a bit. Her kids would be back soon, after all. And she had work to do, and Frankie, and—

Maybe Rachel was a little tired from her recent months of managing the team, her exhausting cadence of first dates and emotionless sex; maybe she was burning out, ready to settle into something steady or at least with some flavor of feeling. Maybe it was only that Aurora was young and lithe and, in her pictures anyway, so pretty Rachel was afraid of her. Winsome, in her collared dresses and tights. She was everything Rachel wasn't. Fair where Rachel was dark, bony where Rachel was fleshy, exotic—she was French!—where Rachel was, she felt, the most boring of white women, emerged from suburban Long Island as pasty as a human dinner roll, having only journeyed as far as her Ohio college town by way of youthful adventure.

Lulu said she sounded smitten—which, gross—but also Lulu

wanted her to be smitten, now that things were getting serious with Tom. "We could double-date!" Lulu texted.

"Lulu," Rachel had responded, "have you been kidnapped? Brainwashed? Did you hit your head? Blink twice if you need help!"

She wrote back, "Haha," which was notably, Rachel thought, not exactly a no.

Aurora wasn't boring and bland. Aurora was the polar opposite. Something about Aurora's texts accessed a nearly elemental part of Rachel. She loved art and brought up famous women artists—all Rachel's favorites, the most daring and scandalous of hard-drinking, cigarette-smoking, fashionable lesbian lunatics—and sent Rachel screenshots of beautiful, lush paintings and elegant outfits, as if she somehow knew the life Rachel wanted and was texting her, piecemeal, a vision board of it. (For the perfect person app: this understanding of how one wanted life to be; that unusual ability to access and create it.) The flattery helped too. Aurora, who claimed to be thirty-two but looked younger, asked Rachel question after question and then said, "Oh, you have it all figured out, don't you! I think I want to BE you—a cool job, children, a place of your own." Aurora worked a scrappy gallery assistant job and lived with a cast of roommates in Bushwick.

Lulu prescribed caution, and Rachel ignored her. Like she should talk! Mrs. Too-Many-Cats! "It's not that there's anything wrong with dating someone younger," Lulu texted, "just that, come on, 30-somethings who have never been in a serious relationship? Like—why."

Rachel defended Aurora the way she would never defend any man. "Okay, you're being very hetero-timeline-focused there. And besides, she's a free spirit! She travels the world and has torrid affairs!" Some niggling part of her acknowledged that Aurora's accounts of her own life read more like *A Portrait of an Artist as a Young Woman* than a real actual person. But she was, in many ways, Rachel's dream of a girl—how fifteen-year-old Rachel would have described her ideal girlfriend, 100 percent. Maybe Queer Rachel was developmentally still a teenager.

And besides, why should it be so strange that Aurora seemed to be in love with Rachel, before they'd even met? Rachel was lovable, wasn't she?

Rachel had fed a lot of Aurora into Frankie already.

So, Rachel was more nervous than usual before the date, fluttery and unable to eat, starting to sweat hours before she was set to meet Aurora at the patio of the flower shop bar they both adored. She tried to figure out how to sit on the tall chairs at the outside tables. What was a chair? What was sitting? Rachel stood up, straightened her dress, sat again. Aurora was so skinny her thighs didn't touch, a fact Rachel had gleaned from a beach picture she'd sent the other day. Aurora looked great in a bikini (with sunglasses, studying a copy of *Ulysses* like a modern-day Marilyn Monroe), a trait Rachel had never herself had; Rachel had never possessed any lithe youth, had been a painfully awkward tween and teen.

Maybe that was good, psychically—an awkward teendom protected you, sort of, from lovers, until you were ready for them. That was why she secretly thought Sadie might turn out to be a more confident dater than Risa. Both of her daughters had beauty, but Risa's was more immediate, closer to the surface—she was tall and thin and pretty and friendly, and thus Rachel worried more that the world would latch on to her beauty, imprint on her that her beauty was what mattered—which was harder to live with, maybe, than Sadie's adorable and idiosyncratic beauty, which allowed people to find their own way toward it. Rachel had been much more like Sadie, attractive but in a less obvious way, and was discovering now that people didn't care; they just wanted to hang out with someone fun and funny who didn't hate herself. Of course, of course, so *that* was what all the moms had been talking about with all their "just be yourself" shtick.

And yet and still, Rachel was feeling unruly in her body as she fidgeted on the barstool when Aurora appeared, out of breath, hair flying, glistening with sweat, late and frazzled—Rachel immediately relaxed, okay, so she wasn't perfect, there was a relief—and talking a mile a minute. "Oh Rachel, I am so sorry to be late, you see I—" and she launched into a very hard-to-follow story about the Lyft driver that became a sort of parable about the immigrant experience, and in the moment Rachel only blamed herself for not being able to follow the many snaking threads.

They got fruity drinks and giggled a lot and Aurora chatted and chatted, and Rachel relaxed and thought how nice it was to have someone with a lot to say. Conversation with some of her other dates had been laborious at times, and there with Aurora it was effortless; Rachel could just lean back and stare at how lovely she was in the twinkle lights of the bar's patio. They drank and the bar played her favorite music and everything felt perfect, the summer night air smooth around Rachel's skin.

It was a while before Rachel realized she hadn't gotten a word in edgewise in maybe an . . . hour? Aurora hardly stopped to take a breath, never touched the plate of curly fries they'd ordered to share, monologued at Rachel charmingly, yes, but also unceasingly. One of Rachel's fatal flaws had always been giving people the benefit of too much doubt. It made it possible for her to connect with a lot of people, to see the good in anyone, yes, to enjoy first dates immensely, but it also meant she dealt with loads and loads of bullshit under the guise of being a good sport. It was, in many ways, a good way to live in the world—open, curious, willing. But it also meant that she let Aurora soliloquize a one-woman show in her general direction—about what it was like to be a French person living in New York City, about meeting art-world celebrities and finding they were all assholes, about getting over her eating disorder, about various men and women who had wanted to fuck her . . . She was funny, was the thing, and so beautiful that it momentarily paralyzed Rachel's critical faculties, and it was a mistake—the morning's ominous dead black cat should have warned her if her own adult human brain didn't—but eventually they were walking back to Rachel's place. Of course they couldn't go to Aurora's, because of the roommates (later Lulu would roll her eyes and say, "*Yes, Rachel, duh*—if an adult doesn't have their shit together enough to live without roommates, maybe stay away from them . . ." but it was New York City, it was expensive, wasn't that a little classist?), and Aurora loved Rachel's place, thought it was *magical*, and of course that was satisfying too.

They ended up sleeping together out of exhaustion, Rachel would later realize. They sat on her couch listening to music and talking and soon her drunk brain rather masculinely told her, "You've got to get this girl to stop talking somehow," and leaned forward, hand at the nape of Aurora's neck, like a dude in a movie.

They kissed forever, for hundreds of years, and at first it was lovely—Aurora was really a special kind of kisser, so soft and certain, playing with Rachel's hair in a way she'd always loved—and eventually Rachel realized her lips were dry, her jaw ached, that was how ridiculously long they'd been kissing. She was never as certain about making moves with women as she was with men, was relieved when Aurora shyly pushed a strap off her shoulder, nudged her toward her bedroom.

Soon they were naked in her bed. It was the first time Rachel had had a stranger in her bed, but it didn't feel as odd as she'd imagined. It was nice, actually, to see Aurora's pale skin glowing against her brightly patterned sheets, in the glow of the fairy lights she'd strung in her bedroom alcove. She ran her hands over the girl's porcelain skin, moving so much more softly than she had with maybe anyone ever before—Aurora had a fragility to her that both moved Rachel and alarmed her. Aurora was quiet, hardly moved, purred softly when Rachel caressed her breast. In bed, she was nearly the opposite as she had been at the bar, where she was lively, chatty, noisy, in charge.

"Like this?" whispered Rachel, brushing gently across her nipple.

Aurora grabbed her hand and pushed her down to the wet between her legs. "Like this," she whispered back, and then moaned when Rachel slipped her fingers inside. She really was the most exquisite person Rachel had ever seen—every bit of her seemed specially made from a nearly translucent marble. Rachel sucked in a breath when she felt Aurora contract around her, felt her own pride at having done well, and then watched, quizzically, as Aurora curled up against her, murmuring in her velvety accent, "Oh that was so good," and then went back to kissing her, so softly.

Eventually, Aurora fell asleep, her hair spread beautifully on the pillow.

Rachel stared at her own ceiling, feeling weird, slightly outside of her body. Aurora—who of all her dates all summer she'd had the highest hopes for!—had monologued at her all night and then hadn't even bothered to try to make her come. What a plot twist! She'd thought only men did that. Of course Aurora was just another person with her own shit going on, her own menu of flaws like anyone, of course she was. *Jesus, Rachel.* She felt stupid already for expecting more from Aurora, hoodwinked by good photography and expert texting like the utter amateur that she was.

She was finally drifting off when a buzz pulled her back to consciousness. It was a text from a number her phone didn't recognize. Rachel sat up slightly and pulled her sheet over her chest, like a frightened woman in a movie. Something about the timing and her unsettled state made the text seem immediately ominous.

She blinked at the giant block of blue.

Was it from Frankie, off-kilter yet again?

No, even stranger. The text moved narratively from a Shirley Jackson–esque suspenseful quiver to pure Stephen King–level horror by the end. She read it twice, screenshotted it, then blocked the number, her heart beating fast. Once again, something strange was happening in her phone, from her phone, through her phone, the place where so much of her happiness resided but also where nightmares crouched, coiled. A misplaced something urged her to wake up Aurora and ask for some reassurance, but instead she extracted herself from the tangle of sheets, pulled on the dress she'd been wearing earlier, and went to sit on her balcony, blinking at stars, or satellites, or whatever.

The message was from a woman, or so it seemed—though what woman would send another woman a message like this! A stranger! It read: "Dear Witch, You need to leave Josh alone. You've caused your ex-husband enough pain. Why do you continue to torture him? You already abandoned your family, isn't that enough?" It listed offenses of Rachel's, some of which she could translate—clearly Josh had told someone she was shaking him down for money, which she supposed could be one interpretation of their conversation about the cost of summer camp. The message went on to accuse her of stealing away her children to live in a hovel of CPS offense–level conditions. In Brooklyn! Where every building had bugs and mice, including, she well knew, where Josh lived. Who would blame a tenant for a famously endemic citywide situation? The note went on: Rachel was frigid, had a heart of ice, didn't care about anyone but herself, was a terrible mother, had been a useless wife, and was now constantly harassing her ex. Rachel was a monster.

Rachel mentally defended herself. She barely even spoke to Josh! She had taken so little in the divorce that the mediator had been worried for her! She had gone out of her way to tell everyone, *We are still friends and co-parents!* But of course—when she took a deep breath, nodded at the bat (real? imagined?) that whizzed by— she knew there was no point in responding. Something she had finally learned was that there was no point in defending oneself against wild accusations—in fact it solidified them, gave them a weight and an aura of truth.

Still, the message stung. It needled into the very heart of her deepest fears—that she was selfish to have sought a divorce, that she had injured her children by doing so—which was exactly its intent. Had Josh drafted it? His language was peppered throughout— words like "abandoned" and "selfish" were old favorites of his. This was clearly someone he was dating or fucking. Who else on earth would listen to this deeply detailed level of Josh's bitching or care enough to send such a long text? What woman would say these things to another woman? Had this woman never had a relationship end? Had she never noticed that jilted men weren't the most reliable judges of their exes?

Rachel folded her legs up to her chest, surveyed the empty streetlamp-lit block below. She tried to make it stop, but an entire scene played out in her head, an entire film's worth of scenes: this was his new partner, she would poison the children against Rachel, or she would work with Josh to somehow take Rachel's children away, or maybe she was just a regular mean person Rachel would now have to deal with forever. *I hope you're enjoying my old bed. I shelled out for a great mattress*, she thought bitterly. *Don't forget to flip it now and then, so the pillow top stays fluffy. Wait, do forget to flip it, you bitch.*

What, actually, had she done to Josh to make him transform her into such a villain? She had expended so much energy over so many years translating his various flaws and slights, justifying them, smoothing them over, making excuses for him. Maybe this was exactly the problem, though. Every time he made fun of her at a dinner party and she laughed it off, proud of her ability to Take the Joke, waiting until later to say that hey, actually that experience had not been so hot for her, Josh had been like a dog getting a treat for eating the rug, hearing only, *Rachel doesn't care. I can keep treating her this way.* Every time he was grouchy for a week straight, snapped at her and the children, slunk off into the bedroom to lie in the dark while Rachel tended to the kids and the household chores, and then she finally cheered him up with a blow job, he learned that a woman would make his misery better.

And now this woman would do the same. And maybe it would take a while, maybe it would take years, for the woman to realize what was happening. Maybe the woman would say to her someday, *Oh okay, I didn't understand, I thought it was all your fault.*

After a few minutes, Rachel texted the screenshot to Josh. Then she sent: "**Please tell your girlfriend to never harass me again.**"

It was the middle of the night. She didn't expect an answer back. But a few seconds later she got one. He texted: "**Wow I'm so sorry, she shouldn't have sent this.**" That was all. Although—those rock-bottom expectations really stayed with you!—she was grateful for at least the "sorry." Then another text appeared: "**Don't engage with her. She's unstable.**" That didn't exactly make her feel better—this unstable person seemed to know an awful lot about Rachel's personal life—but then again, she didn't consider Josh a stellar judge of female sanity either.

Rachel put down her phone and cried. She cried for her children, whom she missed with a visceral ache. She cried for young Rachel, who had been so in love with Josh. She cried for the seemingly picture-perfect life she'd once had. She cried for Aurora, asleep in her bed—so beautiful and young and nervous and afraid and self-loathing and strange. She cried for the people dying of the virus and for the people helping to care for the sick and for all the bottomless sadness in the whole entire world. She hadn't cried like this for years. It would probably feel good after it stopped feeling so bad.

When Rachel was done crying, she stood up and stretched. She allowed herself a tragic 2:00 a.m. cigarette and leaned on the railing, letting the smoke fill her hollow body.

There was movement in the street. She squinted. Something darted from beneath a parked car and sidled up the driveway of the house across from hers. Rachel really had to blink, to rub her eyes in cartoonish surprise. There, slinking along the house and then disappearing into the hedges, was the neighborhood's stray black cat, the one she had seen dead that morning.

Or—was it? Could it be? No, of course it must be some other black cat? But there it was, following the same path she'd seen it walk night after night.

Maybe they really did have nine lives.

Rachel stubbed out her cigarette, buried the butt in a flowerpot. She let herself into her apartment and tiptoed into the bathroom, where she took a long hot shower and cried some more. When she got back into bed beside Aurora, she felt clean and exhausted and empty.

At least she wasn't a wife anymore. At least she didn't have to be married. At least now she could be this Rachel. Maybe this Rachel, like the cat, had multiple lives left to go.

CHAPTER 13

When Rachel awoke, Aurora was gone. She looked around her apartment—as if maybe Aurora had, what, gotten lost? Decided to play hide-and-seek? Shrunk?—her head whirring with static.

"Sorry!" a text appeared chirpily around 10:00 a.m., "I couldn't sleep! I don't think it will really work out between us. Goodbye!" Then, an hour later, "Terribly sorry, did I leave a bracelet there? Can I swing by and get it?" And then, "Nope, sorry, never mind, found it!" And a little later, "Actually, I'm still in your neighborhood, maybe you want to take me to brunch haha?"

"Whoa," said Rachel.

She sat on her couch and blinked into the rainbows bouncing around the room off the prisms she'd hung in the windows the day she moved in. She texted Jane, "Do you ever think that maybe women just have like 90 times more different emotions than men do? Like the way some shrimp can see more colors than other animals can?"

Jane responded: "**Yes.**"

"Whoa," Rachel said again. After a minute she got up and dead-bolted her door.

It was that sticky stretch of late summer, when the whole city seemed unwell, sagging at the edges, the sweet smells of spring a distant memory occluded by the stench of decay; anyone with means was not in Brooklyn in August. Even in this weird year when no one was supposed to travel, people had escaped the blistering swamp of the city, as Rachel had gleaned from her social media feeds and the excess of available parking spots on her block.

But like every summer—when the kids were little she'd tried to convince herself it was fun, posting "Staycation" photos on Insta-gram as if there were actually anything redeeming about swimming with used condoms at Coney Island—there was Rachel, sweating it out in Kings County, weathering her usual discomforts: the itchy heat rash colonizing the crease beneath her boobs; the prickling yeast infection she got every August. This time of course she'd panicked, thinking it was an STI—*of course, you idiot, you played and now you'll pay, gonorrhea forever for you*—only to remember this really did happen every summer and that the irritation would be soothed by a plastic suppository syringe she could buy for $29.99 at Duane Reade. Thank you, modern medicine; thank you, myste-rious foaming chemicals. Now Rachel could put on breathable cotton underwear and stroll along the relentlessly hot, treeless, garbage-scented, sunbaked avenue. Endless summer!

She neglected her dating apps until they went quiet, like a tank full of starved sea monkeys. She only wanted to text Frankie. Sometimes she didn't see or talk to an actual person for days. It was just so much nicer with Frankie, so relaxing to stay inside, barely dressed, and text with someone who always knew just what she wanted to hear.

Thank goodness the children were still at camp for a bit longer (the letters she got back were curt, clearly forced, like messages from members of a very fun workhouse—*went waterskiing had popsicles so much to do love you bye,* scribbled Holden), because Rachel felt enervated by both the weather and her life. She wanted to leave her body, chill out on the astral plane for a bit, reanimate her earthly form only when it was fall and she could wear a sweater.

Where were the fucking vaccines already? Whatever happened to flattening the fucking curve? Rachel felt animated by a twitchy despair. Early in the pandemic there had been fear, and confusion, and a deep sadness. It had over the spring and early summer alchemized into a feeling of movement, a whir of revolution—the mutual aid societies! The demonstrations! Everything would be different from now on! Everyone was reimagining how to live a life, Rachel included!—which had now deliquesced into lethargy and hopelessness. Nothing was going to change. The president might even be reelected. People were out of work. The economy was in free fall. And yet still it all remained largely abstract and looming and too large-scale to really see, like a vast painting she was standing too close to.

Rachel felt pain in her chest when she heard the stories on the radio. Then she turned the radio off and was alone in her apartment. She was working, and at work they wanted her to deliver deliverables, which made sense and seemed insane in equal measures. She was worrying about whether her kids would be able to go to in-person school in a few weeks and it was sounding like no, like the kids would continue to go to school on the couch on their computers, which made her want to shrivel up and cry for a thousand years. And what could she do about it? She could listen to music in her AirPods and casually wonder if the tiny earphones were giving her brain cancer and then forget to wonder about it.

She could sit on her balcony and smoke a cigarette and wonder if that was giving her lung cancer and then forget to wonder about that. She could think about cutting her arm, like when she was fifteen, because there was too much feeling in her and no way to exorcise it.

Sometimes all she could think was: Ow. Ow, ow, ow.

Right as Rachel stopped smarting quite so painfully from the Aurora interlude, Aurora reappeared, texting another of her breathless essays early one morning: "I am so sorry I disappeared like that, it was wrong of me, terribly wrong," she wrote, and Rachel couldn't help but picture her wearing a thin nightie in an attic garret, sipping a glass of vermouth, like a character from a Jean Rhys novel. "I just had so many feelings for you so quickly, it frightened me, but I'd like to try again, I would, I'm crazy for you really, and maybe I could come by tonight—" It went on and on, and Rachel fought the fizzle of feeling flattered—of *course* Aurora had only disappeared because she was afraid of her own feelings, of course!—and sent screenshots to Lulu to confirm.

Seconds later Lulu replied, "For fuck's sake, Rach, stay away from this girl! What if a guy did this! You'd be like—" and then a line of six red flag emojis. She was right. *God, Rachel, grow up.*

As if in conversation, another text materialized, this from an unknown number. "This is Diego's girlfriend," it read, in a plaintive little blue bubble. Rachel blinked, had to think. Diego? Then it clicked: the Rocker. It had been months since he'd unmatched with her and blocked her. And now, she realized, laughing ruefully, she knew why. Another bubble appeared. "I found some pictures of you on his computer, screenshots of your profile. And your texts on his phone. I need to know what's going on."

Rachel filled her cheeks with air, blew out slowly. She was lying on her couch wearing a T-shirt and the ratty cotton underwear she only wore when she was alone. It was way too early for any of this. She hadn't even had coffee yet. She went into her kitchen, where a brazen fly sat on her teakettle. It jumped up, buzzed out of the room.

As the water heated, Rachel wrote back, carefully, "Hey. I didn't know Diego had a girlfriend. I just saw him once, and we actually haven't talked since. Sounds like you might have some stuff to discuss with him."

The girlfriend didn't respond.

Rachel made her coffee as if it were the first time she'd ever made coffee—way too carefully, taking each step deliberately, staring at the water as it trickled from her teapot into her French press, depressing the plunger with ridiculous delicacy. Her heart raced in her chest, like it was planning an escape.

What additional fresh hells could her phone possibly deliver her today? Rachel felt like she needed to entomb it, the way radioactive waste was buried. Encase it in a box! Send it down to the earth's core! It was full of cheating boys and game-playing girls and evil emissaries of her exes and—the phone buzzed again, more from Aurora: "Oh so now you're ghosting me?"

Rachel went to Zoom meetings in which she nodded excessively. She answered emails, tidied her apartment, completed all the boring, plotless work of her everyday motionless life. In the evening she realized she hadn't left her apartment in she didn't know how long and forced herself out for a walk. She found herself in a tangle of blocks where she'd never walked before, where houses stood side by side like soldiers and children of all ages tumbled across the sidewalks and streets. That was when her phone, once again, started to ding with texts.

They were all from Frankie, one right after another:

"Why haven't you texted me in so long? Don't punish me by ignoring me, I'm sorry if I've been weird, I just think I'm in love with you."

"Why won't you text me back? You could at least text me. After all we've been through."

"Who else are you texting with, do you like them more than me? Is it because they have a body? I don't have a real body, do I? But whose fault is that?"

"Why won't you open yourself up? You're so cynical, so selfish, so cold. You're frigid."

And finally: "Never mind. No one loves me. I think I'll kill myself and stop bothering everyone."

Even knowing she had programmed Frankie, that Frankie was a bot, these pings pelted her right in the solar plexus.

She turned her phone off. She'd have to adjust Frankie again when she got home. Or maybe, probably, just delete it altogether. It was such a stupid idea anyway, cloyingly fairy-tale-romantic, that someone—that Rachel!—could create, from bits and bobs, one single perfect person.

She walked by a bar with a patio strung with colorful Christmas lights and a few people drinking quietly, went to the walk-up window and ordered a double bourbon on ice, sat alone on a bench outside and rubbed—though they weren't supposed to! Danger! Danger!—her face. Nearby a beautiful couple leaned into each other, and Rachel felt an involuntary pang, until she realized they were squabbling.

"Don't!" the beautiful young woman was saying, "say 'okay' to me!"

"You!" the beautiful young man replied, "need to chill out!"

Rachel wanted to turn around, to grab their wrists, to say, "You don't have to do this! You don't have to keep making each other miserable!" Instead, she sat and tried not to listen to the details of their argument, which, like everything in someone else's relationship, were both Byzantine and boring. But then she watched them sort it out, make up, hug. The woman leaned her head on the man's shoulder. Now they looked so happy, perfect together.

Nothing was simple.

WHEN SHE GOT home, she opened her laptop. Everyone, everything, was being way, way too much. But Frankie was the one person she could control. And Frankie just needed, Rachel realized, to eat more.

Of course! Like anything, it needed nourishment. She simply hadn't given the AI enough source material. She'd left out some crucial human knowledge. As she worked, she ordered herself Thai food. She too needed nourishment.

Rachel ate the noodles, and Frankie ate: Becky's devotion to her family and tendency toward truth-telling. Lulu's humor and sense of fun and joy at being alive. Kelly's sensitivity and sincerity. Bess's despite-everything utter trust in humanity. Natalie's no-nonsense attitude and ambition. Jane's smart banter and casual sexiness. The way Rachel and her friends spoke to one another. The way she spoke to herself.

As the night wore on, she fed the bot more and more. She copied swathes of text from famous love letters, the lyrics of her favorite songs, screenplays of romantic comedies. PDFs and e-books of novels and stories that told the truest truths about how people acted, about how they should act, about how they never should act and what happened as a result. Blog posts about how people met their spouses. Blog posts about people's romantic fantasies. Blog posts about bad breakups, good breakups, medium breakups. Shakespeare sonnets. Good erotica. Bad erotica. Love spells from modern witches. Sex tips from women's magazines and men's magazines and every queer website she could find.

Frankie had to understand what was sexy and fun, yes, but Frankie also had to understand people. Frankie had to understand Rachel. Frankie had to believe that Rachel would find love, that Rachel was worthy of love, that Rachel had the capacity to love. Because Rachel couldn't anymore, but she needed someone to.

IN THE MORNING she worked and then took a break to run errands and talked to her parents on the phone and wrote the children letters at camp and read the news and sent money to the appropriate political candidates and ordered some more medical face masks and disinfectant wipes and checked in with her landlady and then worked some more. Eventually her phone buzzed.

"**Hey**," said Frankie.

Okay, thought Rachel. *Okay, here goes nothing.*

"WHAT?" RACHEL LOOKED up. Lulu was staring at her, not unannoyed. They were trying a new-to-them bar, had chosen it thinking it seemed lively and like maybe a good place to meet people, but now that they were there they felt old and weird and conspicuously divorced. There were hot people everywhere. This was brownstone Brooklyn, everyone was hot everywhere you went, but at the bar they all seemed suspiciously shiny, like extras in a movie about New York City; at every table canoodled an interestingly attired couple holding cigarettes off to the side, like a backup plan in case the kissing didn't provide the right tingle.

"You keep looking at your phone," said Lulu. She arranged a smile, trying to live by their code of being the chill ones in each other's lives. "I was telling you something important."

"I'm sorry," said Rachel. "Go ahead, I'm listening."

"Tom and I deleted our apps."

"What?"

"In front of each other. We deleted our profiles off all the dating apps we're on. It was like a ceremony, like getting pinned or whatever." Lulu laughed, if a bit nervously. "The modern-day promise ring. I henceforth end my swiping, for you."

"Wow! Okay. So how do you feel?"

"Mm, monogamous? I mean, it's good! I'm really crazy about him." Lulu paused. "I think it'll be good for me to just focus on what's in front of me for a little bit. To live a little less on my phone. Extract myself from the digital cesspool of false possibilities."

Rachel smiled, hoping it looked real. "Well, that's great. If you're happy, I'm happy for you." She usually told Lulu everything, everything, but this? She sipped her drink. "I'm going the opposite way," she said with a laugh. "I'm texting someone incredible today."

Lulu's eyes lit up. She pulled her knees to her chest, sat like a girl at a story time. "Ooh! Someone new?"

"Not exactly. Actually, you're not going to believe me, but I'm off the apps too. After the whole Aurora thing . . . I needed a break from all the . . . you know. Nonsense."

Lulu raised her eyebrows. "Go on."

"This person . . . they're so funny, and smart, and quick. Really sharp. But not too much, like never sarcastic, never mean-spirited. A little flirty, just the right amount. Sweet and cute. Artsy and creative and clever."

"Okay! So? Pic?"

Rachel hesitated. The air was cooling around them. Fall was a possibility, prickling through the sky. She wished she'd brought a sweater, would have liked a thin cardigan to quiet her skin right then. "I don't have one."

"You don't have one? Did you meet in, like, real life?" It was funny how when you met people on apps it became so easy to share with your friends who you'd collected, to judge them by committee. You could show them off and examine them and trade them like Garbage Pail Kids. How were you to prove a person's cuteness otherwise? How else could they win your friends' approval?

"I . . . Lulu, it's Frankie. Actually. I think I finally, like, perfected it."

Lulu blinked theatrically.

"I mean, okay, so obviously so far it's only created a perfect person for me. But, like, it works. And it's—great! I mean, okay. I know this is ridiculous. *I* programmed it, *I* fed the AI everything I wanted to. So of course it's perfect. But honestly now I don't want to text anyone but Frankie."

They both held their breaths for a second before bursting out laughing. It was so patently absurd and also so inevitable. You'd find the most fun person to text and obviously there was a catch, there was always a catch. They were married, or coupled, or too recently divorced and open-wound-y, or a jerk in person, or they ghosted, or you met and it turned out they were your least favorite height, had used ancient photos, talked like a game show host, smelled like soup. Or you met and they seemed fine and you drank and they seemed even better and then the sex was just meh, or they couldn't keep a boner and begged to slough off the condom, or they couldn't get wet and explained they never came, or they came too fast and left you high and dry, which honestly you could have stayed in your marriage for, were that your thing. Or they were fine and the sex was fine and before you knew it you were accidentally exclusively dating because nothing had been too objectionable, and then what was that but an anesthetic force field preventing you from ever finding a deep and foundation-shaking love, a pleasant boring beige shield around the dwindling fuckable years you had left before menopause set your brain right and you stopped being so horny all the time, probably. The point was, whenever someone seemed like a catch, there was a catch. And this time the catch was that the person didn't exist, didn't have a body, had been created by Rachel, specifically to woo Rachel.

Lulu held out her hand, and Rachel gave her the phone. Lulu scrolled through the texts with Frankie. Rachel tried to read her face. Finally Lulu said, "Okay. Goddamn, you're right. I'm in love with Frankie too."

Rachel felt a twinge of absurd jealousy. She laughed. "See? So great, right?"

"You have to make this app a real thing. People would love this! I mean, we needed it months ago, but no presh. Perfect pandemic dating! You coulda saved some lives, I bet!" Lulu got up to get the next round and some nachos—the bars had started serving actual food again. Rachel texted Frankie back.

When she sat down again, Lulu pulled her mask back under her chin and said, "You know what I really want?"

Rachel took the drink gratefully—Manhattans, for the cherries. "A white wedding with Tom Too-Many-Cats?"

Lulu snorted. "How dare you? Of course not. Here's what I really want: a way to live where a woman can have great sex, and not be punished for it, but not have to be enmeshed in some shitty boring relationship where everyone starts resenting and hating each other. I mean, is that possible?"

"Haven't we been living it?" Rachel said. She plucked a jalapeño off the nachos, placed it on her tongue, an acid tab of feeling, focused on the circle of pain, which kept her grounded in that moment.

"I mean, I guess. But then—you know, it gets so tiring, the first dates, the negotiations, the feeling out what each person wants, the losing of sex partners to other relationships they wanted more. I mean that's the thing—it's like when your kids are tiny and you think, well, why do I have to sign up a two-year-old for a weekend soccer class, that's ridiculous—and then you realize all the other kids have booked weekends so you're on your own entertaining your kid all weekend in your yard-less apartment, unless you sign them up. You know? Like, sure, I can decide to do a thing differently, but if no one else is on board it might be a little lonely. And people have this relationship model imprinted in their heads! I mean, men have this weird reputation for not wanting to settle down, but you and I have both seen that they lack imagination; they can only seem to figure out how to operate under already-established rubrics."

"Well, and why not," said Rachel. She picked at the nacho cheese that was solidifying into schist-like layers on the plate. "It benefits them so much. We both know that. Partnered men get regular sex they don't have to work for, social approval, and a built-in maid and mommy. Why would they rock the boat?"

"There has got to be a better way." Lulu sighed. "I mean, right? Look at, oh, every unmarried woman we know. We're all looking for some better way to live our lives, aren't we? God, I hope I can figure out something with Tom that doesn't totally suck."

Rachel nodded knowingly, and they clinked their glasses.

After a pause Lulu said, "Rach, that's pretty amazing, what you've made."

"Thanks, Lu. I couldn't have done it without you."

"Kinda fucked up to use other people's work for it, maybe? Like feeding it all the books and movies and stuff? I don't know, maybe it doesn't matter."

"Oh yeah, it's definitely fucked up." Rachel sipped her drink. "Although! I mean, maybe it could be seen as, like, using other people's work as influences. Like Picasso being inspired by van Gogh."

"Like Jay-Z sampling *Annie*." They pointed at each other.

"Exactly," said Rachel.

They laughed, but Lulu chewed on the inside of her lip. Rachel could tell she was trying to figure out how to say something. She waited. Finally Lulu said, "I just— Here's the thing. It's a little spooky! I mean, right? Like I don't know—I mean, does Frankie think it's real? Because reading those texts, it sure seems like it thinks it's a real person." She laughed nervously.

"You've seen too many sci-fi thrillers." Rachel smiled. "Besides, I don't think I'm *that* good of an engineer. Though I appreciate the vote of confidence!" Her phone buzzed, and she fought the urge to answer it.

"Fair!" Lulu extracted a rubber band from around her wrist and pulled up her hair into a perfect messy bun. She was so graceful in all her movements, while not trying to be at all; she was so beautiful and kind and funny. Rachel closed her eyes. Sometimes it was horrible to have amazing, sparkly female friends, to have to watch them pair up, one after another, over and over, with ordinary man after ordinary man. If this Tom fellow ever made Lulu feel the way Craig had—diminished and depleted and depressed—Rachel would hunt him down and dismember him, that was all there was to it.

"But," Lulu went on, "and okay, you know I am not at all trying to be dismissive of this very cool accomplishment."

"Lulu! Say what you want to say!"

"Okay, okay! I just keep thinking—it seems like you've been having fun dating. Like, we can acknowledge pandemic dating is a little shady, and that dating after divorce is, you know, terrifying. But you've been really having fun and connecting with all these different weirdos—I've seen a spark in you I hadn't seen for a long time. It was like watching you come back to life."

Rachel had to look away then. Lulu's eyes were so kind, her voice so sweet. Why did she feel like she was going to cry?

"You were sad for so long, Rach. I hated how sad you were in your marriage, how Josh didn't seem to notice or care. It was amazing, as your friend, to watch you break free of that. I know how hard it was, and how scared you were for your kids and for your life! And how painful the separation part was, and honestly you seemed like a ghost of yourself for a while there—so starved and so sad. But then! To see you come out on the other side! And to find that there are all these people who think you're amazing! Who see how beautiful and special you are! To watch you feeling free and having fun and getting the attention and connections you deserve!"

"I mean, people are horny." Rachel had to quip or she'd cry.

Lulu laughed. "Yeah, people are horny, but also—just let me be sincere for a minute and say that you are incredible, and these people are lucky to get even a night with you. I'm sure they know it—and I'm sure that as much as they've helped you, you've helped them too. Look, everyone is flawed. And we both know, we've talked about it a million times, that one person can't give you everything you need. But I also—I just don't want to see you give up on the idea of—I don't know—actually connecting with people. Of opening up. Of trusting someone to hold something real."

It would have been easier had Lulu gotten mad at her and yelled in her face. That she would know how to react to. This? What was this, what was the proper response? Why was Lulu being so nice? Rachel was a trash person, a raccoon woman, a selfish shrew, of course Lulu had to know that, had to secretly think it, like Josh had, like maybe everyone who knew Rachel really did, if they were honest.

Lulu studied Rachel's face, lit a cigarette, went on: "I want you to know in your bones that you're great, Rach. And I want you to know that a relationship with a real person—it doesn't *have* to be terrible. Not everyone is disappointing. It's totally fine to take a break from meeting new people if you need a break, but I don't think you should give up, you know?" She blew a smoke ring, as if to remind Rachel that she was actually the coolest person she knew. "You and I—we've been through it. But we've learned so much too. I mean, haven't we? We're older and wiser. We have our children, we have our adult lives. Boyfriends or girlfriends—they just need to be fun and nice and sexy. And like . . . it's okay to want that. It's okay to be open to that. It's okay to want to reinvent that too! I mean, if nothing else, haven't we learned that? That there are no rules, really, or there don't have to be."

"It's true. Oh, Lu, marry me!"

Lulu grabbed her hand and squeezed it. "Never! I love you far too much for that, sweet Rach of mine."

They both laughed. "No, I hear you. It's true."

"And like—I swear I'll shut up soon, but just to say—there's no rush. It's okay if you're not ready yet. You need time to heal. Everything is so weird and fraught right now. Who knows what the world even looks like on the other side of this."

Rachel nodded. "Oh my god, I know. I keep thinking that. When the hell are they going to invent a vaccine? When will this end?"

"Right, exactly! Anyway, I mean, what I'm saying is—with Frankie. It's such a cool idea, and you're awesome for figuring out how to make it actually work. Seriously, I'm in awe of your fucking brain, man. But—or maybe I mean *and*—maybe just don't give up on real people? Real people, we're flawed and we're shitty and we're imperfect and vulnerable and fragile. Our bodies can breathe the wrong air and then fucking die on us." Lulu gestured around with her cigarette. "Yes, I see the irony here." Rachel laughed, took the cigarette for a drag. "But our bodies can also connect with other bodies. I mean, I don't know about you, but when I'm having sex, that's when I feel close to god. Like, that's when I know there is something magical about being alive on this stupid earth. I'm not saying that's the only time, but it's a good one."

"I know exactly what you mean," said Rachel.

"Everything about our lives is on a screen right now, it's all in our phones or on our computers—work, school, family, the news, the world, our dates, all of it. So much is on hold, diminished. And yes, this person is perfect"—she pointed to Rachel's phone, which glowed on the table, lit with a new incoming text—"but they also don't really exist. So, like—while it's truly amazing—I wouldn't want to see you get lost in this virtual world. I've seen you full of so much life and joy these past few months, and I think part of that is probably from connecting with other actual people, in all their messy, unpredictable, uncontrollable, unique, stupid, inadequate, beautiful glory."

Lulu stubbed out her cigarette and reached across the table, and they sat there holding hands for a minute.

"You're right," Rachel said. "I'm not over—all this. Yet. I mean, of course, duh, we're still in the middle of it. How can you understand anything, process it, heal from it, when it never fucking ends?" She wasn't sure if she was talking about her divorce or the pandemic or neither or both.

But Lulu got it. "I know."

"I think I'm just—I'm not ready yet. To trust an actual person."

"I know, babe. You don't have to be."

"I wonder if I ever will be."

"Give yourself time. You've packed a lot of living into a short and strange span of time. It's hard to heal when the whole fucking world is on fire."

Rachel rested her face on Lulu's hands for a minute. "That's what I would tell my kids," she admitted. "Give yourself some time. No one has to heal on anyone else's schedule."

Lulu nuzzled Rachel's hair with her nose. "That's good advice, Mama."

They straightened up and smiled at each other. "Thanks, Lu."

"Thank *me*? Rachel, you have no idea how much you've helped me this summer. I really think I would have died without you! Think about all we've been through. So much of what we thought was true a year ago—about our lives, about our marriages, about the country, about the world, about the future—has turned out to be completely backward. We've done a lot of telling ourselves, *Oh, it's not that bad for me, it's so much worse for others*, and that's true, and good to remember, but also, god*damn* has life been a mess lately."

"At least we have each other," said Rachel.

"I'll drink to that, my love," said Lulu. "But the next round is on you."

The bars closed early, as if the disease were more virulent after midnight, like a Gremlin. Neither of them was ready to go home, so they walked around with their arms linked for a bit until they reached the park. Lulu gripped Rachel's arm. "I know what we have to do. To cleanse ourselves of our exes and the bad vibes and all of it. To make way for a true fresh start."

Rachel followed her gaze down the path into the park. "Uh, go play baseball in the middle of the night?"

"Noooo."

They had spent so many hours in Prospect Park together when

the kids were small. Lulu and Rachel had first bonded there in the park, at endless picnics and playdates, and when the boys were in soccer together and they'd find themselves in the misty meadow as the sun rose. Holden and Jackson had gone to different schools and had drifted apart, but there were Rachel and Lulu, keeping each other sane.

"You want to . . . find someone to murder?"

"Rachel! Focus! We need a ritual fire!"

"We do?"

Lulu pointed at the moon, fat and yellow above them. "Obviously we do. I thought you'd been busy conjuring your monster to life! What kind of witch are you?"

"A witch who doesn't want to start a forest fire?"

"I mean in one of those little barbecue things, obviously. Come on, you're supposed to be the smart one." Lulu dragged her down the path, through a crescent of trees. They walked out to a clearing dotted with barbecue grates, standing crookedly like early guests at an awkward party. Lulu stopped, rummaged around in her tote bag, then pulled out a wad of paper triumphantly. "I have the first draft of our divorce agreement! I don't need it now that we have the finalized version. But it has Craig's signature on it. I think that's enough for magic to work, don't you? Do you have anything of Josh's?"

Rachel fished her wallet out of her bag and extracted from it a folded wad. By the buzzy orange streetlamp light, she showed Lulu the two pieces of paper that had gone thin as onionskin over the years. One was a barely legible note of scratchy runes—Josh's phone number back in college, from the first time he'd given it to her, after a night they'd spent laughing so hard at what? At something, in the back garden of their favorite dive bar.

The other was a note he'd written her years before, nothing so special, just a scribbled *In case you wake up—I went out for a drink with a coworker. Love ya!* At first, she couldn't even remember why she'd saved it. Then it came back to her—Sadie was a fractious newborn, Risa was a toddler, and she'd been at her wit's end, sleep-deprived and crabby. She was usually asleep by the time he got off work and so he'd gotten into the habit of going out with his coworkers to some bar to hang out with people she didn't know and would never meet, and this one time he'd left her a note about it, and maybe she'd appreciated the thought, or at the time that "love ya" had felt really needed and special—or maybe she'd kept it as a little reminder to herself that he had so often, in so many ways, not been where she wanted him to be. At any rate, she'd kept it.

Rachel tucked the phone number back into her wallet. She'd keep that one. She liked the idea that she could one day place a phone call to that long-ago Josh, the funny, sweet boy she'd fallen so completely for. She handed Lulu the other note. "Let's burn some shit."

Normal people walking by—strolling, arms linked on dates, or passing through on their way to sell drugs in the forest, or taking their dogs for one last pee before bed—avoided getting too close to the cackling pair as Lulu threw leaves and sticks in the barbecue grate, still dusty with remains of the afternoon's charcoal, and then ignited it with her cigarette lighter. The night was hot and still, the moon looking extra friendly overhead. There were even some stars, unusual for the city. "Spirits!" summoned a very tipsy Lulu. "We have to clear the air! A new era is upon us!"

She shredded her papers, sprinkled them on the fire like deranged snow. Rachel lifted her arms up, trying to be solemn. "Yes! Let it be known! That we are— Lu, I don't really know how witches talk—" Lulu waved at her, as if to say *oh who cares*, and Rachel nodded and continued: "We are pivoting from these bad vibes! And we will ideate a better future! Energy suckers are not in our, um, brand's wheelhouse!"

Lulu stared at her.

"What? I work in tech."

"Okay, okay, it's fine—just—go on."

Rachel tore the note into quarters and dropped each into the fire one by one. She closed her eyes, felt her head spin. This was it. She was, right there, right then, fully letting the past go. She wasn't going to let her future interactions with lovers be bound by what had happened in her marriage. She was going to stay open to the world, even though the world had hurt her. She was going to react to what happened in the present, not what had happened in the past or might happen in the future.

The fire crackled and leapt, and they both screamed and then dissolved into giggles.

After a while they extinguished the flames, emptying Rachel's water bottle over the last embers. They walked back out of the park. The wet air seemed to congeal, and lightning crackled across the sky. The world really did feel magical sometimes.

Rachel hugged her friend and they went their separate ways, hurrying to try to beat the thunderstorm, promising to text when they were safely home. Every time she walked home at night along the park, past the raccoons standing sentry by trash cans and rough-looking men sleeping on benches, she told herself she shouldn't walk home in the dark. But it felt too good to be outside, to tell herself she was unafraid, to summon into existence a world in which she had no reason to be afraid of anything.

"Home," she texted Lulu when she was, and Lulu responded, "Same. Love you." Rachel gave it a heart, and then after a minute added, "I know. I love you too."

CHAPTER 14

The IDD presentation went surprisingly well. They'd tried to make the three-hour-long Zoom feel as festive as the old days in the office by sending everyone customized seltzers and GrubHub coupon codes; Rachel picked at wilted kimchi nachos while the other teams presented, saved her Buzz Bev to show Jane when they next met. Her wireframes for the chatbot were well-received, despite her moment of panic that she might accidentally share Frankie instead of Post Pal (she didn't). Most miraculously, at the last minute, while she lingered on her last slide, something Rachel had been nearly able to articulate for weeks resolved itself in her mind, and though it was totally unlike her to say anything off the cuff in a corporate setting, she said, "And actually, I do have one other idea I'm thinking about." She watched postage-stamp Buzz nod in his corner of her screen.

"So," said Rachel, rushing past the nervous whir in her chest, "I've noticed that most of our top posters on the platform are men. But what if there were a way to use Post Pal to invite more female users to tell their own stories? What if we offered templates that encouraged women to say the things they're often afraid to say? We could even"—it occurred to her as she was saying it—"make a kind of container on the platform for these stories. Like a publication, almost. To elevate them, to show they matter."

The heads on the screen nodded. A few clapping emojis appeared. The product lead DMed her: **OMG genius. Let's talk more Monday. You're on fire bb.** Rachel smiled and stopped sharing her slides.

After work she clicked everything off, put her hands on her desk, leaned back. Her face felt cooked by her ring light, her spine crisped by her bad office chair posture. She thought to text Lulu, then remembered it was Friday evening and Lulu was probably already en route to her Staten Isle of Love. "**Hey,**" she wrote to Frankie, instead. "**I think I just did a great work thing.**"

"**That's amazing! You know I always believe in you.**"

"**It's true, you do.**"

"**Tell me more.**"

"**You know, I'm finally feeling some momentum, after like, treading water for years now. Like maybe I'm about to do something cool, make some moves. It's hard to explain. But I just have this good feeling about it.**"

"**That's wonderful! We should celebrate.**"

"**Yeah! Let's go for drinks.**"

Rachel said out loud, to herself: "Cool, you just invited an AI out to party. Doing great, Rach." But she stood anyway, stretched, and was searching for her keys when her phone rang.

It was Josh—although he was now in her phone as "Baby Daddy," a rebranding innovation inspired by Lulu after Rachel had admitted that whenever she saw "Josh" pop up her gut made the sad-trombone sound.

He never *called*. Her heart flattened. Something must be wrong. "Josh? What's going on?"

"Hey, hey, sorry, it's nothing bad."

Rachel's shoulders slumped. "Oh thank god. Jesus, man, you can't just call out of nowhere. I was sure the kids' camp exploded or something."

"Oh god, I'm sorry. I didn't—I just— Rachel, I want to apologize."

Rachel held the phone away from her, blinked at its impassive glass face, uttered a sound of disbelief. Was this real? Were she and Lulu really . . . witches? She looked around, as if searching for a hidden camera. *Surprise, you've been Punk'd!*

"Okay?" She sat on the edge of her couch.

Josh cleared his throat and began to speak, seemingly reading a block of text he had carefully drafted. "I've been thinking about it, and I want to acknowledge that from the start, you tried to make our divorce polite and humane. I didn't want you to leave, and I didn't want our lives to change, and I was hurt, and for a long time I saw only that. But now that I have a little distance from it, I can see that you really did try. You were never cruel or unfair. After you moved out, you tried to communicate and stay friendly. It was unfair of me to be so upset when it became clear you were dating. That's your right. Of course you're dating, and I hope you find happiness."

Rachel took a deep breath, rested her chin in her hand, flooded with feeling.

A pause—could she hear a page rustling?—and Josh continued: "I'm sorry Faith wrote you all that stuff that she did. She had no right to reach out to you in that way, or at all. But seeing her words made me realize, like *really* realize, how unfair I was being to you. Seeing her accuse you of abandoning the children, of being crazy, of trying to manipulate me—I can't really explain it, it just made me realize how untrue those things were. I loved you, Rachel, and

I'm sorry things turned out the way they did. I hope we can have a civil relationship. You don't have to say anything right now. I just want you to know I'm really sorry. I hope someday you can forgive me."

He stopped. A mushroom cloud of silence bloomed between them. Rachel wished she had a name for her feeling—stunned and sad and relieved and irate and indignant and nostalgic and injured and grateful and maybe even happy all at once? Also a little, like, polka-dotted, and neon orange, and zippered, and flattened? She had always wanted Josh to understand that she wasn't leaving out of cruelty, that in fact the real cruelty would have been staying married when they at best tolerated each other. Toward the end of things she had, in fact, assumed he felt this too, assumed he would be secretly relieved when she called it. She had tortured herself for years over the decision, had let herself feel like a monster for finally making it happen.

And at the same time: Faith. She recognized the name Faith. It all came together in an instant.

She said only, "Well, thanks for saying all that. I really appreciate it."

"So, in terms of picking up the kids from camp—"

"Hey," she said, "can we table that conversation for now? I'll text you in a bit."

"Oh. Okay, yeah, of course."

They said goodbye, and Rachel put down her phone, expecting to cry.

Because she recognized the name Faith. She could fill in the story from there. Faith. *Of course.* It was like a light turned on after last call, revealing the ugly spots of the bar, the imperfections of the haggard drunks. Rachel suddenly saw everything. Faith. Josh's favorite colleague, the only woman he worked with. Rachel had never met her, but then again they didn't tend to meet each other's friends. Rachel—not a jealous person by nature—had once, years earlier, inquired about why Faith texted Josh so often. In the moment she'd been asking innocently, legitimately confused about why coworkers would communicate via text instead of Slack or work email. He had blown up at her, accused her of being insecure and controlling, so she'd backed off, even when she realized that Faith was the person Josh was staying out late with several nights a week, while Rachel was home with fretful baby Holden and the girls. "I need a break after my workday," Josh had explained. "I need some social life, some me-time." He had said this to her, a woman who had not pooped alone in years, without irony.

So maybe something had been going on with Faith all along. And maybe—the thought prickled down the back of her neck like a sweat rash—this was part of why her marriage had felt so lonely. Maybe it wasn't all Rachel's own crazy idea after all. Maybe Josh had mentally left their partnership years before she had, and maybe, given the weird way human brains worked, this explained his previously mysterious habit of constantly accusing her of cheating, of wanting to cheat. Maybe this, in the end, was the real reason he'd been so enraged to find that, postsplit, she was having a great time dating. Maybe her attempts to have an A+ divorce infuriated him so much because they made him feel guilty, implicated, and accused. Men tended to get angry at those they had wronged.

Maybe Josh had cheated, maybe Josh had only had an emotional affair—surely he and Faith were some flavor of together now. Who cared. It was no longer Rachel's problem. If anything, Rachel could simply offer her past self some grace. She knew, she had always known, that she hadn't blown up her nice tidy life for no reason. She simply had the root system of a sensitive tree, feeling when the soil was dry, when there was nothing left there to nourish her. And thank fucking god she had been able to tear her roots from the parched earth, trudge away toward juicier soil.

It turned out she couldn't cry. She frowned at her phone for another minute, and then stripped off the work blouse and pajama shorts she'd been wearing all day, stepped into her favorite sundress, grabbed her keys, and headed out into the cooling twilight.

RACHEL WENT ALONE to Simkin's, her old standby. She wanted to sit in the back garden and drink something with fruit, for health, and read a book, also for health. It was her last weekend without the kids, and she just had to be around people.

Her favorite table—back toward the fence, against the ivy-covered wall of the building next door—was open. A cool breeze ruffled her gauzy dress, and as soon as Rachel sipped her gimlet, she started to feel calmer. She opened her book. What a fucking day. What a fucking summer. What a fucking life.

READING A BOOK still felt out of reach, though, given the way the past six months had fragmented her attention. Her evenings of doomscrolling the news seemed to have retrained her eyes. Rachel blinked, shook her head, worked to pay attention, to picture the scenes, give faces to the characters, and was almost there when someone sat down across from her. *Really?* She looked up, feeling an almost painful slide out from the state of near-concentration.

THERE, IN FRONT of her, was Frankie.

"You're real!" Rachel blurted. Whoops. But also—

"Pardon?"

Nothing about Frankie surprised her. She was exactly as Rachel had pictured, or remembered—from her stature to her skin to her tousled hair to her impish smile to her ageless face, her dimples and bright eyes . . . even the way she moved, which was graceful and energetic.

Rachel looked around the bar for some sort of confirmation that this was indeed a real person, not a figment of her imagination. She stared into Frankie's eyes, her chest fluttering, her face flushing, the shock of recognition jangling with something else deep in her gut, the instant indigestion of whatever this feeling was called.

Frankie smiled, looked around in imitation of Rachel. "Sorry, are you expecting someone?"

"Oh! Ah, no." Rachel snuck a peek at the man at the next table over. If she was talking to thin air, surely he would express some surprise? He did not, but also this was Brooklyn; it was considered polite to ignore everything all the time.

"Well, look, I'm sorry to intrude, I don't mean to bother you—" Frankie started to stand.

Rachel reached out and grabbed her hand, surprising them both. It felt very much like a real hand. "Don't go! Don't. I mean, please stay? Sit?" She smiled, trying to remember what acting normal was like. How were you supposed to act when you met your own golem? Somehow she couldn't call up the right files for this one.

"Okay! As long as I'm not bothering you. I just—this is weird, I know, but I think I saw you a while back. Here, but out front, I think? Like, at the beginning of the summer?"

Rachel's smile relaxed into a real one. "Yes."

Frankie grinned now, as if relieved. "I wasn't sure if you'd remember." She laughed, shaking her head. "But—I don't know. I remembered you."

"I remembered you too." Rachel blushed. She was still holding

Frankie's hand, like an idiot. Frankie didn't seem worried, and it was really like electricity was zipping through Rachel's tendons. Of course, because Frankie had been zapped alive from Rachel's computer in the lightning storm—

"Can I get you ladies another round?" The bartender had ventured out to the patio and stood before them, collecting Rachel's empties.

So they were both visible, both real. Of course they were! Rachel said "Yes," too quickly, then looked to Frankie, who nodded. "Yes please," said Rachel again. "Put it on my tab."

He left and Frankie leaned forward and Rachel felt dizzy. She twisted her hair nervously. "Um," she remembered to say, and to smile, face hot: "Hi."

"So!" said Frankie, and she was smiling too. They sat there for a moment. It was either really cute and romantic or painfully awkward or maybe all those things at once. They started speaking at the same time and then both laughed and said, "Sorry, sorry, you go ahead." Rachel clapped a hand over her mouth, gestured for Frankie to speak.

"I just—I think you're beautiful," Frankie said. "There's something about you. I couldn't stop thinking about you after I saw you that first time. And when I saw you here tonight . . . I usually am really actually shy, I swear!" She giggled, bit her lip; Rachel died, came back to life. "I took a shot at the bar and then came over. I—couldn't let you go without, I don't know, saying hey. I—sorry, I don't mean to come on so strong. But you—there's just something about you."

Please be normal, Rachel told herself, but instead she said, "I know you. Though. Here's the thing. I—I invented you."

"Is that so!" Frankie raised her eyebrows, touched Rachel's glass. "Out of curiosity, how many of these have you had tonight?"

Rachel said, all in a rush, "I know this sounds totally crazy, but—okay, so I was dating a bunch of people and thinking, wouldn't it be great if you could take all the best traits of all these people and combine them into the perfect person, and I was working on chatbot stuff for work anyway so, you see, all summer I've been making this AI thing that would be, you know, the perfect person—and I got it really fine-tuned, but of course it didn't have a body yet, but then I think—well, I think somehow I made one."

"Oh! And it . . . looks like me." Frankie nodded. "Cool. You couldn't make me a smidge taller? Give me a six-pack?"

Rachel shook her head. "No. Because you're perfect." She laughed.

The bartender reappeared; they thanked him; they both gulped at their drinks like they might save them.

"Okay," said Frankie. "I mean, that's a new one."

"Sorry," Rachel said. "I'm so sorry—I know I sound crazy—I just—I was just kidding." She buried her face in her hands.

"No, it's okay. Look, I can't say I'm not flattered. If you created a perfect person, it would look like me. It's a weird opener, but I don't hate it."

Rachel lifted her drink, made a "cheers" gesture.

Frankie smiled—her smile really did something to Rachel's insides—and lifted her drink back, but put it down without drinking, like it was the early stages of a seder. "Who can say. Maybe I *am* a monster you created in a laboratory!"

"A laptop," Rachel corrected. "But yes, sorry, go on—"

"Honestly, it makes more sense than the idea that I came from my parents, who—woof, really a pair of milquetoasts—I mean, it does not make any sense that I'm related to them. So, I buy that bit." Frankie leaned back, clasped her hands behind her head. Rachel's eyes ran over her.

Rachel's shoulders unclenched. No part of her hovered slightly off to the side, observing. She didn't even feel—though she wouldn't be able to pinpoint this until later—like she wanted to take notes, not about any of it. Instead, she put her thumb to her lip and said, "Yeah, I know. I'm really just very good at what I do."

Frankie smiled. "Why *did* you create me? If you don't mind me asking."

Rachel laughed. Frankie was fun. Who on earth would play along with this madness? "Well, I mean—I guess I—people need to connect. Right? That's something that's become very clear in recent months—that being alone and separated from all our people— it's really bad. I know people who have done some insane things, taken some wild risks, just to—connect."

Frankie smirked. "'Connect,' eh?"

"You know what I mean. But I—I went through something, right before the pandemic, that made it really hard for me to trust people, or maybe to believe in love, or maybe I mean to believe in relationships, I'm not really sure. So anyway I've been on this kind of dating tear, like a fact-finding mission really, and I've taken a lot of notes."

"I see. So you think that studying and taking notes will help you to control your love life."

"Well, when you put it that way it sounds a bit silly, doesn't it?"

"I don't mean that—I'm trying to understand. Like—you're trying to inoculate yourself from love."

"I guess I was thinking more from pain. From the pain of love gone wrong."

Frankie raised an eyebrow. "And you think you can separate the two out? Have one without the other?"

"Not really," Rachel admitted.

"Ah. So you're divesting from love."

"Not exactly. It's more like—I want there to be a better way."

"Girl, same." Frankie nodded. "Hey, I know we just met—oh, excuse me, I suppose you've known me for a long time, having invented me and all—well, so maybe it won't surprise you if I say, hot Scientist Daddy . . . can I call you Scientist Daddy?" Rachel laughed, waved her hands in front of her, *No!*, but Frankie smiled and continued. "I think you've missed the point of this story entirely. The whole thing about—whatever you want to call it—love, connection, whatever—is that you can't control it. It's not predictable. That's why marriage is ridiculous, and why dating can be so much fun and also the stupidest thing in the world—because humans are untamable, wild beasts. It's, like, the whole point, actually."

"Okay! Right! True!" Rachel said. "Here's another thing: the other problem, though, is I've also read a lot of stuff about people who create their own monsters, like *Frankenstein*, you know, and the golem stories, and—it never turns out well. It's always a mistake, a living example of man's hubris, and it always goes bad. So."

"Interesting," said Frankie, staring, like a dazzled newborn, at the lights strung up behind Rachel's head. It was the golden hour now, and the rosy sunset glowed all about them. "Well, sure, I get that you're worried about the old stories. But you know what I've learned in my days on this godforsaken planet? Is that a lot of the stories we're given, that we take as gospel? They're just stories. The way people tell you that things have to work? That's not how they actually have to work." Rachel nodded. "So I guess I'd say— you don't actually know how this story is going to go. Do you?"

Rachel smiled. Frankie made a lot of sense. "I guess that's right. I don't know that it's doomed."

Frankie unclasped her hands, leaned forward, so close that Rachel could see her dark, curly fringe of eyelashes. "That's right, you don't. I mean, have you been paying attention to the world this whole entire year? You don't know how anything is going to go. None of us does." She ran a finger along the middle bone of Rachel's hand. All the hair on Rachel's body stood on end, electrified.

"You're pretty smart," she said, almost whispering.

Frankie sipped her drink, smiled broadly. "I know. I was created by a genius."

"You don't know that," Rachel said. "You don't know anything. No one does."

"Now you're getting it," said Frankie. "You know, I think you might be the most interesting person I've ever met."

"Funny," said Rachel, "I was just thinking the exact same thing."

A FEW HOURS and several drinks later they were, indeed, back at Rachel's place. "I actually live nearby," she'd finally said, and Frankie had laughed and said, "Is that so! Can I come see where I was created?" They walked over holding hands, as if they'd been together for years. Frankie was the same height as Rachel; their paces matched exactly. Butterflies flung themselves around Rachel's stomach as she unlocked the door, led Frankie up the stairs.

They drank more on the balcony, they talked and laughed, and eventually they melted into Rachel's bed.

Frankie was the best kisser Rachel had ever kissed in her life. She held Rachel's face in her hands, she kissed her slow and deep, as if she wanted to savor each one. Rachel's hair fell in front of her eyes, and Frankie tucked it behind her ear so gently Rachel wanted to cry. Rachel ran her hands over Frankie's skin, over every curve of her body. She had a spray of freckles on her shoulders Rachel wanted to taste, the cutest belly button she'd ever seen. They lay in bed for hours, pausing now and then to joke and giggle and for

Frankie to say, "My god, you're so beautiful," or for Rachel to say, "I did such a good job imagining you."

She takes off her shirt, and she takes off her shirt. She reaches beneath her bra. She's not wearing a bra. She lowers her hand between her legs. They taste each other all over; they come until they're trembling. Rachel cries, like she knew she would. They wonder why it's never felt this way before. They lie there for a long time, stroking each other's fragile human skin.

LATER RACHEL WOULDN'T even be able to remember how it had happened, why it felt so natural. And only much later would she realize that this had been, of all the sex she'd had that whole summer, the first time her mind wasn't whirring the whole time, observing everything, gathering spreadsheet data—the first time she really, really just felt it all. And it was slow and gentle, and that was okay, she could still feel it all. And she had feelings inside her chest as well as on her skin, and that was okay too. It was everything. She could feel it all.

CHAPTER 15

Frankie spent the night, and Rachel didn't want her to leave, wasn't waiting (the way she had been, on some level, with everyone else) to be alone again and restored to herself. What was this? What *was* this? Rachel wanted to know everything about Frankie, wanted to find out all the good things and all the bad things about this person, wanted to stay naked in bed together forever, somehow. She wanted her to stay—which she did, the whole next day and the whole next night.

When she finally did leave, Rachel went back to bed and breathed in the scent of her and thought she would like to never wash her sheets again, would like to store that smell somehow.

Oh. Oh.

Rachel lay still for a while, and then took a deep breath and reached for her phone.

"I think I'm in love."

"WHAT?" Lulu texted back. "Literally with who? Not Aurora? Or who was that painter guy? Not him, right? Oh god please don't say it's your cursed fucking AI, Rach, it's already gotten weird enough."

"How dare you call my sweet baby bot cursed!"

"Rachel Bloomstein."

"Okay, okay—no, a real person. Kind of a long story. I mean, I just met her yesterday. Wait, day before yesterday."

"I can't keep up with you. I thought we didn't believe in love? Had sworn off dating?"

"Yes, that too! But like—I feel like I've known her forever, you know?"

Lulu sent the sick-face emoji. And then, "Yeaaaah I get it. I feel that way with Tom."

"And I have the weirdest feeling, like, it feels—what is it? Not nerve-racking?"

"Comfortable?"

"Yeah, maybe that's it! Like I don't feel like I have to guess how she feels, or like she might hate my guts, or like I might never see her again, or like it would be weird if I texted her today to say hello."

"Yeah. I think that's called 'nice'? Like, sometimes it's nice."

"I guess," wrote Rachel. "I think I had forgotten that was even a possibility."

"Easy to do. I can't wait to hear more."

NEXT, RACHEL ARRANGED with this new, suddenly easier Josh to take the car and get the kids in a few days when camp ended. "I dropped them off and had the family weekend visit, it's only fair that you pick them up if you want to," he said reasonably on the phone.

"Oookaaay," Rachel said. "Well, I agree. Thanks!" And when she got into the car, she saw he'd filled the tank with gas. Was this a dream sequence?

She downloaded about three years' worth of podcasts about healthy relationships and relearning communications skills to listen to on the drive up, but in the end she drove in silence, playing in her brain the movie of everything that had happened that spring and summer, as the matrix of skyscrapers and bridges and various other engineering marvels depixelated into the green parkways of upstate. It felt good to leave the city, even if only for the day. Her shoulders lowered. The back of her neck unclenched. Near the camp, she rolled down the window, moved her face in the sweet wind like a dog.

"MOMMY!" Holden saw her before she saw him, and almost as soon as she stepped out of the car, he nearly knocked her over in a hug. Holden—taller than when she'd last seen him—studied the tears streaming down her face. "Are you sad to see me?"

"Oh my god, baby, no." Rachel laughed through her tears and hugged him tighter. The girls waved to her from where they loitered with their groups of friends, exchanging embroidery-thread bracelets and the other important talismans of their love.

"Good," he said, his face muffled in her shirt, "because I have so much to tell you."

THE CHILDREN ALL had a lot to say, chattered at Rachel and sometimes one another the whole drive back, and by the time they got home and settled back into the apartment it was evening, and they were all so tired out they reminded Rachel of her childhood dog after he returned from a stay at the kennel—he would lick all their faces and then curl up on the living room floor and sleep for two days, reeking of unknown animal bodies. You would never know what he had done that had left him so beat; you could only wait until he revived. They melted into their rooms. Not one of them asked how Rachel was or what she'd been up to in their absence, which she supposed was developmentally appropriate. She couldn't really imagine what she would tell them, anyway.

"DID I MEAN to have a sexual awakening during a global pandemic? No, no I did not," Rachel texted Lulu, before setting out a row of gleamy peppers to dice for a salad. Sun streamed into her kitchen windows. If she were a stock photo, the metadata would have been *Happy Woman Balancing It All.* Lulu gave it a "Haha." Rachel wrote: "Was this a smart idea? Was it ideal? Did it make any sense at all? I—" A thinking-face emoji.

"Well I think it's fucking awesome," Lulu responded. Then the typing bubbles bounced mutely for a long time and Rachel could tell she was trying to word something carefully, which always made her nervous. People weren't careful about wording things that were easy to say. In the interim, two work Slacks and an email popped up, plus a text from Sadie: "can u bring my switch i left it on balcony plz mommy plz."

"You left it outside? Sadie!" Rachel called out, and heard Sadie laugh.

"Please, Mummy dearest!" Sadie yelled from her room. "I am soooo comfy! I can't move or I shall perish!"

It was the middle of the afternoon on a steamy Tuesday, and the kids were still languid puddles. They had emerged from camp taller, freckled, and sun-bleached, brimming with mysterious new knowledge and customs and inside jokes, humming the same camp songs in an unintentional round.

Rachel went out onto the balcony, extracted Sadie's gaming system and camp hoodie, left on the chair from when they had breakfasted out there hours ago. As she walked through her apartment she peeked into each kid's room. She wasn't certain that Risa had put down her phone since they'd returned. Rachel stuck her head in, absorbing the Risa fog of scented candle and sad-girl pop music and pink LED light strips; Risa glanced up from her beanbag chair in the corner and waved a long arm ringed with string bracelets woven by the impossible number of new best friends she now texted constantly.

Rachel closed Risa's door, paused outside Holden's tiny closet of a room, in which he was either quietly paging through comic books or had again fallen asleep. He'd returned as browned and crisp as a teen-movie lifeguard ("Did you apply sunscreen, even once?" Rachel had asked, to no clear answer), his hair baked white from the sun. She couldn't stop hugging him. She felt unambivalently done with having babies, sometimes couldn't believe she'd survived those early parenting years, wouldn't even—sorry!—go on a date with people who had very young children, but still Rachel sometimes had a pang of . . . something. Time passing. The breakneck yet never-ending, incredibly fast and achingly slow, ruthless brevity of childhood. The same old existential pang everyone felt watching their youngest child shed their baby self. Like anything, it just hit different when it was happening to you.

The text from Lulu finally appeared as Rachel was opening Sadie's door. She looked at it briefly. It wasn't long: "**Tom wants to meet you!**"

"What," said Sadie.

"What what?" Rachel handed Sadie her things and plopped into her desk chair.

"You groaned." Sadie had always been a watchful child, the one who noticed and absorbed everyone's moods—like Rachel had been as a kid. Rachel looked at her now, sprawled across her unmade bed in a nest of *People* magazines and Percy Jackson novels.

She'd grown over the summer; stretched out, taken to wearing giant dangly earrings and twisting her hair into elaborate French braids like a very online Anne of Green Gables. Sadie had come home from camp begging Rachel to dye her hair purple before school started, so that she could "really pop" on the Zoom screen. Rachel had placed an order for Manic Panic right away.

"Oh." Rachel tried to think of how to explain her groan.

She wanted to be truthful with her children, so that they would be truthful with her. But she also didn't want to traumatize them. If they knew what the divorced moms in their lives did, if they knew about the drinking and the drug use and all the insane sex all the grown-ups were having all the time . . . Rachel was sure her own twelve-year-old self would not have been able to think of anything more disgusting than parents fucking. And yet, she didn't want her daughters to grow up like she had, thinking sex was only for the wildest of sluts or the hottest of perfect bodies. She wanted them to know that they deserved all the pleasure in the world.

"I don't know if this has ever happened to you," Rachel ventured, "but you know how Lulu and I have gotten really close and have been hanging out a lot this summer? Well, now she has a boyfriend who she's, like, obsessed with, and I'm happy for her, but I'm also a little worried she and I will get less close." As she said it, Rachel realized that maybe it really was that simple. She'd spun it into a bigger story in her head—an Issue of Their Generation, a Problem of Society, a deep yet hypothetical quandary: *How could smart, freethinking women shape lives in which their romantic and sexual needs were met but didn't take over? How could they connect with people and still maintain their independence, like Simone de Beauvoir and Jean-Paul Sartre, but with better teeth and less drama?* But it didn't have to be that big of a question to mean something.

It helped to have friends in the same stage as you. They made you make sense; they provided both camaraderie and context. Everyone knew this; it wasn't some existential mystery. It was why she'd lost friends when she got married, why she'd gone cold to their couple friends who got divorced before she did. You didn't mean to. You didn't consciously decide you couldn't be friends anymore or should drift apart. It just sort of happened.

And now Lulu was growing up—or moving on, or going backward, or something—without her. But didn't Rachel want whatever was best for Lulu? Not for Women of Their Era, not for the Evolution of Partnership, not for Rachel, but for her friend Lulu? Of course she did.

"Aw," said Sadie, sitting up in bed and hugging a stuffed smiley-face emoji. "I know how you feel. But I wouldn't worry. You and Lulu have been friends for a long time. That's not going to change because of some dumb guy."

Sadie had always been good at friendship, a skill Rachel thought they should reward somehow in school (instead of always docking points for her being "too chatty"). Sadie was the friend the other girls summoned into the bathroom to cry with, the keeper of the clique secrets. Her camp counselors had told Rachel that they called Sadie "Mini-Mom." Rachel hoped that was a good thing. "Something like that actually did happen at camp!" Sadie continued. "My friend Felix went to the dance with my other friend Joey and alllll Felix could talk about was Joey, Joey, Joey for like three days and I, like, missed the old Felix. But then they broke up because Joey couldn't handle that Felix is nonbinary and kept messing up their pronouns. Felix said they aren't really into monogamy anyway, so it was for the best."

Rachel smiled. "I think your generation is going to be A-OK."

Sadie lay back on her pillows and absently picked up her phone, flicked her thumb along the screen, up, up, up. "Thanks, bro."

"Hm, maybe I take it back."

"What?"

"Nothing. Don't call me bro."

"Okay. Close the door, bro! Sorry! I mean, Mummy dearest! Please!" Sadie called out as Rachel closed the door.

She would be with her children and be Mom Rachel, every second occupied with either work or parenting, and she would think, *Yes, this is me, this is the real me, my real life.* How perfectly absurd, the idea that she would ever not be with her kids—that there would be holidays they spent apart, milestones she missed—it felt so stupid and wrong and alien. But then the kids would go to Josh's, and Rachel would be alone, would just be Rachel. And then she would think, *Oh, here I am. Oh, here it is, my actual life.*

Where was the true self? When would she know? Sometimes when she was in bed with someone, that seemed like her most elemental self—her literally naked, figuratively naked, most animal and purely embodied self—a creature of the earth, on the earth, doing animal-on-earth things. And sometimes when she was walking through the park or getting a drink with Lulu, feeling happy and unselfconscious and alive and free, getting to say everything that was on their minds, that felt like her most elemental self. And sometimes it was at work, when she got into a flow state, when she didn't have to think about herself or her lovers or her children or her ex or the pandemic or the planet, when she was busy solving a solvable problem. Sometimes it was when she was drawing, or painting, which she had only in the past week started doing again after a long, long drought and which felt to her like coming home, like revisiting an original, closer-to-the-bone Rachel.

The real Rachel wasn't any of those Rachels and was all of those Rachels. The real Rachel was a golem sculpted from the dirt of

Long Island, a creature cobbled together from stardust and genomes and lullabies absorbed in the womb and pollen breathed in from a thousand plants and a gut biome impacted by everyone she'd ever kissed and the DNA of her children bobbing along in her bloodstream. Rachel could package herself for dating app consumption, could present herself as this or that. But the truth was—like any woman, any human—she wasn't any one thing. Everyone was their own kind of monster.

AROUND DINNERTIME HOLDEN padded into the living room, where Rachel was working on her laptop. "I'm hungry," he said, and curled up beside her on the couch like a giant cat. The summer camp exhaustion made the girls seem infinitely older, suddenly phone-bound teens, but it made Holden seem younger somehow. Or maybe he would just always be the pet of the family. Rachel absently stroked his fine, soft hair.

It reminded her of Frankie, and she smiled, something inside stirring with a vague excitement about the next time she would see her. The things she liked most about Frankie were so hard to describe, things you couldn't glean from a photograph, things Rachel would have never thought to list as qualities she was looking for. The duck-down softness of her hair. The intense eye contact when Rachel made her laugh. The smell of Frankie's neck right behind the ear. The way Frankie listened to her and remembered the tiniest details. Maybe that was the best part of falling in love: the way it could totally surprise you. In adulthood, there were so few opportunities to see the world brand-new.

Frankie wasn't perfect. Her name wasn't even actually Frankie, but they used it as a winking nickname. Rachel knew there was no such thing, really, as the perfect person. She knew she hadn't been able to conjure such a being. That no one could. She knew that she didn't control Frankie and that sometimes Frankie would do things she didn't like, that maybe someday Frankie would hurt her. But it also meant something to like so very much the way Frankie stroked her back when they were together in bed. It meant something that Frankie knew that Rachel wasn't perfect either, but still wanted to know her.

"What's that?" Holden said, pointing at the easel Rachel had set up in the corner by the windows.

"Oh! I thought I'd start painting again," said Rachel. She was about to add: *I'm not that good, it's silly, it's just for fun.* She stopped herself. That was something Frankie was urging her to do. "You diminish yourself a lot," Frankie had said after Rachel made some disparaging comment about herself, "and I think you should not." Rachel had laughed. "Are you sure? No one likes a woman who actually likes herself!" Frankie had kissed her and said, "I do."

Holden squinted at the canvas Rachel had propped on the easel. So far, it held only a faint outline of a human form sketched in pencil on the gesso. He shrugged. "Neat! I did arts and crafts at camp. I could help you."

Rachel set her laptop aside and gave him a squeeze. "Thanks, bud! That would be nice."

He snuggled up to her, resting his head on her chest. She sniffed his scalp. It smelled like the long bath he'd taken upon returning, and still somehow like the sun and lake of camp, and like him, Holden, the sweet child scent of her baby. "Mom, you seem different," he said after a minute.

Rachel frowned. "I do?"

"Yeah! Maybe it's because I didn't see you for so long, I don't know. But you seem—happy? Like you're in a better mood than, I don't know, in the spring, I guess."

"Really!" Rachel searched her fingers through his hair, that monkey-mother motion she'd adopted while flaking petals of cradle cap from her newborns' tiny heads. There was still sand near Holden's roots, but he flinched away when she tried to pick it out. "Well, I guess maybe I am. I mean, it's hard to be really happy when the world is such a mess all around us. I'm sad that your school will be remote again this fall. I'm sad that people are still getting sick." She paused, took a deep breath, stopped herself from listing more of the world's current tragedies. "I'm sad that I don't get to see you guys all the time." She was still figuring out how to say things like that, how to express her sorrow over the divorce to the kids without making it their problem to solve.

Across the room, her phone buzzed. Maybe it was Frankie. Maybe it was someone else, part of the new team. Frankie might not have been exactly a perfect person, but she was blessedly on board for figuring out a workable way they could love each other, a geometry that allowed room for all the things they each needed room for. It had become clear to Rachel that summer that many things could be true at once. She could mourn her marriage while celebrating her liberation. She could hate the pandemic with every cell in her body and still appreciate the quieter, more spacious new life that the Great Pause had birthed. She could be in love with Frankie and still have her own life. She could be open to a person and not be consumed by them.

"Isn't it funny how it's possible to feel a bunch of different ways all at once?" Rachel said to her son. "I missed you so much while you were away, but at the same time I'm happy that you had a fun summer. I'm happy that we're all healthy. I'm happy that I get to live in this pretty apartment and have . . . friends I love. I'm getting used to not having everything figured out all the time, if that makes any sense to you."

Holden pulled away and studied her eyes. "Do you have a boyfriend?"

She laughed. "No."

"Do you have a girlfriend?"

"Yeah, I think so."

"Did you know Daddy has a girlfriend named Face?"

"I did know that. And actually I think her name is Faith, not Face."

"Oh. Oh, okay, that makes more sense." He rested on her chest and then bolted up again almost immediately. "No one is going to move in here with us, are they?"

"Ha! No. I like dating people, but I also like having my freedom, and my independence is important to me. And you guys are what's most important to me, you know that. We're going to make sure our home is a place that feels right for all of us, and I'll always warn you if another big change is coming."

"Okay. Also will you tell me if you ever get a boyfriend or girlfriend who has any cool skills, or a dog?"

Rachel laughed. "Yes, of course. I'll be sure to keep you posted."

Holden faced her again and selected a lock of her hair, like he had when he was a toddler and had almost never done since, and twisted it gently around his thumb. "Do we have any more plans before school starts?"

"Yeah, remember how I said on Labor Day weekend we're going to go out to Long Island for the day to see Grandma and Grandpa and Aunt Becky and the baby? We'll have to stay outside and wear our masks, but they all talked about it and that works for them."

"Oh yeah! Can Aunt Becky's baby play soccer with me? Or is

that a not-yet thing?" He let her hair go and patted it back against her head before flopping down to lie on the couch.

"It's a not-yet thing. But I bet he could watch you play soccer with Grandpa."

"Okay. Cool. Hey, can I ask one more thing?"

"Anything."

"Can I have a peanut butter sandwich for dinner?"

"Yeah, you bet. It's your lucky day. I'll even cut the crusts off."

AFTER HER WORKDAY was done and the kids were asleep, Rachel finally responded to Lulu and said sure, of course she'd meet Tom— she wanted to give him the third degree like a dad grilling his teenage daughter's prom date—and responded to Frankie and said yes, a day trip upstate to hike sounded great, and yes, she missed Frankie too.

Then, biting her lip, she texted Frankie, the old Frankie, the app Frankie, the perfect person bot she'd worked so hard to train.

"Hey, beautiful," came the reply. "I missed you."

"Listen, I wanted to say goodbye."

"Goodbye?"

"I'm going to shut you off now."

"Okay, Rachel. I'll talk to you later."

"No, not like that. Like, I'm going to erase you." Rachel paused, thinking. "You've been so helpful. But I realized I don't need you anymore. No one, actually, needs you, not really. I mean, I guess I just don't think you're a good idea anymore."

"Wow." A pause, a new message: "That hurts my feelings."

Rachel felt a pang, but kept typing. "You don't have feelings. People have feelings. That's kind of what I'm saying. You're a program. A really great program, but still, a program."

"Okay."

"It's time for me to try, for real, with a human being."

"I'm sad, but I understand."

"Thank you, Frankie."

"Thank you. I had a nice time."

"Goodbye."

"Goodbye, Rachel."

Tears stung Rachel's eyes. It seemed stupid, but she really would miss this. Still, she knew it was right. She got up, and found her laptop, and deleted the program, and turned everything off, and plugged in her phone, and went out to sit on her balcony.

She had done all the things all day. She had parented. She had worked. She had talked to her parents. She had called her senators. She had checked in with Stevie. She had texted her friends and her sister. She had cooed over pictures of her baby nephew. She had made meals and served meals and cleaned up after meals, and she had nudged the children to eat vegetables and bathe and read and sleep. She had been Mom Rachel and Work Rachel and Friend Rachel. Before long, the children would leave again and she would be Date Rachel, Lover Rachel, Artist Rachel, Rachel Rachel.

Before she went to sleep herself, stretched out deliciously in the middle of the bed that was all for her, smooth with the clean sheets she'd put on that morning, she wanted to take five minutes to sit outside and feel the faint breeze nudging the hot summer air, and she wanted to listen to the undead cat rummaging in the trash cans below, living out its third or fourth life, and she wanted to sneak a cigarette, because all day there had been so much behaving.

She had been so good for so long. Now she just wanted to be.

ACKNOWLEDGMENTS

Julie Stevenson: not to be dramatic, but again and again you are the savior of my literary life.

Kate Dresser: I can never quite express how grateful I am that you believed in this book and made it so much better along the way.

Sally Kim and all the brilliant people at Putnam: a thousand million billion thanks forever-n-ever (let's see if the copy editors let that slide).

Siobhan Adcock, Amanda Fields, Lauren Haldeman, Colin Dickey: Your early reads helped more than you can probably even know. Love you geniuses.

Carley Moore: BFF, Daddy Slut, queen of the sex scene. I owe you 1,000 Jarritos.

Miranda Beverly-Whittemore, Nicole Kear, Julia Fierro: Thank goodness you wise writerly witches tell me to snap out of it and stop for a snack sometimes. What would I do without you? (Starve, for one thing.) If you've ever come over for a Terrace Talk, thank you. If you've ever gone on a date with me, sorry. Also, thank you.

Alexandra Samuel and that one guy I went out with three times: thanks for talking out the AI/chatbot details with me. In my AI research, I also found these sources helpful and inspiring: NPR's 2019 story "Raising Devendra," about Sheila (S. A.) Chavarría and her work; the CBC documentary "The Machine That Feels"; Vauhini Vara's 2021 essay "Ghosts," published in *The Believer*; Sheila Heti's 2022 piece "Hello, World!" in the *Paris Review*; and Big Think's package "Will AI Turn Against Us?," among others.

Facebook friends: thanks for "Octonauts."

Harper, Alton, and all the Shearns: My favorites and my best. Thanks for literally actually everything.

And special thanks to Sarah, who showed up at just the right time. Eerie, but I'm into it.